RUNNING
IN HEELS

Read more from Helen Bailey – introducing Electra Brown:

www.helenbaileybooks.com

RUNNING IN HEELS

Helen Bailey

Hodder
Children's
Books

A division of Hachette Children's Books

A Catalogue record for this book is available from the British Library

ISBN 978 1 444 90084 2

Typeset in Berkeley by Avon DataSet Ltd,
Bidford-on-Avon, Warwickshire

Printed and bound in Great Britain by
CPI Bookmarque, Croydon, Surrey

The paper and board used in this paperback by Hodder Children's Books
are natural reyclable products made from wood grown in
sustainable forests. The manufacturing processes conform to the
environmental regulations of the country of origin.

Hodder Children's Books
a division of Hachette Children's Books
338 Euston Road, London NW1 3BH
An Hachette UK company
www.hachette.co.uk

For Madeleine Lecouturier
With love and thanks

The idea for *Running in Heels* first came to me when I was called as a witness in a case of alleged business fraud, and with it the realisation that just as with Daisy Davenport and her family, a comfortable lifestyle can quickly unravel when that lifestyle is built on lies and deception.

Poor Daisy has to deal with some vicious bullying at her new school, and I'm grateful to my friend Lisa for sharing with me her hilarious account of how she finally stood up to her school bully in a showdown at the swimming pool on Hampstead Heath, and which I hope has you cheering for Daisy.

I hope you enjoy *Running in Heels*: a tale of riches to rags, bitches and bullies, liberally sprinkled with fabulous accessories and gorgeous Stud Muffins!

With love,

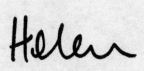

Chapter One

Even if I hadn't woken up this morning to find fourteen missed calls, seven *Where the hell are you when I need you?* texts and one tearful voice mail on my iPhone saying something *totally* terrible had happened and to get my bony butt into town, like, yesterday, as I hurry along the pavement to our Starbucks rendezvous I can immediately tell from Mia's body language she's super-stressed.

She's ahead of me, slumped into one of the silver chairs outside the coffee shop, puffing away on a ciggie in her right hand, stabbing the keys of her moby with her left thumb, a beaded flip-flopped foot jerking up and down like a frog on a hotplate. So violent is the ankle jerking, I'm seriously worried the flip-flop might fly off the end of her foot and hurtle out into the traffic, causing some startled motorist to swerve with shock and crush an innocent tourist against a waste bin.

Not that that would worry Mia. I'd bet my birthday Mulberry Bayswater bag (silver cracked leather, cost an absolute bomb, but, as Mum said to Dad when he went ballistic over the price, you're only fourteen once) she'd pick her way through the carnage, retrieve the stray footwear and carry on with whatever she was doing before the flip-flop fiasco, unless of course said bin victim was a lush lad, and then she might try and flirt with him, even if he was injured and unconscious.

And I'm *totally* not making this up. Mia Howard is the most self-absorbed, screwed-up, flirtatious, bitchy drama queen I've ever met, which makes it well weird that she and I are supposed to be bezzies. And before you think I have something in common with this brunette bundle of bitchiness, I should point out that I didn't *choose* to be best friends with Mia: Dad told me to.

Just over a year ago, Jonathan Howard (Dad's accountant at Aspland & Stratton) confessed he was at his wits' end because his only child had been thrown out of *another* school. Yet again, Mia had committed a long list of expellable offences: smoking in a chemistry class; swigging booze from a voddy bottle in assembly; flashing her sports bra at the games mistress and asking her if she fancied girls. So Dad suggested Mia come to Park Hill, not just because it's a totally fab school with a stylish uniform and stunning grounds, but because they'd also managed to keep my older sister, Portia, from going *completely* off the rails, something that seemed a possibility when she'd come home aged fifteen with a stud in her nose, a ladybird permanently inked on her bum and her blonde hair dyed black and shaved to within a millimetre of her scalp. Dad tried to sue both the hairdresser and the tattoo parlour for not asking for ID, but it turned out Portia had flashed a fake card she'd made in a computer design workshop at school. Anyway, big sis is about to go into the sixth form at Park, the hole in her nose looks like a freckle, and as long as she doesn't flash her butt-bug at an interview, she's on track to go to uni to study art.

So when Dad made me promise to be friends with Mia (in exchange for a twenty-five per cent increase in my allowance), I was lumbered with showing Park Hill's newest pupil the ropes, providing her with an instant social life amongst my group of friends known as The Glossy Posse, not just because we're supposed to be teen models in the making, but because we feel studying style and grooming is just as important as studying for GCSEs.

I say lumbered, but at first it wasn't hard to be friends with Mia. I felt sorry for her when she turned up looking all anxious and vulnerable with her little pale face, long conker-coloured hair and wide brown eyes.

I feel sorry about lots of things: dead birds on the side of the road; old ladies who can't walk very well; a bit of chicken left uneaten on a plate as I fret that the chook has died in vain. But dead birds, old birds and cooked birds don't continually wind up other girls by flirting with their boyfriends or making snarky remarks about their looks, something Mia does all the time. It's been a pretty full-on job being friends with her, but every time I've moaned to Dad about how high-maintenance she is, he's reminded me of my promise – and the extra cash.

'You OK?' I say, touching Mia's skinny shoulder as I sit down.

I scan her face for signs of major crying-induced trauma. There's no hint of redness or puffiness around her eyes, just the usual mega-dose of black eyeliner and smudged mascara.

'Thank God you're here,' she gasps, brushing fag ash off her jeans.

'So, what's happened?' I ask. After a brisk walk, a train journey and more high-speed striding, all in heels, I'm peckish and parched. But Mia's already got a drink (a Frappuccino by the looks of it), and she's in such a tizz, it would seem rude to leave her so distressed for a biscotti and iced beverage.

She grinds her ciggie on to the silver tabletop, slurps a slug of coffee through the straw and says gravely, 'Dom is dead.'

'Oh, Mia!' I can feel tears spring to my eyes as my stomach lurches at this shocking news. 'You poor thing!'

Everyone but Mia loathes Mia's boyfriend of eight weeks, Dominic Harper. Like my boyfriend, Oliver Simons, Dom is about to start Year 11 at Pilgrims College, but unlike Ollie, Dom thinks of himself as a total stud muffin, which is weird given that he's short, squat, has no neck and if he had a ring through his nose he'd be the spitting image of a bull. But just because he thinks he's a hit with the chicks and is challenged in the neck department, doesn't mean I want him dead.

'That's terrible,' I sympathize. 'When?'

'Last night.' She flips open a white and gold packet of Marlboro Lights and shakes a cigarette on to the table. 'We had a row, he stormed off, and *that's* when it happened.'

Both Mia's legs start pumping up and down as she tries to light the white stick. Her hands are shaking so much I'm concerned the flame from her lighter will miss the end of the ciggie and set fire to her long fringe, requiring me to extinguish the flames with Frappuccino.

All sorts of Dom death scenarios are running through my mind: Murder? Overdose? A Spanish matador roaming the streets and mistaking him for an escaped bull, driving a stake through his heart?

'How?' I say, gently touching Mia's arm. 'Unless you don't want to talk about it.'

'Of course I want to talk about it,' she snaps, pulling her arm away and finally lighting the cigarette. 'Why do you think I called you?'

'Soz,' I say, remembering that I'd read in a magazine that people react to death in different ways, and that anger is the third stage of grief, although Mia seems to have got through the shock and denial stage pretty quickly. 'What happened?'

'It started with Cameron Diaz, moved on to you and ended up with Two Ton Jess,' Mia growls.

'Me?' I squeak. I have no idea what possible connection there can be between Dom pegging it, a glossy blonde Hollywood star with legendary lengthy legs, yours truly (long legs, long blonde hair but hardly in the same league as Cam) and Jessica Fawcett, the chubby girl with bright red hair and humungous thighs who rides my pony, Polly, partly because for the last four months all my free time has been spent with Ollie, but mainly because I've lost my nerve when it comes to sitting on top of a quivering beast who farts constantly. 'What's Dom got to do with me?'

Mia takes another slurp of her Frappuccino and sighs as if I should instantly solve this strange leg-themed triangle.

'We went to the flicks last night and before the film came on there was this trailer for some stupid rom-com thing with the Diaz bitch. Dom said he really fancied her, as in, shaggable fancied.'

'So?' I shrug, thinking that a squat-necked fifteen-year-old schoolboy like Dom wouldn't even feature as a blip on glam Cam's radar.

'He wants to shag a woman old enough to be his mother!' Mia shrieks so loudly that some of the other morning caffeine-slurpers and smokers turn round and give us dirty looks.

The pavement tables are buzzing with foreign tourists and the queue is snaking back through the door, but presumably even if you are German, Japanese or from Outer Mongolia, you recognize using the words *shag* and *mother* in the same sentence is pretty shocking.

'And then he says, all right, if you want me to choose someone I'd shag nearer my own age, your mate Daisy Davenport would do nicely. She's babelicious.'

I can feel the skimmed milk from my breakfast wild

berry organic muesli curdle in my stomach at the thought that Dominic Harper has even considered me in that way, and make a mental note *never* to let Mia bring Dom round if we're planning to use the pool and I'm wearing a bikini.

'So, we had this mega row about whether you were sexier than me. You won. I pelted him with popcorn and the manager asked us to leave. Dom stormed off and left me and then snogged that freckled freak that hangs around the stables. Only this time she was hanging around the kebab shop in Copperfield Street, stuffing her chubby chops with a doner and chips.'

Jessica Fawcett goes to Bensham High, a huge mixed comprehensive school in town, but Mia knows her because, although she's not keen on horses, she once had the hots for a stable lad who worked at Pegasus, the place where I keep Polly, until said stable lad made it clear he fancied the horses more than her, at which point Mia told him he was a pervy dwarf who smelt of horse dung and would never find a girlfriend who didn't neigh and wear a saddle.

'And Jessica killed him?' Perhaps I'm becoming dehydrated and hallucinating as, even for Mia, this tale of snogging, slaying and low-rent food seems to have become mega complicated.

'Killed who?' Mia asks.

'Dom,' I remind her. 'You said Dom's dead.'

'Dom's not dead.' Mia screws her face up and looks at me as if I'm nuts. 'Unless the shock of snogging that lump of lard has killed him. The slug rang me afterwards to fess up, only cos some Park girls saw him and didn't buy his excuse that the chubber was having an asthma attack and he was trying to give her oxygen. He said it was just a revenge snog, meant nothing and has put him off the taste of kebabs for life.'

'I thought you meant *dead* dead,' I say, wondering if now that I know Dom isn't dead I could get a drink.

'Oh, Daisy, you're so literal,' Mia says airily. 'Do you think I'd be this unhappy if Dom was in a box with brass handles? I'd be thrilled! The slime ball has stuck his tongue down that chubber's throat, a throat greasy with sliced lamb and chip fat, and expects us to carry on going out as if nothing has happened!'

'Well, it was just a kiss,' I say, thinking how devastated I'd be if Ollie went near anyone else but me.

And then suddenly I panic that with hundreds of miles and several weeks between us, Oll might be doing what Dom has done with Jess, but with someone munching a Cornish pasty rather than a kebab.

He's surfing in Cornwall at the moment, staying at his

family's holiday cottage in Perranporth with his cousins, Lucian and Persephone. I was a bit miffed I wasn't invited too, but Ollie knows I'm scared of swimming unless it's in our heated pool, and even then I freak if some monster bug starts thrashing around in the water next to me and I'm not near the side to grab the edge and clamber out.

Our family holiday was a tense two weeks in a luxury villa in Tuscany when school broke up. Mum was upset she still looked bloated in a bikini despite rigorous dieting and a course of colonics; Portia stayed in bed under protest at being made to come when my older brother Aston was allowed to stay at home; Dad came back early because of a business emergency; and I pined for Ollie, fretting that we'd be apart for four weeks as he went away for a fortnight on the day we flew back.

'Daisy, are you listening to me?' Mia kicks me on the shin. 'Why choose *her* for a revenge snog?' Her whole body is vibrating with anger. 'I'd rather I'd turned Dom gay that have him touch that fugly cow. He said he made the first move, but then she was all over him like a rash and he couldn't escape. *That's* why I want you to sack her.'

'Sack who?'

'The ginger nut!' Mia sounds exasperated that I'm

losing the plot. 'Tell her she's too much of a lardy-arse to ride Polly.'

My fingers start to clench into a fist, so I sit on my hands and clamp my thighs tightly over them.

Now, in the street, with Mia already in a tailspin isn't the time to reveal my true colours, to let the world know I'm not the person they think I am.

Everyone thinks I'm really nice and kind and thoughtful, the sort of girl who on seeing a spider in the bath would carefully rescue it using a glass and a magazine, whispering, 'Come here, incy wincey little spider,' whilst coaxing it to freedom, rather than the sort of hard-hearted cow who would slam a bottle of shampoo on its leg-sprouting body and rinse it down the plughole shouting, 'Die, insect! Die!'

Mostly I am nice and kind and thoughtful and scream for Dad to rescue creepy-crawlies, but at times like these I fantasize about Mia being a black arachnid scuttling around my white roll-top bath before gleefully extinguishing her with a bottle of John Frieda Sheer Blonde conditioner.

But violence with toiletries is only a delicious fantasy and is never going to happen, because I have a shameful confession to make. People *think* I'm confident and glossy, the sort of It girl who has it all, but underneath the naturally perky boobs, butter-coloured locks and Tuscany tan, I'm a quivering wreck of a worrying jellyfish.

Yes, my name is Daisy Davenport and I am a teenage wimp.

I don't mean I slink along with my eyes glued to the pavement watching out for ankle-wrenching potholes, or blush and stammer if someone looks in my direction. I'm not shy; I *love* talking to people, going to parties, having fun, but I've never managed the art of being assertive, of standing up for myself and saying what I *really* think, just in case it upsets someone or starts World War Three. In fact, you could say I'm just a girl who can't say *No*, which is why I'm relieved that Ollie hasn't put me in a position where I really should say *No*, though I'm starting to worry about what I'm going to say and do when his hand wanders to where I'd really rather it didn't.

I know that I need to sort myself out, I really do; I'm just too scared to do it.

Every so often I pop into WHSmith and pull out a book called *Assertiveness NOW! From Wimp to Wonderful* by Wanda-May Rubin. According to the photo and the blurb on the back of the book, as well as having scarily assertive hair that sticks up in a spiky blonde V sign,

Ms Rubin is America's premier life coach who has: *Changed the lives of film stars, international businessmen and homemakers*, though it doesn't mention anything about schoolgirls who find it difficult to stand up for themselves and are worrying about what to do if their boyfriend tries it on.

Ms Rubin predicts that unless I learn to say what I think (in a calm and assertive way, of course), I'll either become Daisy the Doormat and be picked on, Daisy the Diseased (high blood pressure, heart problems, lots of stinking colds and crappy skin due to stress) or Daisy the Destroyer, one of those people you read about who are mouse-quiet and then walk into their nearest Burger King and start brandishing a gun, just because the kid behind the counter gave them a Double Whopper with a gherkin when the order had clearly been: *No pickles*.

So, as well as worrying about not having much confidence and whether Ollie's going to put me in a difficult position, I've now got the added angst of possibly turning into a manky-skinned murderer who'll be bullied in jail, on top of my usual worries about global warming and whether someone from al-Qaeda is going to suicide-bomb the changing rooms of Topshop when I'm trying on a Kate Moss-designed dress. And I know all this is mad, because really, if I could just get greenhouse gases and terrorists out of my mind, I've got nothing to worry about. Courtesy of Dad's luxury-car dealership business we're minted: we live in a fabulous house, I own more accessories than Harvey Nichols, I'm seeing totally gorge rugby captain Ollie and, unlike some teenagers, I never get spots.

But *still* I worry.

About *everything*.

From my snatched browsing I'm sure I'd find *Assertiveness NOW!* useful. The problem is, I daren't buy it in case Krystina, our Polish housekeeper, comes across it when she's tidying my knicker drawer and shows it to Mum, who'd give me the third degree over why I was reading it and thought that I needed it. So it's still in Smith's, hidden between two copies of *West Ham: The Glory Year*, somewhere no one would think to look for it.

As well as chanting one of Wanda-May's Magic Mantras, which she guarantees will give instant results – *I am wonderful! I am amazing! I can become President of the United States!* (she's on dodgy ground with the Trade Descriptions Act if she thinks anyone can instantly become prez just by saying it over and over again) – she recommends writing a diary in a calm but assertive way.

But this gives me another problem.

I daren't.

I'm worried I'd write down all my innermost angst, be run over by a Tesco Home Delivery van on the way home from netball practice, and then Mum would find my diary once I was sparko under a white sheet on a cold metal table in the hospital morgue and, from reading all the stuff I've written, think I hate her. Which I don't – it would just seem that way because Wanda-May had told me to write assertively about all the things and people that bug me, and sometimes my family comes top of that list.

Right now, though, Mia has the number-one slot.

'Belinda Trotter at the stables lets Jess ride her, not me,' I point out feebly. 'And it would be mean. Jess loves Polly.'

'You're not going to do it?' Mia looks murderous. 'For me?'

The last time I saw her looking so angry was when I got the part of Dorothy in the school's production of *The Wizard of Oz*. Mia was furious to be cast as a munchkin, so I persuaded Miss Aplin, our drama teacher, that I'd make a rubbish Dorothy. My plan spectacularly backfired as Miss A kept Mia as a munchkin but made me play the tin man, and I fainted on stage from getting too hot in the costume.

I can feel my body tighten up and I start to freak that this is the Gherkin Moment Wanda-May has predicted, and that I'm about to go mental with Mia's Frappuccino and start stuffing ice up her nose.

Time to defuse the situation for both our sakes.

'Oh, Mia!' I force a false-sounding laugh out of my mouth. 'You and Dom will soon be back together. You'll see.'

'I don't want him back,' Mia snorts. 'I want revenge. Tell Jessica Fawcett she's so fat, if she gets on Polly's back she'll break it.'

'I don't think *that's* very likely,' I say, still keeping with the light-hearted tactic, but removing my hands from their thigh-clamp as they've started to fizz with pins and needles. 'She's got a butt as big as a house!'

A girl in the queue next to me turns round. The most striking thing about her isn't her poured-into-deep-dyed-denim bum, which in truth *is* practically the width of the pavement, but the cloud of orangey-yellow hair piled on top of her head. She looks as if she's wearing a very ripe pumpkin.

'What are *you* gawping at?' Mia sneers at the girl who's watching us with cool, flinty eyes. 'What's her problem?' Mia asks me. 'Other than being a total chubber.'

The girl continues to stare at us as the queue shuffles forward.

'My friend says you have a huge arse!' Mia calls out.

'Mia!' I shriek, giggling. 'You know I was talking about Polly's butt!'

'But she does, doesn't she?' Mia shrugs. 'Makes pony girl look almost anorexic. And check out the back fat. It's flowing over her bra strap!'

This is Mia at her most bitchy, and I'm ashamed to say that I keep laughing, more out of embarrassment than because Mia is being funny. Also the girl *is* huge, not fat, just all over big. Russian Olympic shot-putter-on-illegal-steroids big.

Pumpkin Head doesn't say or do anything, she just keeps watching us. And now Mia has pointed out the back-fat situation, I can't help but stare at the rolls of skin circling her torso.

'Foreign,' Mia decides. 'Probably doesn't speak a word of English or she'd deck us. God, I'd die if I was as big as her. I mean honestly, I'd rather be dead than be fat. Maybe where she comes from they like girls with fatitude. Over here she's just a continental chubby chav!'

Mia does a wildly accurate and hysterically funny impression of the girl by puffing her cheeks out and pretending to be Michelin Man, and then both of us collapse in fits of giggles as the queue moves again.

Pumpkin Head moves forward with the queue, but then turns, catches my eye, draws her right index finger across her throat and mouths, 'You're dead.'

Chapter Two

Seriously freaked that someone has threatened to kill me, I made an excuse about needing to go to the dentist, left Mia sending abusive texts to Dom and went to Smith's, where I dug out *Assertiveness NOW!*, read one of Wanda-May's Magic Mantras, walked around the aisles chanting, *I am powerful! I am powerful!* in my head, decided it made me feel more like a Duracell bunny than a woman of power, and then went to the station where I am now, waiting for a train to take me home to Oldstone.

Fiddling nervously with my Tiffany charm bracelet, I scan the platform for any sign of Pumpkin Head or pupils from Bensham High who think that tormenting girls from Park Hill is a spectator sport.

Even without our cream and brown uniform we're marked out as girls from the costliest private school in the area. In Park's school brochure, Mrs Channing, the headmistress, is quoted as saying: *Girls from Park Hill have an inner confidence* (hah!) *that sets them apart from their peers.*

It's a nice line, but I think it's less to do with inner confidence than outer wealth, and today's get-up of Seven Jeans that cost Dad nearly two hundred quid, the Mulberry bag, an Abercrombie & Fitch T-shirt and a pair of Christian Louboutin silver peep-toes that I've 'borrowed' from Mum, who'd left them by the front door after a party at the golf club last night, means I might as well have *Rich Bitch* tattooed across my forehead.

I was going to wear flats, but these sparkly heels go so fabulously with my bag I just had to wear them, so as long as I get them back before Mum needs them again, she'll probably just think Krystina's tidied them away along with the hundreds of other designer trotters lurking in Mum's custom-built air-conditioned shoe cupboard.

I notice a guy a bit further along the platform, staring at me. He's about the same age as my brother, Aston, eighteen, maybe nineteen, but unlike Aston he's dark-haired, got two armfuls of inky-blue tattoos and a sparkly diamond earring in his left earlobe. Actually, in a rough kind of way, he's rather lush. I wonder what Dad would say if I brought him home instead of Ollie, who's the son

20

of judge Justice Thomas Simons and his wife, renowned psychoanalyst Dr Clara Simons. Not that I would; Ollie's a keeper. But of course if there was a terrible accident in Cornwall involving a shark and a surfboard and Ollie never made it home, Tatt Guy could certainly help me get over my grief.

Oh. My. God! He's coming over! I didn't mean to give him the come on. What do I do now? What if he asks me out? Then I'll get *totally* flustered and might even say *Yes* when I ought to say *No*.

It's happened before.

About eighteen months ago, in a disco on the last night of a school skiing trip to Méribel, I met this lad, Jake Hurley, who, coincidentally, went to Aston's school, Huffman's College. In the dark and sitting down he seemed funny and cute and was an awesome kisser, but when the lights went on, we stopped snogging and he stood up, I realized he was short, a tad chubby and had so many zits on his face and neck it looked as if he'd been attacked by a swarm of killer wasps.

When my friend Isabella Tricket saw him, she pulled me aside and darkly reminded me that as a member of The Glossy Posse it was *inconceivable* that I should have anything more to do with a lad that was a few centimetres short of being medically a midget, and one who would

21

benefit from a dose of strong antibiotics and several hours on a StairMaster. But when in the queue for the coats Jake suggested we met up back in Kent and asked for my number, I gave it to him partly because he was really quite cute, but mainly because I didn't dare hurt his feelings and say no. I then totally freaked that if Izzy discovered I'd gone against her instructions not to date a zitty midget, as Queen (and rather bossy) Glossy she'd oust me from her inner circle, and I'd be left to make friends with unfortunate girls who don't know the meaning of the word style. So to the girls I pretended I'd told Jake to bog off, and when a few days later he texted me to arrange to meet up, I texted back to say that I'd love to see him but unfortunately on the journey home I'd caught leprosy and was in solitary confinement for months. Sorted!

But now I've got the protection of Ollie I can just smile and say, *A date would be great but I already have a boyfriend.* That won't hurt anyone's feelings, although it would be better if I had a sparkly commitment rock on my left ring finger that I could waggle in the air as further proof I'm off limits.

'You're James Davenport's daughter, aren't you?' Tatt Guy says. 'I've seen you at The Gate.'

The Gate is where Donsborough United, our local

football team, play. Dad's the chairman, and Davenport Motors sponsors them, meaning the name Davenport is plastered on their black and white shirts and on signs around the ground.

I nod and smile in what I hope is a friendly rather than flirty way.

'See that?' the man says, stabbing a bulging bicep on which is inked a crest of Donsborough United. '*That's* commitment.'

I can't say I'm heavily into tattoos, but Tatt Guy is very buff and as he's asked me to look at his bulging muscle it would seem rude to refuse. It's certainly impressive.

'Unlike your dad, I can't just wipe it out and walk away,' he says. 'It's with me *for life*.'

'Have you thought about laser surgery?' I suggest, wondering whether he's under the false impression that Dad has had a football tattoo removed. 'Or wearing long sleeves?'

Tatt Guy snorts like a truffle pig. 'When you see your old man, tell him this is what I think of him and his posh cars.'

And then he spits, not exactly at me, more near me, but definitely close enough to see the mound of gob-juice foam away on the concrete platform, just as the train rumbles towards us.

So much for thinking Tatt Guy was going to ask me out. If he gobs that easily he'd be a terrible kisser anyway: much too spitty.

As Tatt Guy gets in one carriage, I get in another and by the time I've sat down, Ollie's cute face is flashing on my phone.

Actually, I'm telling a lie.

It's his bum that's flashing on the screen. He plays rugby for Pilgrims' first team, and after they thrashed arch rivals Huffman's, he and his rugby chums had a mooning competition. Ollie won the prize for the most planet-like butt and he thoughtfully sent me the snap for my moby.

Anyway, I bet he's calling to say he's missing me as much as I'm missing him.

'Daisy, sweets, thank God you've picked up!' he gasps. 'Mum's having a total meltdown. Olga's in hospital.'

'Oh that's terrible,' I say, trying to wrack my brain and remember whether I've ever heard of a rellie called Olga. Ollie has so many aunts, uncles and cousins I keep meaning to get him to draw me a family tree that I can keep in my bag. I've also got a little fantasy that when he hands it to me he'll have added a branch with my name pencilled on it. 'Did she fall off her surfboard?'

'Olga's our cleaner who's feeding the cats!' He sounds

exasperated that I didn't instantly remember his family's domestic staff. 'She tripped over a bottle of Cillit Bang and broke her hip in five places. Without Olga, Aristotle, Plato and Socrates will starve.'

Only the Simons family could name their three rescue mogs after philosophers. There was also a fish called Freud, but Socrates ate him. And I doubt very much if any of the cats would starve; they're pretty massive and could do with a few days of calorie counting.

'So I've told Mum that you'll go round and feed them until we're back at the end of next week, OK?'

What I want to say is, *Ollie, it's not OK. I won't feed your mum's cats. It's not convenient on so many levels.*

Since I started seeing Oll there have been two half-terms, the Easter break and several long weekends where the Simons family has gone away, and for at least part of the time I've been called on to emergency cat-feed.

Not only does cat feeding mean that I've got to beg someone for a lift to Ollie's place in Sherlstone twice a day, but the three 'wouldn't hurt a mouse' darlings his mother dotes on turn from purring pussies into killer kitties when I'm alone with them, even for a millisecond. One minute they're all cute and playful, batting the ends of my hair with their soft padded paws, looking straight out of a Whiskas advert, the next, they're launching themselves at me, fangs bared, claws at the ready and *totally* terrifying. I've still got the ripped Missoni scarf to prove it.

But I don't say any of this, I just say weakly, 'Well . . . OK.'

'I knew you'd come up trumps, sweets,' Ollie says. 'You know where the key is hidden and can remember the alarm code, can't you?'

'Yes, but Ollie,' I whine. 'I'm having a pants day. Mia's annoyed with me, a girl wants to kill me and a tattooed man spat at me a moment ago.'

'Got to go, sweets!' Ollie says. 'We're playing cards and I've just seen Lucian cheating. He's stuck an ace down his backside. I'll ring you later.'

With its pretty little station (five times winner of Best Regional Railway Hanging Baskets) and row of Grade II listed stone cottages, it's no wonder Oldstone was once described by *Kent Life* magazine as one of the loveliest villages in the county. It's a bit of a drive to the nearest Waitrose, and there's no longer a shop or a post office, but there are several estate agents, a pub called The Mucky Pup, where Portia got caught flashing the same fake ID she'd used for the bug tatt, and a village green, which I never walk across because of piles of festering dog poo.

Our house, The Laurels, is about half a mile from the station, but I don't mind the walk, even in high heels. I love sauntering through the lanes with fields on either side, pretending I'm in some romantic TV series set in the country, even if sometimes I have to hold my breath to avoid the smell of manure or jump into a ditch to avoid a passing 4x4. I know some of the girls at school say they would absolutely hate to live in the middle of nowhere, always relying on their parents for a lift, but I love living here. It's quiet, it's safe and—

What on earth?

A crowd of men wearing Donsborough Football Club shirts are milling around the pair of honey-coloured gargoyle-topped stone pillars that flank the entrance to The Laurels. The men aren't the only ones decked out in football souvenirs. The left gargoyle has a black and white scarf around its neck, and the one on the right is wearing a baseball cap at a jaunty angle.

'Can I help you?' I say politely, fiddling in my bag for the electronic dibber that opens the wrought-iron gates. So far my rummaging has produced only a Werther's Original, a panty liner that has become unwrapped and a Mac lip pencil in Spice.

'If you've got a couple of million quid in that bag,' one of them sneers.

'I'm sorry,' I say, finally finding the dibber. 'I've only got about a hundred pounds on me.'

One of the men gives a sarky snort. 'Spoilt cow!' he jeers.

'Derek, drop it,' a man orders. 'It's not the kid's fault her dad's done a bunk.'

My heart flips over, my head spins and I sway on Mum's silver heels.

Dad's left? This is terrible news! Who's going to sort out the spiders and pay my allowance now?

One of the men must have seen the panic in my head cross my face; either that or he thinks I might faint, as he holds my elbow to steady me.

'Your dad's pulled out of the club,' he explains. 'Left Donsborough United penniless.'

'Oh!' I breathe a sigh of relief and lean against a pillar, realizing that *this* was what Tatt Guy was going on about. 'I thought you meant he'd left us for some woman. It's just football.'

'Just football!' the sneery man shouts. 'It's not *just* football! It's jobs! It's our life!'

He thrusts a newspaper towards me. It's a copy of the local evening paper, the *Kentish Chronicle*.

DAVS DROPS DONS SHOCK!

WEDNESDAY 6 AUGUST

Terry Strain: Crime Reporter

In a move that has rocked Donsborough United, with only days to go before the start of the new season, self-made wealthy car dealer and businessman James Davenport, 49, has failed to renew the sponsorship deal enjoyed by the club for the last seven years. The Chron understands that The Dons have tried to find alternative funding, but that the late pull-out of Davenport's has left the club in a precarious financial situation. If immediate investment cannot be secured, The Dons will go into administration and automatically find themselves docked points before even the first kick of the ball of the new season, signalling certain relegation. James Davenport has also resigned as chairman.

A statement by Davenport Motors set out the reason behind the shock move as uncertainty over the future of the luxury car market during this economic downturn. Davenport Motors made ten sales staff redundant in the last six months and predicts that recovery of the market will be slow until consumer confidence returns. No one from Davenport's was available, and neither James Davenport nor his wife Christine, 46, could be reached at their Georgian manor house in Oldstone for further comment.

There's more stuff about Dad, his business and his background, but I don't read it. I just take the paper, say, 'Excuse me, please,' to the men, press the dibber and when the heavy gates open electronically, gallop as fast as I can up the gravel drive.

Darting between the potted bay trees standing outside our red front door, I run up the steps and let myself in.

'Dad! Where are you?' I call out as our black Lab, Bentley, greets me, his entire body wagging with excitement.

I know Dad's somewhere in the sprawling house because his silver Ferrari with personalized number plate DAV 1 is parked outside, next to Aston's vintage purple Lotus Elan, a present (complete with giant white bow on the roof) for his eighteenth birthday last November.

'It's not all about cracking open tinnies and throwing shrimps on the barbie!' booms an Aussie voice from the sitting room.

I put my head round the door to see Dad sprawled on one of the purple velvet sofas, a whisky glass in his hand, watching what seems to be an episode of *A Place in the Sun: Down Under*. He looks terrible: shadowy-eyed and baggy-faced beneath his thick greying hair.

'Dad?' Bentley jumps on to the sofa next to Dad. I

slump on to an identical one facing him, putting my feet on the glass coffee table. 'What's all this about you dropping The Dons?'

He stares at the TV and then says dreamily, 'I wouldn't mind emigrating to Australia, if it wasn't for the poisonous snakes and spiders.'

He gestures towards the telly as a spider the size of a dinner plate scuttles across the wall-mounted high-definition plasma flat-screen. I shudder. Lob a bottle of conditioner at that mega-beast and it might pick it up and toss it back.

'Dad, listen to me,' I urge as spiders make way for snakes. 'There are men outside the gate and we're in the *Chron*.' I wave the paper in the air and then fret about whether I should go and give the sneery man his copy back. 'They're really annoyed with you.'

'We could start again, all of us, somewhere warm,' Dad sighs. 'Terry from the golf club is moving to Thailand, but then his wife is from Bangkok, or so it said on the Buy-a-Bride website. Or what about Dubai? The golf is good in Dubai, but I'm not keen on sand.'

Dad seems in a world of his own, even though the phone is ringing constantly, the gate buzzer is buzzing and Bentley is gnawing on the TV remote control.

I get up, prise the remote from Bentley's slobbery

31

chops and press *Off*, just as some woman is advising viewers to always check their shoes for funnel web spiders before putting them on.

'Dad, what's going on?'

He looks away from the dark screen and gives a deep sigh, as if he's struggling for breath. 'Things are a bit of a mess at the moment, Daisy,' he says. 'The business, the club, *life*.' He shoots me a bleak look. 'If you found out I'd done something bad, something *really* bad, would you still love me?'

'How bad?' I ask. 'I'm not sure I could forgive you if you'd been mean to a dog.'

'Of course not that bad!' Dad laughs. 'Nothing like that. Just bad business decisions, that's all. Trusting people I shouldn't have. That sort of thing.'

'Of course I'd still love you!' I go over and hug him. He smells of dog, whisky and aftershave. 'Why, what have you done?'

'We've been hit hard by this bloody recession,' Dad sighs as I shoo Bentley on to the floor and curl up next to Dad. 'The Russians have gone home taking their tax-free roubles with them, my Middle Eastern clients have stayed in the Middle East and the City bonus boys don't have bonuses to burn any more. We've sold one car in the last three months and that was a yellow third-hand

Lamborghini to a Conference league footballer in Luton.'

'So is that why you've left the club?' I ask.

'Something had to go,' he says sadly. 'It was either this place or The Dons.' He looks around the large room with its high ceiling, white ornate plaster cornices and sunny yellow walls. 'And your mother has always said the only way she'll leave here is in a coffin.'

I pull a face and Dad cracks a smile.

Whereas Dad has always drummed into us that he's proud of his working class roots, Mum prefers to forget hers.

To remind us of his humble beginnings, Dad's often taken us back to the council estate in Woolwich where he grew up with his younger sister, Karen. Of course, we drive over there in a car worth well over a hundred and fifty grand, we keep the doors locked to foil car-jackers and no one dares get out in case the pristine paintwork is keyed or someone nicks the wheels, but still, Dad wants us to know that he went from a two-bedroom flat on the fifteenth floor of a concrete tower block in south-east London to a Grade II listed country stone house complete with gravel drive, tennis court, swimming pool and hand-built Georgian-style conservatory, just by sheer hard graft.

Dad met Mum at a motor show. She was sitting on top

of a Ford Fiesta, dressed in a white fur bikini and draped in a sash on which was printed: *Examine my bodywork!* He was just browsing, dreaming of selling shiny motors from a posh showroom instead of rust buckets from a caravan parked illegally on a bit of waste ground. He didn't come away with any new cars, but he did come away with a date with my mother, a handful of business contacts, and the rest, as they say, is history.

There's the sound of gravel spraying under rubber, a car screeching to a halt outside and the front door opening.

'Jim!' Mum's shriek sends Bentley darting behind the sofa. 'What the hell is going on? Someone has painted our gargoyles black and white!'

Chapter Three

Mum stands in our sitting room reading the *Chron*. Her face is swollen, bruised and splattered with blood, but this isn't because she's been attacked by the football mob at the gates; she always looks this way after her trip to the anti-ageing clinic.

I surreptitiously kick Mum's Louboutins off and try to nudge them under the sofa without her noticing.

'We'll sue!' she snaps, throwing the paper towards Aston, whose mega lie-in was ended by Mum standing at the bottom of the stairs screeching, 'People! Downstairs! Now!'

'Chrissie, it's true,' Dad says heavily. 'I *have* pulled out of the club, and unless they get another backer, they'll go bust.'

'Not that!' Mum snarls as the phone rings for the umpteenth time. 'They say I'm forty-six! I'm only forty-two! They can't even get their facts right!'

She throws the paper at Aston, who's lying on the sofa opposite me, chest bare, lanky legs wide open, which, given that he's only wearing skimpy black Calvin Klein boxer shorts, I'd really rather he didn't.

If there's a chance to be vertical, my brother will take it. I can't believe he sat upright long enough to sit his A levels. Assuming he did manage to cling to the side of the desk in the examination hall at Huffman's, he's off sailing round America for his gap year before going to Brown University in the States to study philosophy. Or is it psychology? I'm not even sure Aston knows what he's going to be doing, other than partying and chatting up American girls.

'You're forty-four,' Aston points out, blowing his pale fringe out of his eyes as he reads the front page. 'I've seen your passport.'

'Where's Portia?' Mum asks, spinning round as if my sister might be hiding behind a sofa or the heavy gold curtains. 'She needs to be here to deal with this crisis. Krystina!'

Krystina appears, grim faced in her pink nylon housecoat.

'Find Portia and send her in here now. Oh, and unplug all the ruddy phones.'

'Chrissie, calm down! This is a crisis for the club, not us,' Dad says as Krystina shuffles off. 'But we do need to tighten our belts and make some sacrifices, just until this recession is over and people are buying cars again.'

Mum looks put out. I expect if her forehead could frown it would, but as it's pumped full of Botox she just looks well odd, as if she has constipation and is finding 'things' difficult.

'I bumped into Mindy Howard this afternoon and she practically begged me to come to Barbados at Christmas. Jonathan has rented a villa on the coast at St James. I *suppose* we could just go for a week, though Mindy seemed desperate for us to be there the whole time.'

I can feel my shoulders sag at the thought of spending Christmas with Mia. There's bound to be some issue between her and someone else involving swearing, drinking, a stolen jet ski and me trying to keep the peace. It's bad enough having a fight at Starbucks without it happening three thousand miles from home surrounded by sand and palm trees.

'Christ, Chrissie! Didn't you hear me?' Dad's voice sounds tight and tense as he glares at Mum. 'I said, we have to make some cuts!'

'I heard you,' Mum says sarcastically, her arms folded defiantly across her chest. 'But perhaps you didn't hear me. I've just suggested I tell Mindy we'll only go to their villa for one week instead of two!'

Dad puts his head in his hands and grinds his eyes with his palms.

'Listen, love, we can't go to Barbados. It's not just about the money. I can't leave The Dons in the lurch and then be spotted swanning off to the Caribbean a few months later; talk about rubbing salt in a very open wound. All of us have got to keep our heads down for a bit, not antagonize anyone or be seen to be flash with the cash.'

I hope this recession is over by the time I'm eighteen. I'm counting on a seriously swish gift-wrapped motor on the drive when I wake up on July 5th in four years' time.

'Well, as you're effectively paying for the Howards' villa,' Mum snaps, 'I think we might as well get some enjoyment out of it.'

Dad looks up sharply. 'What do you mean, *I'm* paying for it?' he says. 'What's Mindy been saying?'

'Nothing!' Mum sounds defensive. 'It just seems unfair that because of all the fees Jonathan's firm takes off the business, the Howard family can afford two weeks in a villa on the Platinum Coast whereas we, their clients, have to freeze our butts off in deepest Kent.'

Portia lurches into the room. Despite it being a warm August day she's wearing scuffed biker boots, ripped jeans, a long-sleeved black T-shirt with *Out of Control* plastered across the front in silver lettering and a black and white skull scarf slung around her neck.

'Where have you been?' Mum demands.

'Gardening with Franco,' Portia shrugs, brushing a green leaf out of her hair. 'He's teaching me about nature.' She spots what I've been trying to ignore. 'Oh put them away, Ast. We don't all need to see your bedroom furniture. What's going on?'

'Christmas is cancelled,' Mum says dramatically. 'We can't afford it!'

'Dad's upset the footie oiks because he's taken the chequebook away,' Aston explains, chucking Portia the paper and putting a tackle-hiding cushion on his lap, not just to hide his bits, but because Bentley has started to sniff him. 'They're bleating like a spoilt brat with a broken toy.'

'Why don't they mention me?' Portia whines as she scans the article. 'They just say there are three Davenport kids. I'd have liked a namecheck.'

'Look, everyone,' Dad says, getting up. 'Business is tough and there are people out there who will hate us for the decision I've had to take. They might even start to cause trouble, spread rumours, begin digging for dirt. We've all got to pull together as a family to get through this.'

He begins to pace around the room, body-swerving the sofas and the coffee table, whisky slopping in his glass.

'Daisy, you've enough accessories to last you a lifetime; Portia, it's time you got a Saturday job; Aston, sell your Lotus to raise some funds for your gap year and Chrissie,' he walks over to Mum, who's leaning against a bookcase looking absolutely horrified at Dad's *economies* speech and puts an arm around her, 'I love you even with wrinkles and grey hair.'

Oh dear, it was all going so well, other than Dad clearly not understanding the whole essential-accessory scenario.

'What are you saying?' Mum shrieks, shrugging him off. 'That I'm turning into a sad old trout?'

'No!' Dad realizes he's just lit the blue touchpaper. 'I'm just saying I don't think you need to spend thousands of pounds a year having sheep's placenta or whatever it is pumped into your face.'

'I'll let Polly go,' I volunteer. 'If it helps.'

At the back of my mind this would mean that not only could I stop feeling guilty about having a pony I never ride, it would solve the problem of Mia and Jess. Perhaps Jess could buy Polly off Dad? That would be perfect.

'There's no need for that,' Dad says. 'Polly can stay.'

'I don't mind,' I say. 'Honestly.'

'Keep her,' Dad insists.

'But I never ride her,' I try again.

'Forget about the wretched pony, Daisy!' Dad shouts.

I'm shocked. The last time he raised his voice to me was when I was about eight and I drew a rainbow on the side of a car in Davenport's showroom using a selection of colourful but indelible magic marker pens. I think my lip wobbled and my eyes watered, just as they're doing now.

'And *I* don't need some poxy job,' Portia announces. 'I can save you, like, thousands of pounds a year.'

We all stare at her.

'I'll ditch school,' she says simply. 'Save you a packet.'

'Absolutely not!' Mum erupts. 'Education is not something that can be economized on. We're not even going to discuss it, are we Jim?'

'Well—' Dad starts.

'I'm not saying I'll actually, like, leave *all* school,' Portia butts in, biting the cuticle of one of her black-painted fingernails. 'Just Park Hill. I could do A levels at Friar's Tech in town, or the sixth form at Bensham High. I'm *sooo* over elitist private education. It's immoral!'

I don't think Portia has suddenly developed socialist principles, I think it's more likely she fancies going to a school where there are boys.

'You'd be eaten alive,' Aston drawls, scratching himself under the cushion. 'A Park Hill girl at Bensham would be like throwing an injured fox to hungry hounds. They'd run you out of town, *if* they didn't break your sparrowy legs first.'

Portia looks defiant and juts her chin out. Unlike me, she's never had a problem with being assertive.

'They, like, *so* wouldn't dare,' she snarls.

'We'll discuss it after your GCSE results,' Dad says. 'When are they due?'

'The twenty-first,' Portia pouts. 'A week after the As.'

'It's not up for discussion,' Mum insists. 'If I have to, I'll cancel the automatic bug-skimmer I've ordered for the pool.' She sighs and adopts a tone of voice that implies that this will cause her immense hardship. 'But I am not, I repeat not, letting my bob get straggly or my highlights fade.'

She sweeps out of the room followed by Portia and Dad, the three of them bickering over whether it's really necessary for Portia to go to a posh school if she's just going to paint murals on the side of buildings for a living and become the new Banksy.

'I've got to go out,' Aston announces, stretching and removing his crotch camouflage, revealing what Mia would sniggeringly call his plate of meat and two veg.

'Can you give me a lift to Ollie's place in Sherlstone?' I ask, looking away. 'I've been press-ganged into feeding his cats, *again*.'

Given that Dad's been on the whisky and Mum's in a foul mood, Aston is my only method of transport.

'OK, but I'm going in five,' Aston replies. 'I've got to see a man about a dog.'

'Talking of dogs, have you seen Bentley?' I ask. There's no sign of the slobbering hound, but I can hear a gnawing noise.

I twist round to look over the back of the sofa.

'Bents!' I jump up and wrestle a silver Louboutin out of his mouth. 'Oh my God! What have you done?'

As the hound looks up, wagging his tail, I inspect the damage.

It's a footwear massacre. The right shoe is swimming in slobber, the heel is chewed, the bright red sole is covered in fang marks and the silver leather bent out of shape. The toe isn't so much peep as full frontal. I should *never* have borrowed them without asking, especially as a trip to see Mia in town hardly warranted

43

the temporary theft of designer shoes.

'They cost hundreds of pounds!' I wail. 'Mum will go mental when she finds out I've borrowed them.'

'So don't tell her,' Aston says simply. 'Then she'll never know and just blame the mutt.'

Dressed in a grey T-shirt, three-quarter length khaki shorts and brown leather flip-flops, my brother is waiting for me outside, leaning against Dad's Ferrari, swinging the keys.

'We'll go in this,' he says. There's a bleep, the indicator lights flash and a soft click as the door locks release. 'Mine's blocked in.'

'You can't!' I say, standing my ground, which is easier now I've changed into cream leather ballet flats. 'Dad won't let you.'

'He's gone for a lie-down,' Aston shrugs, climbing into the driver's seat. 'Saw him go into the bedroom. If you don't get in now, I'm going without you.'

This puts me in a difficult position. I hate going against Mum and Dad's instructions, but if I don't get a lift with Aston I'll either have to spend money on a taxi (hardly the economy Dad's suggesting), or leave Clara Simons' cats to starve to death. Forget ditching the football team, Cat Killer would really get the locals hating us.

I get in, put my seat belt on and flip my Prada sunnies down. The car roars into life and we head off down the gravel drive lined with towering glossy-green laurel bushes.

'What if those guys are there?' I say, starting to fret there's going to be some kind of ugly confrontation involving saliva and football fans. 'Someone spat at me earlier.'

'Then we'll gob back,' Aston says, without joking. 'We'll blast them with body fluid.'

Outside on the lane, more Dons fans are milling around.

Aston opens the gates and edges the Ferrari towards the men who stand in front of the exit, despite furious horn blaring.

'Out of my way!' Aston shouts, flicking his right hand at them as if he's swatting a fly. 'Move!'

'Aston!' I whisper. 'Don't upset them. Remember what Dad said.'

I love my brother because he is my brother, but I'm not blind to the fact that he can be an arrogant toff-head.

'We just want some time with your father!' one of the men calls out. 'To see if we can work something out.'

'You mean to see if he'll open his wallet again?' Aston

shouts above the sound of the revving engine. 'It's typical of you lot. Our old man has pumped hundreds of thousands of his own money into your poxy little club, and the moment things get tough and someone takes away your toy, you turn on him.' He nudges the car forward and I freak that we might run over someone's toes. 'Now eff off!'

My phone rings. I reach into my bag, pull out the dog-mauled silver shoes I've stuffed in there until I can work out where to hide them from Mum, and see Ollie's pale round moon-butt flashing on the screen of my phone.

'Ollie!' I say, as Aston swears and gives a V-sign to the fans, accelerating the car and forcing the men to jump into the hedges on either side of the lane. 'Am I glad to hear from you!'

'Have you fed the cats yet?' he asks, as at G-force speed we leave The Laurels behind. 'Were they OK?'

Chapter Four

Infuriatingly, I break a nail trying to prise out the fourth brick up and tenth brick along from the left of the start of the wall, the hiding place for the spare front door key, which is hidden not for emergency cat feeders but because Ollie's dad is always going out and forgetting his.

It seems strange to me that Judge Simons can recall huge chunks of criminal law and tiny details in ancient murder cases, but can never remember to put his key in his pocket. I also think it's rather inappropriate that a man who sends people to jail for breaking and entering houses practically invites criminals to burgle his Edwardian rectory, because as well as the not so hidden key (there's no mortar around the brick so it looks really obvious), the alarm code is 1234.

I stab the numbers into the panel by the front door,

and, after locating the store of food in the utility room, feed the cats, a process that involves sitting on the pine kitchen table with a couple of tins of cat food and a silver fork, throwing food in the general direction of the moggies whilst occasionally pretending to shoot them with a gun made out of my fingers, picking one puss off after the other as they circle the stone floor like furry sharks.

Doof! 'So long, Aristotle!'

Doof! 'Au revoir, Plato!'

Doof! 'Adios and goodnight, Socrates!'

I'll worry about going round to clean up another time, although the way these furry beasties are devouring their organic, wild, line-caught salmon with spring vegetables, they'll probably lick the floor spotless.

I lob a final few fishy chunks towards the other side of the kitchen, re-enact a rather satisfying *Doof! Doof! Doof!* Western-style shoot-out with both hands, hurriedly fill their water bowls whilst they gobble down the last morsels, and then dart back out of the kitchen, through the black-and-white-floor-tiled hall, set the alarm, close the stained glass door, stick the key back in the wall, push the loose brick in and then head back to the drive where Aston is waiting in Dad's car, rock music and the growl of five and a half litres of turbo-charged engine filling the air.

'Drop you home?' he says, backing the car out of the drive.

I think of the atmosphere at The Laurels and the footie mob at the gates.

'Can't I come with you?' I say. 'I could sit in the car and wait.'

Aston laughs. 'Don't think so, baby sis.'

'Is it a girl?' I press. 'Are you going to see some chick?'

Despite me thinking he's a stinky layabout, girls go nuts for my brother. Almost every Sunday morning a new leggy blonde appears at the kitchen table wearing nothing more than one of his T-shirts, a sheepish smile and last night's party make-up. We don't even bother to ask their name any longer: we know we'll never see them again.

Aston shakes his head. 'I'm meeting my mate Charlie.'

'Well, why can't I meet Charlie?' I shout above the noise.

He stops the car and turns down the music.

'Look,' he says. 'I'll only be half an hour or so. Why don't I drop you at Izzy's and pick you up later?'

'The Trickets are at their apartment in Marbella for August,' I grumble.

'Beatrice?'

'The Staffords have rented a *gîte* in Provence.'

'Well, Clemmie then.' Aston sounds irritated. 'The Burkes never go abroad, not after their plane made that emergency landing on water in the dark.'

'She's at her nan's in Scarborough,' I say. 'And before you mention it, I don't want to see Mia. She's got boy issues and I just don't feel strong enough.'

'Right, in that case, I'll drop you at Pegasus,' he says. 'You can see that mule you never ride but Dad won't let you ditch.'

As Aston pulls the car into the stable yard, Belinda Trotter rushes from the tack room, then stops dead in her jodhpurs. Belinda always appears harassed, as if all the horse-related problems of the world are resting on her meaty shoulders, but today the ex-three-day-event Olympic champion seems über-stressed, even for her.

'Oh, it's you,' she says, her face falling as I clamber out and Aston roars off. 'I heard the car and thought it was your father.'

'Dad?' I query. 'When does he come here?' He's even less interested in Polly than I am.

'Um . . . to sort out bills.' Belinda tugs anxiously at her thin grey ponytail. 'I read the stuff about The Dons in the paper,' she says practically yanking the hair from her scalp. 'Tell your dad . . . tell him . . . oh . . . nothing.'

And then she scuttles off back into the tack room.

Belinda has turned well weird, I think to myself as I walk across the stable yard where, along with half a dozen other ponies craning their necks to see who's arrived, Pol's peering at me suspiciously over the half-door of her stable. Even her eyes seem to be saying, 'Come on over, wimp! Bring it on, *if* you dare.'

I feel terrible that there must be girls who would give their right arm to have a pony like Polly, even if losing a limb made riding her difficult. The problem between Polly and me is I never wanted her in the first place, Mum did, but it wasn't Mum who had to sit high above the ground on a bundle of muscle intent on causing trouble.

Eighteen months or so ago, a horsey friend of Mum's came to the house, saw me on Dobbin, the antique rocking horse that sits in our hall by the window, said I had a great seat, would look *fabulous* in full riding kit, and Mum started dreaming of having coloured rosettes fluttering in the kitchen and cups on the mantelpiece. So, without consulting me, Mum contacted Belinda and Belinda found Pretty Pollyanna, a seven-year-old 14.2-hand-high palomino mare. With her golden chestnut coat and flaxen mane and tail, she looks like a peroxide blonde with a deep spray tan, a sort of chav of the horse world with a bossy gobby attitude to match.

Pol knew from the off I was scared of her and took great delight in bullying me: spooking at plastic bags in hedges; shying when a dog barked; bucking at every opportunity, leaving me either flat on my butt or hanging round her neck, clutching the reins, sobbing.

We won prizes: Mum made *sure* we entered competitions. I got firsts for Prettiest Pony and Rider, Best Turned Out and Neatest Plaited Mane and Tail, but we never got a sniff of a rosette if the competition involved any actual riding. So I stopped riding Polly, kept on visiting her, mostly with Mia during her stable-lad-lusting phase, but when I started seeing Ollie the visits stopped altogether.

I'm pathetic, I think to myself. Wanda-May Rubin wouldn't be afraid of a pony.

I stride over to the stable door with my head held high, repeating *Calm and assertive, calm and assertive*, over and over again in my head.

'Hello, Polly,' I say in what I hope is a calm and yet clearly assertive voice. 'How are you?'

I put my hand towards her and she nudges it with her velvety nose, blowing warm breath on to my outstretched palm.

This is good, I think to myself. I'm channelling my inner Wanda-May and it's working. Polly the palomino knows who's boss. But just when I think how nice it all feels, Polly's long yellow teeth nip my skin.

'Right, that's it!' I cry, pulling my hand away. 'You're going to a new home.'

'No!'

I jump, Polly neighs and from below the stable door, up pops Jessica Fawcett's freckle-head.

'Jess!' I gasp. 'You could have given me a heart attack! What on earth are you doing?'

'Seeing to Polly's hooves,' she mumbles, avoiding my eyes. 'They needed oiling. What do you mean, going to a new home? Are you moving?'

'Um, well . . .' This is going to be difficult. I'm not a good liar. 'Dad says we need to economize, and although I really don't want to, we might to have to sell Polly.'

I'm determined that rather than cut down on accessories, Polly will be my economy, whatever Dad says.

'No!' Jess says urgently. 'You can't!'

'There's no other way,' I say, hiding the Mulberry round my back. Clearly I could put the bag on eBay and make enough dosh to keep Polly for another couple of months if I really wanted to. 'Maybe you could buy her? I could have a word with Dad if you like. You could pay us back bit by bit.'

'We couldn't afford her,' Jess says sadly. 'Mum's out of work.' She eyes me suspiciously. 'Are you *sure* you can't afford to keep her?'

'Quite sure,' I say. 'It's not because of Mia.'

I could kick myself. *Hard.*

Jess gives me an odd look. 'Why did you say that?' There's a pause and then the sudden dawning of why I've mentioned Mia. 'Oh my God! That lad said he was seeing your friend. She knows about him and me, doesn't she? I am *so* dead!' Then she suddenly sags over the top of the stable door, hanging there by her armpits like some busty rag doll.

'Well, she's not happy,' I admit, as a rather disturbing image of Dom the Bull and Jess the Freckle exchanging chewed meat pops into my head. 'But I know that Dom must have started it.'

'He did.' Jess bites her lip as she drags herself off the top of the stable door. 'He just sort of pounced on me and mugged me with his mouth, right in the middle of my tea.'

'Didn't you yell, or push him away?' I ask.

Jess shakes her head. 'I was too scared,' she says. 'And shocked.'

'Oh, Jess,' I say sympathetically. 'You really need to

stand up for yourself, be more assertive. There's a good book I can recommend you read. It's called *Assertiveness NOW!*'

Chapter Five

'No way!'

As I'm standing in front of the mirror brushing my hair and wondering whether I might be more assertive if I put my hair up like Wanda-May, Portia bursts into my bedroom wearing just a white T-shirt and black knickers, her silver BlackBerry clamped to her ear.

'Like, no way!' she shrieks again. 'Straight up? No way!'

I frown as she points excitedly at the phone then jabs a finger at me before throwing herself on my bed, where she lies on her back, drumming her feet on my white duvet cover with excitement.

'God, it'll be everywhere within hours.' There's a pause. 'Oh sod it.'

She tosses her phone on the bed. 'That total troll of a woman Mitzie works with has told her to bin the call.'

She sits up cross-legged. 'Anyway, you'll never guess what's happened!'

'Mitzie's been arrested for stalking Robert Pattinson *again*?' I suggest, remembering that earlier in the year, Mitzie MacDonald's parents had to drive to London in the middle of the night to haul their eldest daughter from a hotel foyer where she'd set up camp by the reception desk and was refusing to move until she saw R Pattz and he'd sucked her neck.

'No,' Portia says dismissively, hugging her knees. 'Mitzie says you and Aston are, like, *totally* famous. You know Mitz is working in that poxy newsagent's in the hols? Well, she saw the papers come in this morning and you're in the *Kent Journal*. Big picture, front page, full colour, the works.'

I can feel every drop of blood draining towards my toes.

'Why?' I croak.

Portia snorts. 'It's still all that crap about Dad ditching The Dons. Someone took a snap of you and Aston leaving here yesterday on their moby and sent it to the *Journal*. Mitz says you look a *total* snobby cow in the picture.' She scrambles off my bed and pads over the cream deep-pile carpet to my MacBook open on the desk. 'Mitz says the paper has a website so you might even be a web sensation!'

As my stomach starts to churn, Portia begins tapping on the keyboard.

'Oh. My. God!' she gasps. 'You *do* look a complete and utter snotty rich bitch.'

With trembling legs, I go to the desk and stand behind Portia, who's staring at the screen.

Under the headline **PUTTING THE LOUBOUTINS** is a picture of me and Aston in Dad's Ferrari. Aston is curling his lip and giving a V-sign, and I'm laughing and swinging Mum's red-soled shoes in the air, the silver Mulberry sparkling on my lap, the Prada sunnies across my nose.

Portia's best friend is right: I *do* look a total bitch. If I saw that picture of a girl, all long blonde hair, swish car and designer accessories, looking as if she's laughing at the fans, I'd despise her.

'Whilst last night fans of The Dons contemplated the bleak season ahead, Jim Davenport's pampered kids were still living the high-life, driving a two-hundred-thousand-pound car and flaunting shoes worth more than four hundred pounds,' Portia reads out. 'When asked to relay a message to their father, Aston Davenport, eighteen, swore and accelerated his high-powered vehicle towards the group of concerned supporters, leaving them frightened and shocked. The full video of The Dons versus The Davs can be seen on YouTube. Parents of youngsters are warned that Aston Davenport's language is particularly foul and that Daisy Davenport, fourteen, laughed as fans ran to escape injury. The incident happened late yesterday afternoon when Little Lord Snobby and Little Miss Snooty left their million-pound-plus des res—'

'Stop! Stop!' I cry as Portia starts to scroll down the screen. 'I wasn't laughing at what was going on, I was smiling because Ollie's bum was flashing on my phone!'

'And the shoes?' Portia asks. 'What's with Mum's shoes?'

'I borrowed them,' I say weakly. 'They were on top of my phone in my bag. I was hiding them because Bents chewed them.'

Portia swings round in the chair and looks as if all her Christmases have come at once.

'Oh, my perfect little sis, you and Aston are in *so* much trouble,' she smirks. 'Mum and Dad are going to go thermonuclear. The two of you are going to positively glow with radiation.'

And boy was she right. Whoever said all publicity is good publicity is either wrong, or hasn't told my parents.

This wasn't just the usual sort of nuclear-angry parental showdown I'm used to witnessing, such as the time when Aston thought his girlfriend in the lower sixth might be pregnant (false alarm), or when the police turned up with Portia, who had collapsed on the village green, smashed on alcopops having vomited into Mum's Alexander McQueen scarf. This was Chernobyl-style shouty-crackers, a nuclear explosion the size of which has never been seen at The Laurels and has never, *ever* involved me.

'What the hell did you think you were doing?' Mum snarls at me and Aston standing in the kitchen whilst she brandishes my MacBook in our faces. 'How could you have been so stupid as to borrow my shoes and your father's car without asking?'

'Chill out, peeps,' Aston yawns. He goes to the cupboard and pulls out a jar of Nutella. 'It's not like anyone's died. In forty-eight hours no one will care about what I drive or what Daisy wears.'

He waggles an index finger in the jar and sticks a lump of brown goo in his mouth.

'I'm sorry,' I say, trying to hold back the tears. 'I just saw the shoes, they went with my bag and I never imagined . . .'

Even in my wildest worries I never thought that I'd

borrow Mum's swanky heels and find them not only plastered over the front page of the local newspaper, but also starring in their own YouTube video.

'And the Ferrari was, like, a totally bad idea, as it turns out,' Aston admits, going back into the jar for a double dip. 'I should have moved it and taken the Lotus.'

'They don't even mention me, *again*,' Portia grumbles. 'It's like I don't exist in this family.'

'Don't you kids understand?' Dad bellows, ripping the Nutella jar from Aston's hands and slamming it on to the granite work surface so hard the stainless-steel Gaggia cappuccino machine rattles. 'It's not taking the ruddy car or waggling those ridiculous shoes, it's your attitude that is at fault! Those are hard-working loyal fans and you've laughed in their faces!'

'Actually, *I* didn't laugh,' Aston points out, pointedly (and suggestively) licking each one of his fingers. 'I swore, but I didn't laugh. Daisy laughed.'

'But not at the fans!' I squeak.

'Lover boy's arse was lighting up,' Portia adds, not entirely helpfully.

Dad's face looks like an overripe blueberry about to explode and splatter over the clotted-cream coloured walls.

'Right!' he yells. 'Until further notice, you're all under house arrest!'

Despite being several miles away and therefore well out of mauling distance, Aristotle, Plato and Socrates are still stressing me out.

I tried to tell Dad that I've promised Ollie that I'd feed the cats, but he just repeated his *No one leaves this house* mantra and said that he didn't care if my boyfriend's mother's cats live or die, which I don't believe but daren't challenge, so I've spent all day worrying about what I'm going to do.

I toss my phone from one hand to another, as if it's a hot baked spud. It's almost five. I'll have to ring Ollie and tell him that due to circumstances beyond my control but partly of my making, I am unable to leave The Laurels and feed expensive fish to the furry philosophers.

Bentley follows me out through the conservatory and into the garden, as in my head I practise my call to Ollie.

Hi, Oll! Uno major problemo with the moggies' munchies. Dad's forcing everyone to stay at home until football fans stop spitting at us and the papers stop writing about us so, unfortunately, unless you can get someone else to feed them, they'll have to try to kill the odd pigeon or mouse . . .

No, I can't do it. I could have done it if I'd been brave enough to buy and read more of *Assertiveness NOW!* but I can't let Ollie's mum down and possibly ruin their holiday by sending her flying into a feline-feeding-induced panic. I'd never get my own branch on the Simons' family tree then.

I flick through my phone looking at the names of my friends. Everyone is either away or lives too far from Sherlstone to ask.

Except Mia.

Dare I ring Mia and ask her to feed Ollie's cats? I'm really surprised that I haven't heard from her, given that the Davenports have been plastered over the paper twice in twenty-four hours. Word and the Internet site has spread quickly, even abroad, as several members of The Glossy Posse have already texted to say that my hair looked fab and where did I buy those amazing shoes?

The Howards live in a small modern house in Potter's Bottom, not that far from Sherlstone, practically walking distance as long as you're not in silver peep-toes. Anyway, I never ask Mia for anything whereas she's always leaning on me, and although she's bitchy, she's totally honest, so it's not like she'll go in to feed the cats and leave with the Philippe Starck lemon squeezer in her bag.

I dial her number.

'What?'

It's a man's rough and growly voice. I must have pressed the wrong speed dial. I apologize and start again.

The same thing happens. I glance at the screen. There's a picture of Mia with a whole packet of lit ciggies in her mouth. It *must* be her number.

'Um . . . sorry. I was after Mia. Mia Howard?'

There's heavy breathing at the end of the phone, and for a moment I freak that she's been kidnapped by some pervo paedo and is being held hostage in a lock-up by a grunter.

'It's her father,' Mr Howard snaps.

'Oh!' I breathe a sigh of relief that it's a parent, not a paedo. 'It's Daisy. Is she there?'

'She's in her room and can't talk to you.'

'Oh.' This and a seriously grumpy Mr H on the line has rather thrown me. 'It's just, I was hoping that she might feed my boyfriend's mother's three pussies. The Simons family? They live in The Old Rectory, in Sherlstone.'

There's a pause and then, 'Judge Simons?'

'That's the one,' I say, watching Bentley sniff around the edge of the garden, cocking his leg by every bush. 'Cos of the stuff in the papers Dad wants us to stay here and keep our heads down, just until things blow over.'

'Very sensible,' Mr H says, sounding perkier. 'You don't want to be speaking to the press or listening to busybodies, do you? Text the details and I'll make sure the cats are fed and watered.'

'The only thing is,' I say, 'could you ask Mia to keep schtum about it? I don't think Ollie's mum would like a stranger near her precious kitties.'

'Whatever.'

And then Mr Howard cuts the call, and I stand in the garden, in the warm late afternoon sunshine, texting the moggy-minding instructions, wondering why Mia's father has committed the unforgivable parental sin of answering her phone. In the end I decide that she must have behaved badly, asked the vicar whether he goes commando under his robes or something, and Mr Howard has impounded her moby and sent her to her room as punishment.

Clearly, we're both in the doghouse with our parents.

At the bottom of the garden Bentley is barking, no doubt going mad at some furry critter who's sitting in a bush taunting him. I follow the barking to the end of the garden where Bents' bum is sticking out of the laurel hedge, his tail wagging.

'Come on,' I say. 'Get out of there, you daft hound.'

I plunge my hand into the mass of laurel leaves to grab Bentley's collar but, instead of leather, get a fistful of something lumpy.

'Yeow!' A man comes staggering out of the undergrowth, holding his crotch. 'You nearly castrated me!'

'Oh, I'm *so* sorry,' I gasp as the man stands rubbing his bits with his hands. He's solid-looking, almost totally bald and has a pale round head like a freshly-boiled potato.

'I'm your new gardener,' Spud Head says without missing a beat. 'I was spreading rotting manure.'

I might be a wimp, but I'm not stupid. Nothing stinks, there's no sign of a spade and no one muck-spreads in grey trousers, a white shirt and polished black shoes, plus, Bentley is slyly trying to remove a silver Dictaphone sticking out of the man's trouser pocket.

'Franco's our gardener,' I say, backing away. 'He's young and Spanish.'

'OK, you got me,' Spud Head shrugs. 'You must be Daisy. I'm Terry Strain from the Kent Newspaper Group.'

Ohmygod! There's a journo in the bushes snooping for a scoop! Dad will go abso mental if he sees me talking to him. I'll be grounded for life! Will Ollie still want to see me if I become a prisoner in my own home, never able to watch him play rugby or go to the cinema? You can't go out with someone if they can't actually go out, can you?

'Please go,' I say. 'I'm in enough trouble already.'

'You don't seem like Little Miss Snooty,' Spud Head says. 'In fact, you seem like a lovely girl, even though you obviously don't like me.'

'Oh, it's nothing personal,' I assure him, although I'm not sure I could ever be friends with a veg head. 'It's just, some of the stuff you printed in the paper was wrong. It's upset everyone.'

'Well, we can easily sort that out,' Spud Head says. He prises the Dictaphone from Bentley's mouth and wipes the dog-slobber off on his trousers. 'You just tell me what we got wrong and I'll put it right.'

I anxiously look around to see if anyone else is about.

'It'll all be on here, in your own voice, so there's no chance of you being misquoted or me jotting down the wrong facts,' Terry presses.

Come on, Daisy! I think to myself. *Stop being such a wimp! Tell Tel the Spud to shove his gadget where the sun doesn't shine, in a calm but assertive way, of course.*

'It's your chance to put things right, to paint your

family in a better light. And I won't say it was you who told me.'

Well, put like that . . .

I lean towards the silver machine.

'OK, well the first thing is that you said Mum was forty-six and she's only forty-four,' I gabble as the red light blinks. 'And Aston doesn't own the Ferrari, it's Dad's car, but Aston needed to see his mate Charlie and I needed to feed some cats and the Ferrari was blocking his Lotus in, so he took it, without asking.'

Terry the Spud shakes his head and whistles. 'Bet your dad wasn't happy about that.'

'And them some,' I agree. 'And Mum was livid because the shoes in the picture weren't mine either. They were hers. I'd borrowed them from her without asking and then the dog chewed them so I was hiding them in my bag.' I look at Bentley, who's at my feet chewing a stick. 'That mutt chews everything. Oh, and I wasn't laughing at the men. My boyfriend, Ollie, was on the phone. He's the son of a judge. He sent me a photo of his bare bum and I was laughing at it.'

'That all?' Terry says.

I nod.

Spud Head looks around. 'It must be lovely having all these grounds, a swimming pool, a string of ponies . . .'

'There you go again!' I say. 'I don't have a string of ponies. I have one, Polly, but she's not here. She's stabled at Pegasus, near Sherlstone.'

'You don't have, like, twenty or something?' Terry asks. 'That's what I heard. That the Davenports owned a load of top showjumpers.'

I shake my head and laugh. 'I think I'd know if we did.'

'Well, thanks,' Spud Head says, slipping the Dictaphone back in his pocket. 'You've been very helpful.'

'And you promise you'll say that the other stuff was all a mistake?' I say.

'Promise,' he says, as with a rustle of leaves his butt disappears into the hedge and I hear a car in the lane start up and drive away.

I spent the next few days totally stressed out that I shouldn't have mentioned Ollie to Terry the Spud, freaking that he might write something about a top judge's son being an exhibitionist flasher who goes around taking pictures of his private parts before texting them to young girls. But I needn't have worried. Not one word of anything I'd said to him appeared anywhere. The Davenports were knocked off the front page by a woman whose body was found stuffed in a wheelie bin in Wincheap, and, just as Aston predicted, within a couple of days everything went back to normal, which is where life has stayed and is just how I like it.

Aston got four A*s, got drunk and has either been in bed or out partying. A week after Aston's stellar results, Portia surprised everyone by getting ten good GCSEs. Dad went back to work, Mum cancelled the automatic bug-skimmer and The Dons lost their first three games of the season and are at the bottom of the table and about to go bankrupt.

Bee and Clemmie came back from their holidays and, along with some other girls from Park, we lounged around our pool, made cupcakes and played tennis.

But the best thing of all was that Ollie came home from Cornwall with an enormous box of clotted cream fudge, and we spent so long on our reunion snog in the conservatory whilst everyone was out I got chapped lips and a stiff neck.

The only odd thing was, despite ringing her, emailing her, poking her on Facebook and trying to message her, I didn't hear a squeak from Mia.

Chapter Six

I sit bolt upright in bed.

The buzzer linked to the main gate is making one long irritating noise, as if a swarm of angry wasps are riding mini motorbikes around our hall. It's no wonder Bentley is barking his head off at the front door.

'Jim! Ignore them!' Mum shrieks.

I might just have been able to put a pillow over my head to drown out the buzzer and the barking, but Mum's voice is capable of piercing a vacuum, let alone John Lewis's top of the range pillows filled with down from rare-breed organic geese.

I squint at my alarm clock. Barbie's fluorescent arms are telling me it's six in the morning.

As clearly I'm not going to be able to get any more beauty sleep, I swing my legs out of bed, put on my fluffy white towelling dressing gown swiped from The Ritz in

71

London, where we stayed after seeing *Wicked* (I *honestly* didn't realize it wasn't mine to take away until Mum told me, and by then we were home), and pad out on to the landing, just as Portia emerges from her room wrapped in a beige towel, looking surprisingly perky given that she's been woken early too.

'What the hell is going on?' she yells at me above the sound of buzzing and barking.

We go down into the hall where Mum and Dad are facing each other, Mum in a full-length cream satin nightie, Dad in a pair of canary-yellow boxers and an oversized Homer Simpson T-shirt.

'We think it's those wretched football hooligans again,' Mum snaps. 'The club officially went bust last night.' She turns on Dad. 'Jim, I know I said ignore them, but I've changed my mind. I am *not* having our Bank Holiday Monday ruined by yobs.'

She pushes him to one side and presses a finger on the intercom panel by the door. 'Go away, you horrible little men,' she shrieks. 'Go away or I'll call the police, do you hear me?'

'This is the police,' a male voice crackles through the speaker. 'We have a warrant to search these premises. Open up.'

* * *

I've never seen so many cops in one place in my life, not even on the telly.

Men and women pour through the front door and begin swarming through the house like uniformed ants, scurrying here, there and everywhere, busy busy busy in fluorescent yellow jackets with POLICE emblazoned across their shoulders, just in case we need reminding who they are. A couple of police dogs arrive, huge hairy big-nosed German Shepherds straining on short leads. Bentley stops barking but starts circling the hall, his hackles raised as he growls at the canine imposters.

Remembering I'm wearing lifted goods, I clamp my hand over the embroidered gold Ritz logo.

'You OK, miss?' a policewoman asks. 'You're not having a panic attack or anything?'

'I'm fine,' I say weakly, watching the chaos unfold before me.

'What on earth is going on?' Mum screams, her head swivelling around as if she's possessed by evil spirits. I expect under the circumstances even Wanda-May Rubin would lose her calm-assertive approach and go ape.

A tall dark-haired good-looking man in a grey suit steps forward.

'DCI Tim Long. This is our warrant.' He flicks a piece of paper in Mum's face. It could be his shopping list for all I know. 'We know what we're after.'

Oh God! Is he after my dressing gown? Has the hotel checked the room, looked at the bill and tracked it down to The Laurels? Are they searching for other unpaid-for souvenirs? There's a mountain of mini Molton Brown toiletries in the guest bathroom and an ashtray from The Savoy on the white wrought-iron table on the patio. We are *so* sunk!

But DCI Long doesn't stare at what I'm wearing. He fixes his eyes on Dad who's standing green-faced and sweaty, looking as if he feels *really* carsick.

'James Davenport?'

Dad nods and says quietly, 'That's me.'

'James Davenport, you are under arrest on suspicion to defraud Her Majesty's Customs and Excise, forgery of documents, false accounting and money-laundering. You do not have to say anything but it may harm your defence if you do not mention when questioned something you later rely on in court. Anything you do say may be given in evidence.'

For a moment there's total silence. Then Mum gasps, 'No!' and Portia screams as a policeman brandishing a pair of silver handcuffs pushes Dad's arms together and snaps the cuffs shut around his wrists.

'Dad?' I croak. I feel as if I've got a whole pond of

frogs stuck in my throat. 'Dad, what's happening?' This is obviously going *way* beyond putting a handful of tiny bottles of bubble bath and body lotion in your washbag.

'It's OK, Daisy,' Dad assures me as the frogs scuttle down my throat and start tap dancing in my gut, a feeling *way* worse than butterflies in your tummy. 'It'll all be OK. We'll get it sorted. It's all one big mistake.'

'I'll ring our solicitor,' Mum says briskly. 'Is it still that Cohen chap? The one whose wife had the obvious face lift?'

Dad nods.

'And I'll ring Ollie,' I say. I turn to DCI Long. 'My boyfriend's father's a top judge,' I explain. 'He wears a white wig and everything.'

I turn to run up the stairs to get my moby, but a burly policeman body-blocks me.

'Steady on, love,' he says, pushing me back into the hall. 'You're all to stay here, in one place, just until we've searched everywhere.'

I am nuclear furious!

I've been woken up early, Dad is in handcuffs, I'm parading around in front of strange men in a stolen dressing gown without a bra and knickers underneath, and now I've been manhandled!

'Oh, sorry,' I say, shuffling back to the centre of the hall where I lean against a polished-wood round table with a huge display of pink and white lilies in the centre. 'I didn't realize.'

A female police officer descends the stairs clutching the arm of Franco, our gardener. Strangely, whilst Portia is wearing a towel, Franco is wearing my sister's pink and white striped dressing gown.

'We found this one hiding in a wardrobe in a bedroom,' the policewoman says, a dirty smirk cracking across her face. 'Butt naked.'

'What were you doing in my daughter's wardrobe?' Mum asks Franco.

Looking at semi-starkers Portia and inappropriately dressed Franco, even I can guess the swarthy Spaniard wasn't in my sister's bedroom just to prune her spider plant.

Franco stares at his feet. Portia looks coy and tightens her towel.

'He's our gardener,' a crimson-faced Mum explains. 'He's from Barcelona.'

'And as his employer, do you have paperwork to back this up?' the policewoman asks. 'A photocopy of his passport for instance?'

'Well, no but, Franco, you must have documents and

things, don't you?' Mum's eyes are pleading with Franco to say *yes*. I suspect that she'll forgive him for being in the nuddy in my sister's wardrobe, as long as he was hiding there legally.

Franco looks sheepish. 'I have no paper. I tell Mrs D I from Spain. She give me cash. I really from Argentina. I am illegal in Ingerland.'

'Oh my God,' Mum groans, running her hands through her hair. 'This is a nightmare!'

I wish it were a nightmare as then at least there would be a chance of waking up sweaty and upset, but back to normal. When this is all over I'm binning every hotel souvenir I can find, even my collection of plastic shower hats.

'Mrs Davenport, you'll be charged with employing an illegal immigrant and this young man will be deported,' the policewoman explains to Mum.

'He will not!' Portia explodes. 'I'm sixteen! We'll, like, get married and then he can stay in the country legally. Franco! Ask me to marry you *now*!'

Wow! I wouldn't even dare ask a boy out, let alone to marry me. Wanda-May Rubin would be *so* proud of my sister.

'I already have wife in Buenos Aires,' Franco admits with a shrug. 'And a little girl, Graciella.'

Portia's face is a picture, and not a very pretty one.

'You two-timing foreign freak!' she yells. Then she turns to the policewoman. 'Either deport him or I'll kill him and bury him under the tennis court!'

A yawning Aston wanders downstairs. Only my brother could sleep through World War Three breaking out in our hall. I'm just relieved he doesn't have some pillow-lipped chick in tow.

'Some plod has just chucked me out of my pit,' he drawls, ruffling his hair. 'What's up?'

Mum's arguing with DCI Long, Dad and Franco have both been taken away to get dressed and Portia is sitting on the floor, semi-naked and sobbing, so it's up to me to fill in the details.

'Dad's been arrested for cooking the books; Mum's going to be arrested for employing an illegal alien; Franco the illegal alien has been sleeping with Portia even though he has a wife in Argentina, and Portia's going to kill him and dig up the tennis court.'

As I reel off what's happening, I can hardly believe it myself.

'Oh, and one of the police dogs has cocked its leg against the antique sideboard, but Mum doesn't know.'

'So none of that affects me then,' Aston shrugs as he

leans against the wall and scratches his crotch through his boxers.

'Lovely.'

For a moment I think the policewoman is referring to Aston's hand-to-ball co-ordination, but when I turn round she's staring admiringly at Dobbin.

'I always wanted one of these as a kid but it wouldn't fit in our flat,' she says. 'Had to make do with riding my little brother. He was OK about it, until I forced him to wear a bridle made out of old tights.'

The policewoman gives Dobbin's dappled backside a push, sending the wooden horse into more of a fast canter than a slow trot. Backwards and forwards Dobbin lunges, stirrups jangling, mane flying. If Mum weren't so busy having a fit at a policeman looking in the coat cupboard, she'd have a tantrum to see her antique horse going mental on its rockers.

And then a small plastic bag of white powder falls out of one of Dobbin's flared nostrils and plops on to the hand-tufted Chinese rug.

'Christ . . .' Aston mutters under his breath, his hands flying up to cover his face.

'Gives a whole new meaning to the phrase cokehead doesn't it, sonny?' the policewoman says sarcastically, picking up the bag and holding it to the light.

'I want to see a solicitor,' Aston says. 'Until then, I'm saying nothing.'

Dad comes down the stairs wearing a suit, shirt and tie. Unlike the rest of us he now looks calm and controlled, as if he's going to a business meeting wearing handcuffs instead of cufflinks.

One of the policemen opens the front door.

The drive is packed with police cars and vans. Dad's silver Ferrari is swinging in the air as it's winched on to a low-loader.

'It'll be fine,' Dad assures us over his shoulder as the cop leads him down the steps towards a police car, its left-side passenger door already open, a blue light flashing. 'I just need to speak to my solicitor. Tell him a few facts.'

I watch as the man guides Dad's head under the car roof before slipping into the back seat next to him.

A shiver runs through my entire body, and not just because I'm standing hardly dressed on a stone step in bare feet early in the morning, but because what's unfolding before my eyes *suddenly* hits me.

This isn't an episode of a soap or a bad dream. The police haven't come to hunt down my bathrobe or confiscate bubble bath.

They've come to take my father away.

My lovely, kind, gentle father who's so honest he won't even break the speed limit or do a U-turn in the road if the sign says *No U-turns*. The sort of man who when finding a pound coin on the pavement pops it into the nearest charity box.

And now he's been arrested on suspicion of fraud.

Something has gone *terribly* wrong.

The police car starts to move slowly away from The Laurels.

'Stop!' I yell, racing after it, tiny stones piercing my toes. 'Please don't take him! Please!'

I jog alongside the car, pleading with the driver to stop, banging on the window, sobbing as I run. Next to me but divided by glass, Dad's crying, tears rolling down his whiskery grey-green face. I've never seen Dad cry before, not even when he impaled his thigh on a blue biro that had been left on the sofa, requiring a trip to A&E, several stitches and a new pair of Armani dove-grey trousers. To see him so upset breaks my heart.

I'm sporty, but running on gravel in bare feet is hard and the police car soon edges ahead of me. As it passes through the open gates I can see Dad looking out of the back window, wide-eyed and frightened. I run towards him, still waving, still pleading with the car to stop, but it's all in vain. By the time I reach the gates, the car has accelerated down the lane and out of sight.

And then the click of a camera shutter goes off in front of me.

Pointing a silver lens at my face is Terry Strain.

The journo in the bushes.

NOW THE SHOE IS ON THE OTHER FOOT!

TUESDAY 26 AUGUST

Terry Strain: Crime Reporter

Only weeks ago Daisy Davenport, fourteen, was living the high life of the well heeled as shocked fans of Donsborough United stood bewildered at the gates of The Laurels, the luxury home of the Davenport family. Now it's Daisy who stands tearful and desolate outside her home as police carried out an early morning swoop yesterday on the Oldstone property of her multimillionaire father, luxury car importer and dealer James Davenport, 49. Computers, mobile phones, paperwork, cars and laptops were removed from the property during the thirteen-hour search of the house and grounds. Raids were also carried out at the premises of Davenport Motors on Ash Road, and at Pegasus Stables in Sherlstone, owned by ex-three-day-event champion Belinda Trotter, as well as inquiries at the offices of Davenport's accountants, Aspland & Stratton.

According to police sources, two arrests have been made, a 49-year-old man and a 55-year-old woman. Both are currently helping police with their inquiries, but at the time of printing, no charges have been brought. It is believed that the raid followed several weeks of investigation into fraud involving the false preparation of paperwork, conspiracy to defraud HM Customs & Excise by false VAT reporting and money-laundering.

David Cohen, solicitor for the Davenport family, strongly denied any wrongdoing by his client and attributed the raid to misinformation given to Kent Police.

In a separate development, Aston Davenport, son of James Davenport, was arrested and charged with possession of a class A drug and has been bailed to appear at Canterbury Magistrates Court next month.

Chapter Seven

'I just wanted to tell your mother how sorry I am about all this nastiness.' Mia's dad is standing on our doorstep, his nose twitching. 'Can I come in?'

He doesn't wait for a reply, but scuttles straight towards me. To avoid body-contact I step back, and before I know it Jonathan Howard is in our hall.

With his carroty hair and yellow buck teeth poking through his grey and ginger beard, I've always thought Mr Howard is the spitting image of a weasel. A suit-wearing, round-shouldered, bad-tempered little mammal. It's not just me who can't stand Jonathan Howard; from the little Mia says about her dad, she's not his greatest fan either. I sometimes think it's why she behaves so badly, just to wind The Weasel up.

'Mindy and I were shocked when we read the paper and saw your picture,' he twitters, his eyes darting hungrily around the paintings, the furniture and the knick-knacks, as if he's looking for a mouse to eat or a bird's-nest to rob. 'Someone must have tipped off the press. Any idea who?'

'My picture?' In my sleep deprived and anxious state, I vaguely remember a camera being shoved in my face.

The Weasel opens his briefcase and hands me a copy of this morning's *Kent Journal*.

The snap is a close-up of me with unbrushed hair, in flood of tears, two snot rivers oozing from my nose and The Ritz written across my chest. I can't imagine The Glossy Posse complimenting me on *this* shot.

For one dreadful moment I think The Weasel is going to lunge forward and kiss me, so I'm mega relieved when he reaches towards me, not to plant a smacker on my cheek but to give me the post he's holding.

'I met the postie at the gate,' he explains, handing me a pile of envelopes and pizza delivery leaflets. 'Is your mother around? I didn't see her car outside.'

'The police took it,' I say. 'And all the others. I'm sorry, Mr Howard, but I don't think Mum's up to seeing anyone at the moment.'

Aston came back from the cop-shop just after lunch having been charged with possession of cocaine, then fell asleep on the sofa where he lay dribbling on the purple velvet all afternoon, even though at one stage the police actually lifted up the sofa to have a look underneath.

Portia stayed in her towel but sat by the pool making an alarmingly realistic figurine of a man holding a spade and a bunch of carrots out of Blu-Tack, before ripping its head off and hurling it into the water.

Mum came back by taxi about midnight last night looking grey, shattered and haggard. She said Dad's solicitor would be working everything out, but until then she needed a hot shower and a good night's sleep and that we'd talk in the morning.

As Krystina had the Bank Holiday off anyway, I'd spent the day making tea and tuna and mayo sandwiches for the police, who were actually really rather sweet, even when they were rifling through my knicker drawer and peering up my rag doll's dress.

And now it's ten in the morning, and whilst I've been up for hours helping Krystina put things back exactly as they were before the police moved them around, there's been no sound from anyone else's room.

'Jonathan!' An immaculately made up Mum stands on the landing, her arms outstretched, like an angel in Armani. 'How sweet of you to come.' In a flutter of cream silk and pearls, she sweeps down the stairs and into the hall, kissing The Weasel once on each cheek. 'Coffee?'

I'm staggered. It's as if she's wiped from her mind that this time yesterday Dad was in handcuffs, Portia was in tears and Aston was in trouble. She's just carrying on as if *nothing* has happened. In fact, she was in more of a state when a nervy Mindy Howard dropped a glass of red wine on the cream carpet in the sitting room last Christmas, but I expect she knows Dad will come out of jail, whereas, despite Krystina spending hours on her hands and knees with cans of Vanish and a wet cloth, the stain has never come out and we've had to put a rug over it.

'I'd love some coffee,' Jonathan says eagerly. 'If it's not too much trouble.'

'Of course not, come through.'

Mum heads to the kitchen, past the pot of Fair Trade rich-roasted organic coffee from Nicaragua, which Krystina has set up on the side, and towards the kitchen table. 'Daisy, be a darling and bring some over, will you?'

Mum and Jonathan sit down. At warp speed I bung sugar and spoons on a tray, slop coffee into two mugs, grab a milk carton from the fridge and take the whole lot over to them. The Weasel gives me the creeps but I want to find out what's really going on. About four in the morning, going through everything in my mind, I'd remembered the conversation Dad and I had on the purple sofa, the one where he'd asked me whether I'd forgive him if he'd done something wrong. Is this what he was referring to?

'So, how is Jim?' Jonathan asks, his nose twitching, his voice as pinched and weaselly as his face. 'Is he bearing up?'

I put the tray on the table and sit down opposite Mum and next to The Weasel.

'I haven't seen him.' Mum rolls her eyes at the fact I've put the milk carton on the tray rather than pour it into an Emma Bridgewater spotty jug. 'They were still questioning him when I left. David Cohen is sorting this whole mess out, including,' she lowers her voice, 'all that stuff with Aston and Franco. It's nothing that can't be sorted.'

I feel relieved that someone is trying to get Dad out of jail. Ollie has been a complete let-down. He finally rang on the house phone late last night to say his dad couldn't do anything, and even if he could, he wouldn't.

'You do understand, sweets?' Ollie had said. 'Dad doesn't want to be put in an awkward position. Even you asking me to ask him was a bit dodge.'

I told Ollie I was sorry that I'd asked him to ask his dad, and then got off the phone and squeezed a lemon in the fruit bowl so hard a pip flew straight through the yellow peel and hit me in the eye.

'And you're sure this Cohen chap is the right man?' Mia's dad presses. 'He's got a good reputation for this sort of thing?'

'Absolutely,' Mum nods. 'David says that most successful businessmen have had a run-in with the law at some point in their careers. Disgruntled staff, jealous rivals, that sort of thing. We think it's just an angry football fan causing trouble, spreading rumours. David's going to ring me when Jim's released. It's a pain they've taken my car though.'

'You can use Mindy's motor whilst yours is being held,' The Weasel gushes. 'I'll tell her to leave it at my office with a tank of petrol.'

'That is so sweet, Jonathan. Thank you.' Mum reaches across the table and pats his arm.

Beside me Jonathan Howard gives a tight little cough, as if he's about to chuck up a hairball. 'Um . . . the police asked me a few questions, but of course I couldn't tell them anything.' He shuffles in his chair and does the hairball thing again. 'I did actually have a falling-out with Jim over him pulling out of The Dons.'

I glance sideways. Mr Howard's nose has gone into twitch overdrive and he's wringing his paws as Mum begins to flick through the letters I've put on the table, opening them with the handle of a silver teaspoon.

'I felt he should have warned me what was going to happen, just in case there was a backlash. We had words—'

'Damn!' Mum interrupts The Weasel. 'Park Hill have written to say Jim hasn't paid the fees for the start of the new term.' She tosses the letter down and starts opening others. 'I'll get him to sort it out when he's back later.'

School fees are the least of my problems. I'm phoneless and it's as if I've lost a limb.

'Can you find out when we can get our mobiles and things back?' I ask. The police took away my iPhone and my MacBook in plastic bags and I just know that there will be millions of texts and emails from the girls, asking how I am, commiserating with me on how rank my hair looks in the newspaper photie, wondering about The Ritz dressing gown.

In the hall, the house phone rings. Krystina puts her head around the door.

'A Mr Cohen?' she queries, holding the cordless phone towards Mum.

'I'll take this in another room,' Mum says, getting up. 'Jonathan, lovely to see you. Thank Mindy for the car and maybe see you both for drinks soon?

Daisy, can you see Mr Howard out?'

I immediately spring up hoping this is a signal for The Weasel to scurry back to his den, and feel relieved when he gets up from the table. But as he walks through the kitchen, he stops and leans against one of the counters and begins to look slowly around, staring at the green Aga, the central black-granite-topped island with its restaurant-standard gas hob, the rows of copper pans and shiny silver utensils. I just hope his eyes don't stop on me and look me up and down in the same way he's looking at our fridge right now. He's practically drooling, stroking its stainless steel door and running his mottled hand lightly over the silver letters S M E G.

Finally, Jonathan Howard stops salivating over the kitchenware and says abruptly, 'I'm off.'

Followed by a waggy-tailed Bentley, who loves everyone, even weird weaselly accountants, Jonathan Howard scuttles to the front door and out on to the drive, where his car, a black soft-top BMW identical to Mum's, is parked with the roof down. Business must be good at Aspland & Stratton if their staff, even senior staff, can zoom around in top of the range sports cars.

'Is Mia OK?' I ask, as Mr Howard gets in. 'I haven't heard from her.'

'She's working hard,' The Weasel says curtly, starting

the engine. 'Always in her room, studying.'

That doesn't sound like Mia, especially when it's the holidays. But I don't have any time to question Mr Howard further as he slams the door shut and, spraying my ankles with gravel, roars off down the drive.

Back in the house I notice that the light on the base unit of the phone in the hall isn't lit. Mum must have finished her call with Dad's solicitor.

'Mum!' I call out. 'What's the news about Dad?'

Silence.

'Mu – um!'

Not a peep.

I look in the kitchen, the sitting room and the dining room. I knock on the door of the downstairs bathroom, check Dad's study, which has been stripped bare of files and papers by the police, then the games room and the conservatory. I look outside by the pool and skirt round the tennis court but don't bother with the garage as there are no cars to park in them at the moment, and with still no sign of her I go back into the house.

I'm just about to dart up the stairs to see if Mum's in her room when I notice Bentley scrabbling and whining at the cloakroom door. I didn't look in there because unless you're ten and in trouble for peeing in the

Christmas punchbowl during a party (Aston), or fifteen and too drunk on smuggled cheap cider to get up the stairs to bed (Portia), no one hides in a coat-filled cloakroom. But something is worrying the hound.

I pull the dog back by his collar and open the door.

'Mum!'

She's slumped on the floor, surrounded by Ugg boots, muddy wellies and pink Crocs, clutching the phone in her right hand, looking shocked and shaking like a jelly.

I rush in and bend down to try to pick her up but she doesn't move, even when Bentley licks her face. This really freaks me out as Bentley's breath is so rank it's capable of rousing the dead, let alone a slumped shaking mother.

'Mum, what is it?' I'm really scared now, and it's not just because sitting on the floor in cream silk is such an un-Mum-like thing to do. Her teeth are chattering as if she's been left outside on a freezing mountain in the depths of winter, except it's the end of August and she's in the depths of our cloakroom, which has under-floor thermostatically controlled heating.

'I – I – didn't – want – you – to – to – see – me – like – this,' she says, gasping for breath between each word. 'Sor-ry.'

'Is it Dad?' I ask.

'Yes,' she gulps.

'Is he dead?' I cry. 'Is Dad dead?'

Now *I'm* shaking. Lying in the dark last night, one of my sleepless nightmares had involved Dad being throttled in the shower by a mad Dons fan already inside for murder and with nothing to lose.

Mum shakes her head. 'Worse – than – dead.' She can hardly get her words out. 'Much – *much* – worse.'

What on earth can be worse than being dead? The only thing I can immediately think of is being un-dead. Has Dad morphed into a weird-eyed zombie?

Still shaking and now crying, Mum looks up at me. She's got a green Barbour draped over her head, a hockey stick poking out from behind her back and Bentley has started to mount her leg. She looks barking mad, like Wee Woman, the homeless old lady who wanders around town smelling of wee, pushing her stuff in a Tesco trolley, her scruffy white dog perched on top of a pile of black bin bags.

'Your father is guilty,' she croaks.

I stare at her, the conversation on the purple sofa flooding my brain.

'Guilty. Guilty. Guilty,' Mum parrots, in case one *guilty* isn't enough for me.

My head swims, my legs go to jelly and I have to grab

a handful of coat material to steady myself. I feel as if I'm being dragged backwards at high speed into a long black tunnel. I wouldn't be surprised if I was sucked up into the sleeve of a random Puffa jacket and deposited in a heap on the shelf above me.

Did I hear right? Dad's *guilty*?

I haven't been sucked into a sleeve, but I feel light-headed and my legs won't hold me up any longer, so I slide down next to Mum, pull a yellow flip-flop out from under my butt and lean against the coats, the sound of blood rushing in my ears, my heart banging in my chest so hard I'm convinced it's about to explode.

'Are you sure?' I ask, willing Mum to say that there's been a terrible mistake, that Dad has been set up or tortured into a confession. 'When he was arrested he said all this was a mistake.' I'd been clinging on to his words, sure that he wouldn't lie to me, telling myself that our sofa conversation had been about football, not fraud.

'Quite sure.' Mum pushes Bentley off her leg and he starts on me. 'For some reason he changed his story.'

She drops the phone in her lap and wipes her nose with the back of her hand. 'His solicitor rang to say that, against his advice, your father has pleaded guilty to all the charges: fiddling the VAT; forging documents; taking money out of the company he wasn't owed;

money-laundering, you name it.' She sighs, sniffs back snot and shakes her head. 'He'd have confessed to global warming and the demise of the ruddy dodo if they'd asked him.'

'And who was the woman the paper mentioned?' I ask. 'What's she got to do with this?' Could Dad be having an affair on top of stealing money? Was he nicking money for some foxy mistress?

'Belinda Trotter from the stables. He was using her to launder the money and she was keeping a cut of it. She confessed once he did. They're both facing jail sentences; David Cohen thinks several years, at least.'

So *that's* why Belinda was all stressy the day I saw her. Dad being in the papers had obviously freaked her out.

'There must be something we can do,' I say, panic rising within me. 'Someone Dad knows. A better lawyer, one who costs more money, or—'

Mum puts her arm around me.

'Daisy, we have no money. I'll have to discuss it with Jonathan, but it seems we owe hundreds of thousands to the bank, to the mortgage lender, your school, tax, the VAT people, the list is endless. The police will be freezing our bank accounts to get back the money your father swindled from the revenue. It's not only the football club that's gone bust; *we're* bankrupt. This life of ours here at

The Laurels is finished. Your father is going down and he's dragging us down with him.'

DAVENPORT CHARGED

WEDNESDAY 27 AUGUST

Terry Strain: Crime Reporter

Well-known local businessman and ex-Donsborough United chairman James Davenport, 49, has appeared in court this morning charged with forgery and fraud. Davenport, of The Laurels, Oldstone, has been charged with conspiring to defraud HM Customs & Excise, ten counts of forging paperwork, eight counts of fraudulent use of documents and ten counts of money-laundering.

All the offences are alleged to have taken place during the last twelve months.

Belinda Trotter, 55, of Pegasus Livery Stables, Sherlstone, is charged with forging paperwork and money-laundering.

Pleas of guilty by both parties were entered when Davenport and Trotter appeared in court.

James Davenport was refused bail. Belinda Trotter was allowed conditional bail.

A date for sentencing has been set for 11 November.

Chapter Eight

Dad's not coming home, possibly for about two years.

The judge won't let him have bail because he thinks if he lets him out before he puts him away again he'll run off to live on a Brazilian beach with a woman in a thong, or maybe it was a woman with a Brazilian in a thong on a beach, or at least that's what Mum said when she came back from court via the offices of Aspland & Stratton, where she had a meeting with The Weasel and collected Mindy Weasel's car, a maroon Porsche Cayenne 4x4 with a green pine tree air freshener dangling from the rear-view mirror.

Jonathan Howard has confirmed that we *are* bankrupt, in other words, we owe more than we own, and what we do own is about to be owned by other people.

Mum needs to find a job. She also has to catalogue all her jewellery and the antiques so they can be sold and the money given to a long list of people who are waiting for their bills to be paid. Worst of all, we have to pack up and leave The Laurels as soon as possible because the bank is about to repossess it. Thank goodness we didn't spend needless money on that automatic bug-skimmer after all.

And now we're all sitting in the sitting room (except Aston who's lying on the floor with his feet on the coffee table), trying to make a list of people who might lend us money so that we don't end up like Wee Woman, or if we do, that we use a trolley from Waitrose.

So far Mum – still puffy-faced and prone to sudden bouts of spontaneous sobbing – has discounted the bank (we already owe them zillions), her parents (too poor), Dad's parents (too dead) and Aunty Karen on my dad's side (never talked about, but last heard of running a tattoo parlour in Goa with a woman called Illusion).

And when we tried to think of a job that Mum could do straightaway without any training or qualifications, the only thing anyone (Portia) could think of was becoming a prostitute.

'We're just like Roberta, Phyllis and Peter,' I sigh. 'The same thing happened to them and they had to leave their big house for a tiny cottage.'

'What the hell are you talking about?' Portia sneers

at me. 'More losers you know?'

'*The Railway Children*!' I squeak. 'Their father got sent to jail! Don't you remember Bobbie running along the platform shouting, "Daddy! My Daddy!" when he came home?'

Remembering the heartbreaking scene starts me off sobbing. It's like me running after Dad in the police car, but of course I was dressed in a stolen white towelling dressing gown rather than red flannel petticoats or whatever Bobbie was wearing.

'The difference, you idiot,' Portia snarls, 'is that *their* father wasn't guilty, whereas ours is guilty as hell.'

Portia hasn't taken the news that Dad is taking a long holiday in one of Her Majesty's prisons very well, though she did cheer up when she spotted a slim silver lining in an otherwise dense black cloud, which was that with no money for school fees she could leave ruinously expensive Park Hill for A levels at Friar's Tech or Bensham High after all. She's also got it into her head that having a relative in jail could be seen as rather cool by the punk brigade, though I'm not sure that fiddling the VAT counts as system-busting anarchy, just theft.

And Aston?

I don't think it's dawned on my brother just how serious this all is. When Mum told him what was going on he just yawned, scratched his bits and muttered, 'Bummer.'

I hope he's a bit more pulled together when he appears in court next month charged with stuffing drugs up Dobbin's hooter or the judge will think he's still snorting the funny stuff. Actually, I hope he'll manage to stay upright long enough to stand in the dock. As it's his first offence he won't be sent to jail, but he will have a criminal record, so his hopes of going to uni in America have been shattered as he can't get a visa. Only now do I realize what he meant when he said he was going to see his mate 'Charlie'.

'But still, their dad was in jail,' I point out. 'Same problem, different century.'

'And did their mother sell her body to survive?' Mum asks.

Good grief! What sort of mother thinks *The Railway Children* is a tale of prostitution?

'Their mum wrote stories, sold them and bought iced buns for tea,' I explain, trying to sound bright.

'I failed English at school,' Mum says glumly. '*And* pretty much everything else. Exams weren't my strong point.'

Now Mum's mentioned school, I decide to mention one of my major worries (global warming and terrorist bombs seem insignificant at the mo).

'Will I still be able to go to Park Hill next week?' I ask, remembering the letter on the thick cream paper. 'Can we afford the fees?'

Mum noisily blows her nose.

'I'm not sure,' she says, as my stomach hurtles towards my feet. 'Jonathan thinks we might be able to get some sort of hardship bursary for both of you. I've got a meeting with Mrs Channing tomorrow, at nine-thirty.'

My stomach stops performing circus acts at this fantastic news. The thought of leaving fabulous Park Hill with its stylish uniform, beautiful grounds and wood-panelled assembly hall, not to mention The Glossy Posse girls, had been so gutting, I couldn't even think about it without wanting to hurl myself in the bug-infested pool and hold my breath. But now there's a chance that when term starts I'll be back in the assembly hall with its stained glass windows, belting out the school song and planning what I'm going to choose for lunch. There's a fabulous salad bar where the chef cuts the cherry tomatoes and cucumber into water lilies and tulips. I'd *really* miss those flowery salads. And when Mum meets Mrs Channing, the headmistress is bound to make a special case for me.

I've always been a model pupil, first up with my hand

to be a hamster monitor even though the ratty thing was renowned for eating fingertips, or volunteering to stir the whiffy paint in art class because it gave our teacher a migraine if she so much as sniffed a molecule. I even put myself forward as a real-life Resusci Anne when the rubber doll we were supposed to be using in first aid didn't turn up. It was all going so well until Tilly Nash practically burst my boobs by pumping on my chest so hard, I had to go and lie down in the first aid room and take painkillers. Of course, Tilly came in and was all sobby and sorry and pretended it was a mistake, but everyone knows she really fancied Ollie and was narked when he asked me out at the inter-school disco, so I wouldn't put it past her to have bounced on me in an act of jealous revenge.

'Remind her I was Resusci Anne,' I urge Mum. 'Remind her my boobs almost exploded.'

'I'll do my best,' Mum promises. 'For both of you.'

'Don't worry about me,' Portia sniffs. 'I'm never going back to that bourgeois bastion of middle-class educational values, not even if Alicia Channing begs me to.'

'So, what did Mrs Channing say,' I ask, practically ambushing Mum at the front door. It's nearly two in the afternoon and given that her meeting at the school was first thing, I thought she'd be back hours ago. 'Is there a bursary?'

'There is,' Mum replies, putting Mrs Weasel's car keys on the sideboard and dumping several green plastic shopping bags on the floor. 'There's one bursary not yet allocated.'

Oh, happy happy joy joy!

I knew it! Despite not being able to sleep last night for worrying, deep down I just *knew* Mrs Channing wouldn't want to lose me, a girl who for the good of the school would risk injury from hamsters, stinky paint and jealous girls. Being tall, I'm pretty handy on the netball court too, so perhaps she took that into account. Oh, and this sounds really awful, but I know for a fact that several people said I looked really good in the picture they used of me holding a test tube in the chemistry lab in the school brochure. It's not everyone who can carry off safety goggles, but I'm proud to say I made those goggles look as good as designer sunnies.

I skip around the table in the hall with delight, and, quite frankly, having not heard from Ollie or the girls I need some good news.

'But not for you.'

I stop mid-skip, as if my body has been instantly frozen. I'm aware that I'm impersonating a flamingo in our hall, but I don't seem to be able to get my left leg to move.

What's Mum saying? That there's money for a year of school fees floating around, but Mrs Channing thinks someone else should get it?

Who?

Who do I know who just days before the start of a new school year has found themselves in the position of being penniless, possibly homeless with their father in jail?

Who else could *possibly* be as unlucky as me?

'For Portia,' Mum says. 'I'm really sorry, Daisy.'

'Portia?' I gasp, my foot finally hitting the floor. 'But Portia's going to Friar's Tech!'

'Nooo,' Mum says slowly. 'Portia *wants* to go to Friar's Tech, but Mrs Channing and I agree she'd do much better finishing her education at Park Hill. They let the pupils come and go at Friar's, whereas Park will keep an eye on her, make sure she realizes her potential.'

I can't believe I'm hearing this. I can't believe that Mrs Channing has chosen to give money to my wayward sister rather than me! When did Portia ever volunteer to have her chest battered or her fingers bitten? Has Portia even set foot on a netball court in the last year, unless it was to have a crafty fag away from the teachers, let alone to set up too many goals to count?

'Did you remind her I was the stand-in rubber doll?' I croak, slumping against the table and almost knocking over the vase of wilting lilies. 'Has she forgotten about all the stuff I've done?'

'Of course not,' Mum assures me. 'Mrs Channing says she'll be really sorry to lose you, but that you'll do well whatever school you go to. You're popular, you work hard, keep your head down, stay out of trouble and will easily fit in somewhere new. Portia is trickier; she needs more guidance, less distractions, especially since . . .' she looks around the hall and up the stairs and whispers, 'Franco.'

Ger-rate. I'm being punished for being a model pupil. Clearly if I'd slept with an illegal married gardener, put holes in my nose and hacked at my own hair with nail scissors in English lit, Mrs C would be practically pushing cheques in my direction.

'Anyway, Mrs Channing was very helpful. She made some calls, pulled some strings and has got you into another school at *very* short notice. They start on Monday but you don't have to go in until Tuesday, so they can really look after you.'

'But I don't want to leave Park!' I cry under my breath. 'It's not fair!'

'Daisy, don't give me a hard time.' Mum's heard me. 'I've got enough to deal with at the moment.'

I want to scream and rant and rage. I want this to be my Gherkin Moment, the moment where I stamp my feet and start pulling over the reproduction Ming vases and scribble on the watercolour paintings, and let everyone know that Daisy Davenport isn't going to leave Park Hill without a fight.

'OK,' I squeak, fighting back the tears and ramming my clenched fists into the back pockets of my shorts. 'Sorry.'

'I popped in and met the head there, a Miss Birch. Not the same style of leadership as Alicia Channing but, well . . .' Mum's voice trails off. 'There's your navy blazer and a new black jumper.' She nods towards the bags. 'You've got lots of white shirts and you can wear the black Marc Jacobs skirt you wore to Granddad's funeral.'

Asda are selling school uniforms? Since when did you pop a sliced white and a blazer in your basket? The uniform at Park Hill was sold in a special shop where you had to queue for hours and then pay masses of money for a brown blazer edged in cream silk piping. They even supplied matching brown velvet scrunchies for our hair. What sort of school sells their uniform along with a bag of frozen petite pois?

'Where is this school?' I ask, trying not to let too much bitterness creep into my wobbly voice. 'Where have you and Mrs Channing decided to send me?'

Mum bites her lip and takes a deep breath.

'I'm sorry, Daisy. If there was another option at this stage, believe me, I'd take it. You're starting Year 10 at Bensham High next week.'

'The school for chavs?' I gasp, as Mum trudges up the stairs with the bags. 'You're sending me to Chaverama High?'

Not for the first time in the last few days I wonder if I've had a bang on the head and am actually unconscious and having weird nightmarish dreams. Perhaps at any moment I'll wake up in a hospital bed covered by starched white sheets, listening to bleeping machines, look up at the light and hear someone gasp, 'She's come round! Daisy's out of her coma! To think we nearly switched off the ventilator!', and Dad's not on remand in jail awaiting sentencing for fraud, but bending over my hospital bed looking relieved. Or perhaps I've been sucked through a wormhole and have entered the Davenport Dimension, a strange parallel world where, instead of life being peachy, *everything* goes horribly wrong. I just need to turn round three times and say the magic phrase (Dolce & Gabbana? Harvey Nicks?) and I'll be deposited back in my usual life of expensive schools, tennis courts and designer accessories.

But my life isn't a dream, it's shocking reality. Portia screaming at the top of her voice that she doesn't want to go back to Park Hill confirms I'm awake and living the nightmare.

What was it Aston said to Portia about Bensham High? *The Bensham Bitches would run you out of town, if they didn't break your sparrowy legs first.*

I look down at my legs. They're not as skinny as my sister's, but I'm quite fond of them. They not only keep me upright and keep me moving, they look quite good in shorts. They're not going to look as good or work as well with a couple of great white plaster casts stuck on them.

What on earth am I going to do?

How am I going to cope with the Bensham girls if I can't stand up to Mum or Mia or even Ollie's mum's cats?

Who's going to help me now?

Mrs Channing has let me down; I haven't heard from Mia; Ollie is more worried about embarrassing his dad than comforting me; Portia will be cocooned in Park Hill; Mum's up to her eyes in her own problems; Dad has let *everyone* down; and Aston is barely awake enough to know what's going on at the best of times.

There's only one person who can help me now.

One person who can prevent my legs from being broken.

One person who can show me how to stand up for myself in an Asda school uniform.

One person who can turn me from timid to tough, maybe even make me president.

Wanda-May Rubin. The woman with the scary hair.

Now, more than ever, I need that copy of *Assertiveness NOW!*

Chapter Nine

I practically sprint to WHSmith.

It doesn't close until six and it's only four, but I need to start the Wanda-May regime asap. No furtive page flicking or casual chapter-surfing for me. I need to invest £9.99 to buy *Assertiveness NOW!* if I'm to become as fearless as Ms Rubin by Tuesday morning. And I no longer need to worry about Krystina finding the book hidden at the bottom of my scanty drawer as, after five years of being with us, poor Krystina has been given a bottle of Scotch, the pick of the freezer, a glowing reference and the sack, there being no money to pay for a housekeeper because within weeks we'll have no house to keep.

I shoot through the door of Smith's, and then, slowing my pace so as not to attract unwanted attention, saunter casually to the sports section and make a beeline for the football books. There are still two copies of *West Ham: The Glory Year*, but no sign of Wanda's book nestled between their claret and blue spines. Sweating slightly, I pull out the books, look on either side of them, even search between the rugby titles below, but Wanda-May has vanished.

Not to worry, for once. She must be back where she belongs in the self-help section, sitting alongside books about getting over miserable childhoods or mending shattered hearts.

Except, she isn't.

I've done the whole A–Z-of-authors sweep twice, once with my sunglasses on and once without. I've looked between books on giving birth and books on dying, behind a huge hardback about graphic gynaecological things, and a tome about conquering depression by eating potatoes, but *Assertiveness NOW!* has vanished. Obviously someone more assertive than me has bought it, and, quite frankly, if someone is assertive enough to buy it without taking weeks to pluck up the courage, they don't need the book as much as I do.

'Can I help you?' A woman in a blue-checked shirt is standing beside me.

She looks so kind, so helpful, so sympathetic, she makes me want to collapse on her checky shoulder and sob, 'Yes, please! Can you help me get my father out of jail, stop me going to a scary school and sell me a winning lottery ticket, even though I'm not yet sixteen?' But I suspect she just means help in a book-searching rather than life-changing way.

I hesitate for a moment. This woman works in Smith's, a shop that is flooded with newspapers. I've been on the front of said newspapers at least twice in the last few weeks. It was bad enough coming up here on the train, wondering if people recognized me despite my cunning disguise of tied back hair, massive tortoiseshell sunnies and a brown and white tweed trilby I found in the cloakroom, but do I really want Mrs WHSmith knowing Daisy D's a wimp and possibly selling her story to the papers? Not on your life.

On the other hand, I need that book, badly.

'Miss?' the woman enquires.

'I'm after a book,' I practically whisper. 'It's by Wanda-May Rubin and it's called *Assertiveness NOW!*' I try to emphasize the NOW! without raising my voice. 'You used to stock it.'

'And you've looked on the shelf?' Check Woman asks, as if I've just marched into the shop and demanded the book without even bothering to look for it myself.

'It's gone,' I say. 'I mean, it's not there.'

'Tim!' Check Woman screams across the shop. 'We got a book called *Assertiveness NOW*? This young lass is after it.'

Just tell the whole shop, won't you? I think, feeling my cheeks flush. *Just stick a great big neon sign over my head saying: Wimp!*

Tim starts tapping away on a keyboard, and to prevent more loudhailer type announcements across the shop floor I head towards him.

'Out of stock,' Tim says in a nasally voice, keeping his speccy eyes on the screen. 'But we can order it.'

I think for a moment. I'll try somewhere else. If I don't get it by Saturday, thereby giving me at least two days of reading time, it will be too late, as when the book finally arrives I won't even be able to walk to the shop to pick it up because by then my legs will be busted by the Bensham Bitches.

'It won't take long.' Tim peers at me through his milk bottle lenses, which have a pale pink sticking plaster wrapped around the left hinge. 'A few days, max.'

Really, someone should take him to Specsavers and point him towards the disposable contacts. Without the rank glasses he'd be OK, *if* he also lost the pudding-bowl haircut and sorted out the rampant razor rash on his turkey neck. The pointy ears might need surgery

114

though, unless some girls are heavily into the Trekky Spock look.

'Would you like to place an order?'

Just say: No, thank you, I think to myself. Tim isn't asking me out for a pizza or to go to a Star Trek convention with him. He isn't going to go home and cry just because I didn't order the book.

But what if he's on commission and the book makes the difference between affording contact lenses or sticking with the mega specs? What if he always has to wear broken milk bottles because I didn't order the book? No one will ever go out with him and he'll end up leading a sad and lonely life *all* because of me.

'Yes, please,' I say feebly.

'Your name?' Trekky Tim asks.

I panic. What am I going to do? If I say *Daisy Davenport* that will really give the game away. I might as well take off my hat and glasses, throw them in the air and shout, 'Yes, it's me, Daisy! Daughter of the car conman!'

'I need a name and telephone number,' Tim presses, his bony hand hovering over the keyboard like some alien claw. 'Then we can let you know when the book's in.'

This is tricky. Not only will Trekky Tim have my name, he'll have my details to ask me out, and then I'll be in trouble. I mean, even though I haven't heard from him, I'm going out with Ollie who's my *Just Say No* date shield, but this Tim really does look like the sort of lad who would be crushed if, having picked up enough courage to ring me, I knocked him back. And knowing me I'd end up saying Yes and then be ill with worry about how I was going to get out of the date and keep it all from Ollie.

It's leprosy-gate all over again.

I can see how these bigamists get into trouble. They probably didn't mean to be married to more than one person at the same time, but when the second one asked it must have seemed so rude to say No, especially if they'd gone to all that expense and bother of choosing a ring.

'My name's Ollie Simons,' I say. 'Short for Olivia. And my mobile number is 07973 . . .'

I get out of Smith's before I agree to order something else I don't want under a false name, like a book on extreme ironing. I'm going to have to ring Ollie and tell him that if a man called Tim phones to say there's a copy of *Assertiveness NOW!* waiting for him in WHSmith, it's actually for me. Quite how I'm going to explain why I used him as a cover and what I'm doing ordering a book like that, I'm not yet sure. Now I've got to hotfoot it to Waterstone's to see if they have Wanda-May in stock. I'm going to end up with two copies and spend twice as much as I intended to.

This book had better perform miracles.

'Daisy!'

'Ohmygod!'

'Poor you!'

It's The Glossy Posse: Beatrice Stafford, Clementine Burke and Isabella Tricket. They're standing in front of me, jumping up and down, shrieking and flapping their hands in the air like three demented Bratz dolls.

Bee and Clem are a bit like bug-eyed lollipops, tiny with big heads wobbling on the end of their skinny necks, but Izzy T is a babe: glossy dark hair, wide eyes, white smile, the total package. Mrs Channing used her on the cover of the school brochure, and I know for a fact that several boys pretended they were parents of girls and wrote in asking for a copy.

'God, things must be mega rough for you,' Izzy says, touching my arm. 'But we're all here for you, aren't we girls?'

The other two make sympathetic noises and, just like with the woman in Smith's, I want to cry. But whereas I couldn't blub on to a complete stranger's uniform, Izzy will understand if I rest my face on her slim brown shoulder and let it all out.

I go to hug her, knocking my trilby off and bumping her nose with my sunglasses.

'Daisy!' she cries, stepping backwards. She jabs a finger towards her face. 'Remember!'

Izzy had her beak straightened during half-term because she *said* she had breathing problems, but everyone knows she had a nose job. Apparently, when she went to see the plastic surgeon he gave her a photograph album full of celebs and asked her to point out which nose she fancied. She chose a Dannii Minogue.

'Sorry,' I say, rummaging around Clemmie's French-manicured toes for my hat. 'By the way, if you think I've been blanking you, the police still have my phone. I'm totally ex-communicado.'

'No probs, it's been, like, *so* mental with going to Marbella all summer and then catching up with everyone,' Izzy gushes, flicking her hair. 'I bought, like, sooo many things, I don't know when I'm going to wear them. I bought this, like, *mental* scarf, fuchsia pink covered in skulls, cost, like, zillions of euros but the colour is *so* me, even Ollie said so.'

'Ollie?' I say, my heart leaping. 'When did you

see Ollie?'

Clemmie and Bee stare at the ground, embarrassed. Clemmie even flushes scarlet.

'Is he in town?' I look around as if Ollie might pop out from behind a bus shelter and yell *Surprise!*

'I had, like, a bit of an *I'm back* do yesterday,' Izzy admits. 'Very caz, like, nothing maj, just a few burgers from Iceland and disposable barbies on the lawn. Ollie popped by.'

'Oh!' I say, trying to keep my voice light, even though I feel physically wounded that I wasn't at the barbecue with everyone else. I know full well that even though Izzy and Ollie live close, no way would Oll just 'pop by' on the off chance that Izzy was back and throwing a party. Izzy obviously invited him. 'Was Mia there?'

'I left a message but she didn't come,' Izzy snorts. 'Sooo rude.'

'Did you try my house phone?' I ask. I can't believe that Izzy would invite Mia and Ollie but not me. 'I was in all day.'

Izzy clears her throat. 'Actually, Daisy, I didn't ring you. You're, like, blacklisted.'

I stare at the trilby in my hands, trying to get my eyes to focus on the tweed. At the moment it's just one big swirl of hairy brown soup.

'It wasn't Izzy,' Clemmie butts in. 'It was her parents. They're a bit freaked about your dad.'

'And Aston,' Bee adds. 'Cos he's a druggie.'

I clutch the hat so tightly my knuckles turn white.

Is *this* my Gherkin Moment?

Am I about to go mad and stuff the trilby up Izzy T's cosmetically enhanced nose, thereby wrecking her sleek and expensive beak?

'It's the others that are in trouble, not me,' I say weakly. 'I've done nothing wrong.'

Izzy shrugs and wrinkles her Dannii. 'Daddy's got to be squeaky clean at the mo,' she purrs. 'He can't have even a whiff of scandal around the family.'

'He owns Bug Busters!' I protest, hoping my tone of voice implies that I can't possibly see why a man who's made his money from nuking carpet beetles and bed bugs wouldn't want me at his house.

Izzy gives me a haughty glare. 'Daddy's expecting to be selected as the Conservative candidate for Donsborough and District in the next election,' she explains. 'You partying *chez* Tricket might look *très* sleazy.'

Before I can bristle at being called a sleazebag, Clemmie shoots me a sad look and gives me hug. 'See you at school on Thursday?'

Oh. God. I haven't told anyone I'm changing schools.

How could I? I've only just found out myself.

'Um . . . I'm not coming back to Park Hill,' I say, biting my lip. 'Portia's going into the sixth form, but I'm going to Bensham High.'

'Daisy!' Clem grabs my hand and looks as if I've just told her I've been diagnosed with terminal cancer. 'I am *so* sorry!'

'I can't believe you're going to become a Bensham Bitch!' Bee squeals. 'Their uniform is mega minging. They mix black and navy! You'll look like a big bruise!'

Izzy looks as if she might throw up at any minute.

'I would, like, just die if I even had to set foot in that place,' she shudders. 'In fact, I would rather slit my wrists than go to Chaverama High.'

And then Izzy grabs Clem and Bee and, arms linked, the three of them saunter off, giggling and gasping, leaving me standing on the pavement, surrounded by hundreds of other shoppers, feeling completely and utterly alone.

Chapter Ten

'Well, good luck, darling.'

Mum reaches over to the passenger seat to hug me, except I don't want her to hug me, I want her to tell me that some long-lost rellie has unexpectedly stumped up a shedload of readies for my school fees and we're doing a tyre-burning U-turn straight back to my old school where I feel safe, secure and stylish. Term at Park Hill doesn't start until Thursday, but I'd sleep in the car park for forty-eight hours if I had to.

'Go on, Miss Birch wants to see you at eight-thirty, before school starts,' Mum presses. 'You don't want to be late on your first day.'

Late doesn't even come close to it. I might have to stay in the car for ever, not just because I don't want to go in, but because physiologically I can't move. I'm actually frozen with fear to Mindy Howard's cream leather car seats. I honestly think that to get me out someone's going to have to remove me *and* the seat and carry me in. That's going to create a great first impression with the Bensham Bitches, isn't it, being carried into school like I'm some princess on a sedan chair, unable to walk even the short distance from school gate to front entrance. Of course, if I end up with the broken legs Aston has predicted, I'll have to be carried to class anyway. Seems like a lose–lose situation to me.

To cheer myself up, I've put my school stuff (pencil case; full make-up kit; hair brush; mirror; phone – back from the police – address book, etc.) in the large Louis Vuitton shopper Mum and Dad gave me last Christmas, scooped my hair back with a tortoiseshell bulldog clip, and borrowed (with her permission this time) a pair of Mum's Prada patent leather flats with a shiny silver buckle. I think my choice of accessories says trendy and classy without pushing the ex-rich bitch thing too much.

Mum gives me a nudge. 'It'll be fine, Daisy,' she says gently. 'You've always been a popular girl at Park. Everyone here will love you.'

I look at the girls hanging around the school gates where Mum has parked the Porsche. They're laughing and joking and pushing each other around and stabbing the keys of their phones and doing exactly the sort of thing Park Hill girls do, except our uniforms are cuter, our phones are posher and we can't possibly look as terrifying as this mob.

'What if they pick on me?' I say. Now my MacBook's back from the cops I spent last night surfing the Net, torturing myself by reading horror stories of girls going to new schools and being tied to goal posts and pelted with stinky eggs. 'What if they stick rude notes on my back and snigger?'

'Daisy, don't be ridiculous.' Mum's dropped the caring, gentle-mother routine and has reverted to her current default mode of snappy irritation, though I suspect it's because she's as tired and emotional as I am. 'You're not the sort of girl to be bullied. You're bright and pretty. Now *go*, or Portia will be late for her sixth-form induction day.'

Of course, we mustn't make Park Hill Portia late, must we?

I turn round to see my sis in the back seat, earplugs in, iPod on, bobbing her head along to music, unconcerned that I'm about to be thrown to the chavvy hounds whilst wearing an unflattering navy nylon blazer whose sleeves are too short.

Private school cow! I think, and then feel amazed that

already I seem to be thinking like one of the Bensham Bitches who bait Park Hill girls.

Mum's giving me the evil eye and actually looks as if she might push me out of the car, so with sweaty hands I unclip the seat belt, prise my butt from the leather and haul myself on to the pavement.

My legs are like lead, my stomach is churning and I can feel the corners of my eyes pricking with hot tears.

'I'll pick you up here at just gone three-thirty!' Mum calls out as I slam the car door. 'Good luck!'

And then she drives off, leaving me alone in the wilderness.

Except – not quite.

As I clutch the LV shopper I can feel the outline of *Assertiveness NOW!* beneath the brown and tan leather. I managed to find a copy in Waterstone's, and over the last few days I've read it cover to cover *five* times.

Wanda-May assures me that the only thing stopping me becoming the woman I want to be is confidence. As well as the Magic Mantras, she recommends thinking of a role model, someone you admire and look up to, and in difficult situations (job interviews, discussing a pay rise with your boss, taking back a faulty DVD player) pretend to be them. In other words: Fake it till you make it.

So with a pounding heart, sweaty armpits and heavy legs, I walk through the gates of Bensham High comprehensive school, pretending to be Cheryl Cole.

'Can I help you?' A woman with short grey hair and dangly silver earrings looks up at me from her desk in an office partitioned off from the entrance hall by a glass window.

'Aye.'

Good heavens! I really *have* channelled my inner Cheryl Cole. I'm speaking with a Geordie accent. I'm talking Cheryl.

'I mean, yes, I'm Daisy Davenport,' I say, rummaging in my bag for the letter I'm supposed to hand over. 'I'm seeing Miss Birch at eight-thirty.' I glance at the clock on the office wall. It's already eight-thirty-one. 'I'm sorry I'm late.'

I wave the letter as the woman gets up from her desk and bustles over.

'Daisy, of course! I thought I recognized you,' she says, smiling as she slides open the glass window and takes the envelope. 'I've seen your picture. I'm Mrs Cassidy, one of the school secretaries.'

'Um, hello,' I croak.

'You must be feeling rather lost,' Mrs C says kindly.

'But we'll look after you here. Bensham is a very friendly school.'

My already damp eyes refill with tears. I do hope that people don't keep being nice to me. All this sympathy makes me want to cry, which would be a total disaster on my first day. Not only would blubbing underline the fact that I'm a complete wimp, I've just a hint of non-waterproof mascara on. I thought if I wore it, firstly it would make me look a bit better, a bit more Cheryl-like, but also because I'm hoping the threat of panda-eyes will stop a few tears turning into a raging torrent.

'Just take a seat over there and I'll ring through to the headmistress's office and see if she's ready for you.'

Mrs Cassidy motions to the fake leather chairs lining the corridor and, grateful for a chance to sit down, I perch on the edge of one, clutch my bag to my chest for safety and look around.

Everything at Bensham seems so flat and grey. The car park in front of the school is laid with grey tarmac; the walkway to the entrance is lined with grey paving slabs; inside the chairs are grey; the walls are grey; the floor tiles are grey. I know Bensham has been around since the 1970s (no glossy brochure but quite a good website), but that's no excuse for looking so shabby. Park Hill is in a building dated 1845 but, compared to this

127

pile of grey concrete, it looks box fresh.

What sort of school did the Goddess Cheryl go to?
I wonder.

I glance at my watch. Any minute now, Mum will be driving Portia through the gates of my old school, past the green lawns and tall trees to the red-brick mansion some people describe as a Victorian gothic monstrosity, but which I love because I think it looks straight out of a vampire movie and I can pretend at any moment some hunky lad with strange eyes and odd dental work will burst into history class, knock the teacher out of the way, sweep me off my feet and run off into the woods with me. Quite what happens after that, I daren't think.

But I'm no longer at a vampire-magnet mansion. I'm a nervous new girl at Chaverama High.

Cheryl! Cheryl! I remind myself.

'Daisy?' a booming voice enquires. Without looking up, it's difficult to know whether it's male or female in origin. 'I'm Barbara Birch, the headmistress. Welcome to Bensham High School.'

I gawp at the enormous woman standing in front of me. She's about six feet tall, has a shock of feather-cut bright yellow hair, big round eyes and a slash of red lipstick across her mouth.

It's Big Bird from Sesame Street.

She couldn't be more different from Mrs Channing, who wore little round-necked Chanel suits, pearl earstuds and always had an immaculate dark bob and pale glossy lips, even when walking her dog after school, a primped-up apricot poodle called Gloria.

'Hello, Miss . . .'

Oh. My. God. What did she say her name was? I was too shocked to find my headmistress is a mega puppet to concentrate. I can only think of the letters BB. And she's wearing some mad psychedelic tent of a dress that is practically hurting my eyes.

'Mizz Birch,' Mizz Birch reminds me, holding out her hand.

'Hello, Mizz Birch,' I say, standing up and shaking her hand, which is like sticking my mitt in a vice and pumping it up and down. 'Pleased to meet you.'

Which of course is a big fat lie.

'Likewise. Do come on through.'

She leads the way and for the first time this morning I find myself trying to smother a giggle.

Walking behind the headmistress, I see she even has a butt and feet like Big Bird.

Compared to the dreary corridor, stepping into the headmistress's study is like jumping headfirst into a kaleidoscope. It's an interior-design version of the woman herself, full of life and colour and odd knick-knacks. There's bright artwork on the walls – oh, actually it's a year planner with multicoloured stickers – a gurgling tank filled with tropical fish, framed photographs of Mizz Birch in bright dresses meeting grey-suited bigwigs, and on her desk a rainbow-striped mug, with BOSS written across it, crammed with coloured pens and pencils. There are real pot plants and fake flowers made out of modelling clay, a huge papier mâché butterfly suspended from the ceiling and what looks like a shrunken head on a stick in the corner.

Big Bird perches on a black chair behind her paper-littered desk.

'Now, Daisy.' She leans forward. 'How are you doing, my dear? Are you finding things difficult?'

'Well . . .'

'I had a long chat to your mother last week, and to Alicia Channing. Alicia and I went to Durham together, so we go back years. You must be very confused by everything that's happened to your family in such a short space of time.'

Oh no. Here we go again. Sympathy alert. I can't cry. I just can't.

Panda eyes! Panda eyes! I chant in my head to remind

myself of the disastrous consequences of blubbing.

'Once you've settled in, perhaps we can discuss some extra help for you, maybe some counselling with one of the support groups the county runs?'

Stop! Please stop! Any minute now I'm going to resemble a burst water main as tears start spurting from my eyes and completely drown all those papers on Mizz Birch's desk. Think Cheryl! Think Cheryl!

'We'll do everything we can to support you and, when she's free, Mrs Wilson, Head of Pastoral Care for Year 10 girls, will have a chat too.'

The Panda Eyes mantra isn't working. Cheryl isn't helping. Quick, what else would Wanda-May suggest?

Distraction. That's another Wanda-May technique.

If it all gets too much and you feel overwhelmed, concentrate on something and examine it in minute detail until the feeling of panic passes and the feeling of inner strength returns.

Desperately I stare straight ahead at the outside strand of the double row of beads around Mizz Birch's ample chest and start counting down the beads in my head: *blue bead, red bead, green bead. Blue bead, red bead, green bead.* This is good, I no longer want to cry. I can feel the panic ebb away, just as Wanda-May promised it would. *Blue bead, red bead . . .*

I'm transfixed by a strange bead-shaped bulge.

Oh God, is that a bead or an enormous nipple?

It's green but it's a different sort of green to the others, more dress-green than bead-green, but it's so hard to differentiate between the swirly-patterned dress and the multicoloured necklace. Oh no! How has this happened? Wanda-May never warned me about getting stuck between trying to decide between a bead and a nipple.

Move on! Move on!

'Do you like them?'

I look up to see Mizz Birch looking down, her hands spread across her chest. Is she asking me about her beads or her boobs? I feel panic rising but I can't control it without thinking *Blue bead, red bead, nipple bead.*

'Um . . .'

'One of the Year 8 pupils made them for me. I think they're rather splendid!'

'Oh!' I gasp. 'You meant your beads not your boo—' I stop myself just in time. Never mind the beads around this Big Bird's chest, beads of sweat are running down *my* chest I'm so nervous.

'Anyway, my dear, to make things a little easier, we've assigned you a chaperone for the next few weeks, just to ensure that the transition from Park Hill to Bensham is as seamless as possible for you.'

'A chaperone?' I have visions of someone following me

around, carrying my books, tasting my lunch, unpacking and packing my gym bag. Perhaps they think we had servants at Park Hill? Perhaps they're giving me a servant just to make me feel more at home! It's a bit OTT, but I can live with it.

'A Bensham chaperone is a cross between a monitor and a mentor,' Mizz Birch explains. 'She's one of our Year 10 pupils who's taking the same subjects as you. She'll make sure you find your way around, get to know the ropes, introduce you to the others, that sort of thing.'

I feel *much* better. OK, so it's not a servant, but it'll be a friendly face helping me to fit in, just like when Mia first came to Park Hill. In those first few weeks I took Mia *everywhere* with me, even to the loos, which is why I'm rather narked she hasn't once been in touch to wish me luck or see how I am. I can't believe she's studying *that* hard in the holidays, and for what?

'That's great,' I say, smiling at Mizz Birch. 'Thank you.'

'And Melanie's a lovely girl,' Mizz Birch continues. 'Her hand shot up as soon as I went into the form room yesterday to ask for volunteers.'

Behind me there's a knock at the door.

'Ah, here she is!' Mizz Birch waves towards the door.

'Melanie, come in and meet Daisy Davenport. Daisy, this is Melanie Grabowska.'

I swivel round in my chair and get the shock of my life.

My blood freezes in my veins, my stomach hits the floor and my head swims with panic.

I feel even worse than when Dad had the handcuffs snapped around his wrists or I heard I was being sent here.

Standing at the door to the headmistress's study is Pumpkin Head.

My chaperone is the girl outside Starbucks who threatened to kill me.

Chapter Eleven

Mizz Birch is burbling in the background about school-related stuff and getting an ID card done, but I'm not taking anything in because I'm even more panicky than I was when I was counting beads and dodgy nipples. I'm desperately thinking back to that day in August with Mia, trying to remember what I'd done to my hair and whether I was wearing sunnies. There's a slim chance if I had my hair loose and my sunglasses on Big Mel won't recognize me as the girl on the table outside Starbucks who stared at her back fat whilst Mia made sarky remarks. I can remember the shoes I was wearing – the wretched silver Louboutins – but I can't remember whether my sunnies were on my nose, my forehead or, in a rare moment of slack summer accessorizing, in my bag.

'Any problems, speak to Melanie first,' Mizz B says,

getting up. 'Or your form teacher, Mr Pirbright, or ask for Mrs Wilson. And have a wonderful first day.'

Oh no! This means I have to leave the safety of the headmistress's office and head out into the jungle with my killer. Can't I stay here and clean out the fish tank or dust the shrunken head or something?

'Thanks!' I say as brightly as I can. 'I'm sure I will.'

'I'll look after her,' Melanie smiles. 'She's in good hands.'

'So, Daisy,' Melanie says as we negotiate our way through the crowded corridor, swerving the shrieking bodies. 'I've seen you before.'

Oh. My. God. I am *so* dead. I might as well just lie down here and let everyone trample me before Big Mel gets her hands around my skinny neck. She knows I'm Starbucks Girl.

'From the papers?' she explains, guiding me around a corner. 'Dad's a big Dons fan so we had all the rags.'

I can feel my shoulders sag with relief under the weight of my LV tan-leather hand-stitched straps. Of *course* that's where Melanie has seen me, the same place that Mrs Cassidy saw me. I've been a front-page picture. I've got to stop being so para that my chaperone is a killer-in-waiting and start making friends with her.

'Aye, it was all a bit mental,' I admit. 'The whole Ferrari and shoe-gate thing.'

A slight hint of fake Geordie sing-song has crept into my voice. I must stop! I want to *look* like Cheryl, not *sound* like her.

'Those shoes looked pretty damn mint,' Melanie says.

She may be a potential murderer, but I'm mega grateful she's chaperoning me around these endless corridors or I'd never make it to registration.

'Is it true they, like, cost four hundred pounds?'

'And then some,' I smile. 'More like closer to six. Oh, and the dog chewed them!'

'Wow!' Melanie giggles. 'We've only got a hamster who nibbles electric cables. Your dog had a chew-toy worth six hundred smackers! That is *well* mad!'

'I suppose,' I giggle back. 'But Mum has shedloads of others. Bentley could probably eat one pair a week and there'd still be masses left!'

We both laugh.

'Will you bring them in?' Melanie asks. 'I'd love to try them on. I've never worn anything that spendy before.'

'Of course,' I say, glancing at Melanie's rather wide feet and wondering whether they'll fit. 'I'll dig them out.'

'Awesome!' she says, sounding excited. 'And your

skirt.' She nods towards my legs. 'That's *never* from Primark!'

'Marc Jacobs,' I say proudly, holding it out and doing a little curtsey. 'From Harvey Nicks. The blazer is Asda though.'

This is good, bonding over accessories. Mia, Izzy, Clem, Bee and I used to spend hours online in the school library looking at the Tiffany website, deciding what we'd like next. Maybe Melanie and I will connect over Cartier or become friends because of Fendi.

'Grabowska is an unusual name,' I say, feeling much more relaxed. This whole Confident Cheryl routine is working really well, if only I could ditch the sing-songy accent. 'Where's it from?'

'It's Polish,' Melanie replies. 'Mum and Dad came from Poland yonks ago, but I was born near Gravesend. We moved here about five years ago.'

'That is *so* weird!' I gasp, thinking that I'm getting on better with a Bensham Bitch than I could ever have imagined. 'Our housekeeper is Polish. She was with us for five years.'

'Really?' Mel replies. 'What's her name? I might know her. The Poles are quite a tight-knit community round here.'

'Krystina . . . er . . .'

And now I'm stumped. I don't know her surname. It was long and unpronounceable so we never bothered to learn how to say it. But I can't let Melanie know we were lazy on the foreign surname front.

'. . . Polski,' I lie. 'Krystina Polski.'

'Right.'

There's something about the way Melanie stiffens and says *right* that makes me wonder if I've said the wrong thing, and that Polski in Polish actually means Polish slut or something terrible.

'I mean, she doesn't work for us now. She had to leave because of all the trouble.'

'So, where is she?' Melanie asks. 'This Mrs Polski.'

'Eating lamb chops and a black forest gateau, I expect,' I say. 'We let her choose what she wanted from our freezer before she left.'

We're climbing stairs now. Up to one landing, up another. I noticed earlier lots of the girls wear trousers rather than skirts. Perhaps I could add a bit of interest to my uniform by wearing a skirt one day and Mum's Chloé black wide-legged butt-flattering trousers another? And does she have a navy cashmere V-neck? I doubt it; she's more of a pastel kind of woman. But Dad might, and he's not going to need superfine sweaters made from the soft underbelly fur of mountain goats in jail, is he? And maybe if I showed these girls just how good a well-cut uniform could look, it might change the way they feel about school, even improve their grades. I could become a school stylist!

A posse of lads saunters towards us, laughing, joking.

'Wow, he could butter my muffin,' Mel whispers as they pass by. 'He's super cute!'

'Which one?' I whisper, turning to look at them.

'Blond, black leather jacket – don't stare!' she squeals, grabbing my arm.

'Daisy?'

The lad Mel's got the hots for has turned round too. He's staring right at me.

'I thought it was you,' he says, wandering back towards us, leaving his mates to carry on loping along the corridor.

I smile and think that perhaps being in the papers isn't such a bad thing after all. At least it doesn't mean I have to go through the butt-clenching new-girl embarrassment of introducing myself to everyone; they already know who I am and what my dad's done.

'Yes, it's me, Daisy Davenport,' I joke. 'Front-page news. The girl with the silver shoes.'

I'm not surprised Mel has the hots for this Stud Muffin. She's right, he is *totally* heaven on a stick: tall; blond surfer-shaggy-type hair; obviously works out; fab white gnashers; and, from the look of the badge on his blazer underneath his jacket, a sixth former. Beside me, Melanie is practically hyperventilating with lust.

'You've no idea who I am, have you?' The Stud Muffin says. 'Not a clue.'

Mel laughs as if he's made a joke.

He looks at her as if she's nuts.

I look at him again, which is no hardship.

He seems vaguely familiar, like I might have seen him before, but I'm not sure.

'You've been in the papers too?' I suggest.

The Stud Muffin laughs. 'How's the leprosy?'

'Jake?' My stomach hits the floor as I realize this gorgeous creature was once the lad in the disco in France I dumped on Izzy T's orders.

'You've had leprosy?' Melanie gasps, taking a step away from me. 'You're a leper?'

'Um, well . . .' I start, staring at Jake, wondering how on earth the chubby lad with the spots turned into this sixth-form stunner. He must have been mainlining Miracle Gro as he's shot up like a weed and if you look like that, who cares about a few zits?

'We were going to go out but then poor Daisy suddenly got sick,' Jake says. 'Where was it you caught it?'

141

'Méribel,' I mutter. 'But I'm fine now. I thought you were at Huffman's?'

'I was, but it got too expensive and science is better here,' he says. 'I've just started. Anyway, it's good to see you've recovered.' He winks at me. 'See you around, I guess.'

'Did you really have leprosy?' Melanie asks as we race towards the form room, in danger of being late because of Jake ambushing me.

'It was just an excuse to dump him,' I say. 'Honestly, he looked nothing like that. He used to be short, spotty and almost as chubby as Big Bird.'

'Big Bird?' Melanie queries as we keep going along endless grey corridors.

'Mizz Birch,' I say, giggling at the thought of the school being run by a mental monster puppet. 'She's the spitting image. Surely you've noticed?'

Melanie stops and pushes open a fake-wood door with a rectangular glass panel running down it. Before it's even fully open, I can hear the racket coming from within.

Then it's as if an *off* switch has been flicked.

There's stony silence whilst everyone gawps at me, looking me up and down like some two-headed baby pickled in a glass jar.

'If it isn't Little Miss Snooty,' a black girl chewing gum sneers as Melanie leads me to a desk and pushes me into a chair. She's got evil slanty eyebrows, which either means she *is* evil, or her bronze and black braids are pulled too tight. 'So where's Daddy hidden the millions then? The Bahamas, Bermuda or under the pool tiles?'

Everyone laughs.

Except me.

My face starts to burn and I feel so shocked I want to run out of the classroom, all the way down the stairs and out of the school gates. I expected a bit of staring and nudging, some whispering behind my back and, once I'd met Melanie, death, but I never thought that anyone would be so openly hostile to me.

'Button it, Deez,' Melanie barks at the girl, who shrinks back across her desk. 'Ignore Deeza,' she adds to me. 'She's like my nan's dog, Stinky; always a bit funny with new people, but once you get to know her, she's fine.'

Some of the other girls get up and crowd round my desk, but they're not looking at me, they're gawping at the Louis Vuitton, touching it, staring at it, cooing over it.

'Is it a fake?' someone asks, worshipping at the shrine of LV. 'It looks too lush to be fake.'

'Nah, not with her old man's nicked millions,' someone else says. 'Pukka, isn't it?'

'Um . . . er . . . yes . . . it's real,' I admit, as Melanie strokes the leather. 'It was a present, *and* I've got the matching purse.'

I get out the rectangular monogrammed purse to *Oohs!* and *Aahs!*

'Pirbright's coming!' someone yells as kids scuttle back to their desks.

In walks Mr Pirbright: tall, thin and round-shouldered, wearing a brown corduroy jacket, scruffy black trousers and gold-rimmed glasses.

'Good morning, everyone,' he says cheerily.

I rise to my feet. 'Good morning, sir.'

Giggles and sniggers ring in my ears.

I look around.

I'm the only one standing up.

The only one in a class of about thirty students not convulsed with laughter.

'Um . . . at my old school we always stood up,' I explain in a squeaky voice before my knees give way and I sink back down on to my grey plastic chair, my entire body burning with humiliation. 'Sorry.'

'And I think that's a very good tradition.' There's a smile in Mr Pirbright's voice, but I have no idea if there's one plastered across his face, as I daren't raise my eyes from my desk. 'You must be Daisy Davenport.'

'Um . . . yes,' I mumble into my chest. 'I am.'

'And I gather Melanie is looking after you?' he enquires.

'Um . . . yes . . . she is.'

'Splendid!' he says. 'Now, let's get on.'

Chapter Twelve

Other than total humiliation in registration, the morning hasn't been so bad, I think to myself as we stream out of the gates at lunchtime. The classrooms might be less stylish at Bensham than at Park, but the lessons have been pretty much the same. I mean, just because you pay thousands of pounds in fees doesn't change the French language or the answer to a maths question, does it? It just means that you have better lunches, a more elegant car park and Farrow & Ball paint on the walls.

Some of the girls I've come across like Deeza and another called Sonja have glared daggers at me, but most of the others have wanted to know what it's like to have loads of designer labels in your wardrobe, how much the Mulberry bag in the photie cost and did I have a boyfriend? A few pics of Ollie looking all hunky seemed to impress them, but I kept back the one of his bare butt as I'm not sure it shows him in the best light.

Quite frankly, the boys in my year are a total disappointment. They all look about ten, with bum fluff, spots and braces, and bombarded me with questions about whether Donsborough United would start up again, the top speed of a Ferrari and how much money Dad nicked, none of which I could answer. But Mel has been an absolute sweetie, making sure I've got everything I need, even suggesting I come out with her and some of the girls at lunchtime to get a burger from a place near school. I can't believe that I've actually sort of enjoyed my first morning here. The way things are going, if I can get my uniform sorted out I'll be pretty much settled in by the end of tomorrow.

In my head I start composing another letter to Dad in HM Prison Dover Court:

Dear Dad,

Everything's going really well at Bensham High. Most of the girls seem nice, and once I've shown them how to accessorize their uniform to maximum effect . . .

Maybe this time he'll reply. Mum said he's in bits with guilt and doesn't want any of his children to see him in prison until he gets his head in a better place. She's been to see him once since his court appearance and took in a letter from me, but he hasn't written back yet. Perhaps if he knows I'm happy at school he won't feel quite so bad about what's happened.

'Let's swap phone numbers,' Mel suggests as she sees me getting my phone out of my bag whilst we're queuing. 'Then if you get lost or need something, you can just phone me.'

'Oh thanks, that would be great!' I say, noticing I've had texts from Ollie, Clemmie and Mum. 'What's your number?'

'I'll stab it in,' Mel says. 'Give it here.'

She swipes the phone from my hand, fiddles around and then stares at the screen.

'So this is what you and your Park Hill friends call us,' she says crisply, holding the phone in front of my face.

I peer at Clemmie's text:

Surviving the Bensham Bitches at Chavarama High?

Luv The GP xxx

Oh. God.

'What does she call us?' one of the girls at the back of the queue yells out.

I'm not sure who she is, but she was in maths and one of the glary girls.

'Apparently we are Bensham Bitches and this school is

148

Chavarama High,' Mel announces, raising her eyebrows.

'I didn't say it, it's my friends from The Glossy Posse gang,' I gabble. 'They're just joking, you know, having a laugh.'

The other girls aren't laughing. They're looking menacing and muttering under their breath choice phrases such as 'Stuck up cow' and 'Freakin' posh bitch.'

My legs feel wobbly and I start to go off the thought of a burger and long for something fresh and tomatoey and shaped like a flower.

'You'd better watch your back,' someone behind me growls, 'or else.'

'Or else you'll have *me* to answer to!' Melanie snaps at the girl before turning back to me. 'I've put my number in and texted yours to mine.' She tosses the phone towards me and I catch it with shaky hands.

'Thanks,' I say, scrolling through the menu to read Ollie and Mum's texts.

But when I get to my inbox, *all* the messages have gone.

Every single one of them.

The one from Ollie I haven't read; the texts from Ollie I've read but like to keep; the unopened one from Mum; and one from Dad. Dad's is nothing special, it just says:

Thanks, Princess! Dad xxx and was in response to me wishing him happy birthday last June because he'd gone to work before I got up. I've kept it because I never got round to deleting it, and now it's the only text I've got from him and I don't know when I'll ever have another.

Tears career down my cheeks like searing hot streaks.

'What's with the salties?' Mel asks, nudging me in the ribs a little harder than necessary.

'My texts,' I gasp, flicking through every function I can think of on my iPhone. 'They've all gone!'

'*All* of them?' Melanie queries.

'Every single one!' I croak, looking at the blank screen through wet eyes. 'Even one from Dad.'

'Oh God, Daisy, I am *so* sorry,' Mel gushes. 'It must be my fault! I'm not used to such a posh phone. I deleted the *Chavarama* one cos it would be terrible if the girls got to see it – you know, mugged you for your phone to get it. I must have wiped the others by mistake.'

I sit on the loo, look at the empty inbox on my phone and want to howl like a dog. My texts have gone, I'm missing my old school, my father is in jail and I'm starting to wonder if my chaperone is as unfailingly sweet and light as she makes out.

I'd like to believe Mel, I really would. I'd like to believe that she innocently destroyed all those texts just to protect me from Clem's message falling into the clutches of a Bensham Bitch, but there was something in her voice that was so phoney, so put on, I'm convinced she did it on purpose. But I can't prove it, and even if I could, what would I say to Mizz Birch or Mr Pirbright? I got this text from my friends at Park Hill calling everyone here chavs and bitches, and I'm upset Mel's deleted it, even though she said she did it to protect me?

Yeah. Right. That's really going to go down well, isn't it?

I left the girls at the burger bar and came back to school. Mel made a great fuss of saying she'd come with me, but I said I'd be fine, I wasn't hungry, and that I'd just hang around until English lit after lunch. She's arranged to meet me outside these loos at one-thirty.

I hear the door to the toilets squeak open and several sets of footsteps come shuffling in. Someone tries my door, but finding it shut, goes into another cubicle. There's the sound of zips being pulled and make-up bags being rummaged through.

Through the crack between the door and the door frame I spot a group of girls clustered around the mirrors over the basins. I recognize one of them as red-haired

Kaylee from my French class this morning. She seemed quite warm and smiley when I met her. I even wondered if we might become friends.

'So, have any of you met that posh bitch Daisy Davenport?' someone asks. 'You know, the one whose dad's a total tea leaf? Apparently at her old school she was in some gang called the Glossy Girls or something.'

I hold my breath.

'Yeah,' Kaylee replies. 'The snotty cow was in my French class this morning being all *Ooh la la*, tossing her hair and telling Madame Bradders how she'd been to France, like, loads of times, bleating on about Coco Chanel, trying to show us all up.'

No! It wasn't like that! I want to scream, pulling my knees up to my chin so I can't be identified under the door by the Prada buckles. I didn't waltz into class crowing: *Ha ha, I've been to France more than you, you sad losers!* Madame Bradley *asked* me if I'd ever been so I told her I had – loads of times. And when she asked each of us what was the best thing to come from the great garlic country, how was I to know that everyone else would say things like fries, letters, sticks and plaits, *after* I'd mentioned Coco and her fabulous designs?

'I'd like to shove that snotty bird's bonce in the bog,' a voice says over the sound of a torrent of pee coming from the cubicle next to me. 'Then she'd stop being Miss Better than Us.'

I can hear the loo flushing accompanied by a sickening peal of laughter. My stomach does a back flip. I'm *that* close to anxiety-vomming, but I can't risk them hearing me and battering the door down to force my head round the U-bend.

'The snobby cow thinks she's so ruddy wonderful,' Pee Girl snarls as she leaves the cubicle. 'Mel said even her skirt was designer. What a shame if it got covered in Tippex.'

There's cackling and the sound of shoes shuffling away from me, and then silence, except for the thud-thud-thud of my heart battering in my chest.

I look at my watch. Just under five minutes until I'm meeting Mel outside. In five minutes I have to go into a class with these girls, girls who hate my guts because they think I'm a stuck-up cow who's waltzed in wearing expensive clothes.

In a panic, I pull out Wanda-May's book and start manically flicking through the chapters.

Here's one entitled: *What Doesn't Kill You Makes You Stronger*.

Yeah. Right.

Or what about *Sticks and Stones*?

It's all very well for America's premier assertiveness guru to remind me that I might get broken bones but calling me a snobby cow won't hurt me, but I'd rather not have broken bones, thank you very much. And I am hurt, *very* hurt.

Remember your Magic Mantra! Wanda-May reminds me in one of the little shaded boxes dotted through the book. *You are a wonderful human being! For an instant confidence boost, remind yourself just how wonderful you really are!*

Despite Pee Girl's claims, I don't think I'm wonderful at all, quite the opposite, but it's worth a try.

In my head I start chanting: *I am wonderful. I am wonderful.*

Nope, not feeling wonderful. Still feeling shaky and rank.

I am wonderful! I am wonderful!

Ooh! Still not feeling wonderful, but I am a *teeny* bit less shaky. Perhaps my inner Cheryl is starting to return.

I am wonderful! I am wonderful!

Yes, definitely better, more just OK than wonderful, but I'll take what I can. And I must look at the mascara situation. The tears will have wrecked the Maybelline.

I get off the loo, wait for my bum to wake up and stop tingling pins and needles and continue chanting in my head as I open the door and head to the mirror.

I am wonderful! I am wonderful!

I lick my left index finger and run it underneath my eyes, wiping away the dark smudges as the bell goes.

I am wonderful! I am wonderful! Like Cheryl Cole! Like Cheryl Cole!

It's time to go back out to all those girls who hate my guts, but do I care? No I don't because I've just reapplied the mascara, added a touch of clear lip gloss and thought: 'I am wonderful! I am wonderful! Like Cheryl Cole! Like Cheryl—'

'I think you're a snobby rich bitch who needs to be taught a lesson.'

Melanie's face stares back at me in the mirror.

She's at the door, and I haven't chanted my mantra silently in my head. Without meaning to, I've said it out loud.

Melanie Grabowska thinks that *I* think I'm the mutt's nuts, and there's nowhere to hide.

'It's not what you think it is,' I gasp. 'I can explain.'

'Can you?' Her eyes glitter with contempt.

'Yes!' I swallow hard and start backing towards the toilet I've just come from. 'It's from this book, this book about how to be assertive?' I desperately rummage in the Louis V to find Wanda-May. 'She says to recite a Magic

Mantra when you're worried, and I *was* worried!'

Melanie steps towards me. 'You should be worried,' she says darkly. 'Coming here, strutting around, thinking you're so wonderful!'

'It's the book!' I panic. 'It's all in here!'

I wave my copy of *Assertiveness NOW!* in the air.

Melanie snatches it from my hand. She doesn't even look at the cover or Wanda-May's scary hair on the back, she just tosses it past my shoulder where it lands with a thud and a splash in the toilet behind me.

'Now, fish it out,' she orders. 'Stick your hand down the bog and get the book.'

I go over and peer into the toilet. Wanda-May is looking up at me through slightly murky water, still with that inane grin on her face. Clearly this is a test, a test to see whether I'm strong enough to get the book out, or just a wimp who'll say, *Oh let it drown, I'll get another copy.* Actually I have got another copy on the way. It should be in WHSmith by now. I wonder if they've phoned Ollie to tell him? Maybe that's what his text was about.

'Get it!'

I roll up my sleeve, gulp and plunge my right hand into the cold water to retrieve the soggy tome.

When I turn round, Mel is in the loo with me, leaning

against the closed door, filling the cubicle with bulk and pumpkin hair.

'You thought I didn't know who you were, did you?' she hisses, jabbing her finger in my face. 'You thought I'd forgotten about you and your bitchy little bezzie outside Starbucks, laughing at me, making fun of my butt, calling me a continental chubby chav, didn't you?'

'No! Yes! I don't know!' I gasp as *Assertiveness NOW!* drips on to Mum's Pradas and I fret about whether the buckles will turn rusty.

'Well, *I* hadn't,' Mel hisses, her face almost next to mine. 'I recognized you from the papers and when I heard you were coming here it was like, bingo! I've got the snotty bitch right where I want her!'

'You've got it all wrong!' I plead, the backs of my legs pressed hard against the cool porcelain toilet rim. 'It was a girl called Mia who was being mean about you. We were talking about Polly's backside, not yours!'

'Oh, so it's all right to talk about Polly behind her back-fat then?' Mel growls.

'Polly's my pony!' I squeak. 'I didn't say anything about you!'

'But you laughed, didn't you?' Mel's face is black with anger. I'm practically bent over backwards to keep away from her but I can still smell her burger-breath. 'You

157

laughed *with* her *at* me, a couple of stuck-up rich bitches looking down their noses at a girl you thought couldn't understand what you were saying.'

'I'm not rich!' I plead. 'We've lost everything, the cars, the pool—'

'Yeah, right,' Mel cuts me off. 'You really expect everyone to believe that whilst your dad is banged up, you and your lot are slumming it?' She curls her lips in disgust. 'You pulled up in a swanky tank, the papers say you live in a mansion, and,' she kicks the Louis on the floor, which makes me wince, 'you bring your books to school in a bling bag and stick your spendy purse under everyone's nose. *Everyone* knows the money is sitting in a bank somewhere, just not anywhere the cops can get to it.'

'That's not true,' I sob. I'd been trying so hard not to cry again in front of this bully and ruin my reapplied make-up. 'We're broke. Even Mum might have to find a job.'

My stomach sinks as I realize how that must have sounded.

'People like you make me sick, Daisy Davenport,' Melanie sneers. 'Five years and you didn't even know your cleaner's surname. You called her Mrs Polski, Mrs Polish, and thought you could buy her off with a bit of lamb and few brandy-soaked cherries. And as for that whole leprosy stunt with my lad Jake—'

'Please . . .' I beg. 'Please leave me alone.' My back is breaking from bending backwards. 'Jake's yours, I don't want him.'

Mel steps back and leans against the door, folding her arms over her large boobs. 'But I can't leave you alone, can I?' She grins sarcastically. 'Because I am the chosen one, the one who has been asked to make sure you are never alone, and believe me, I'll always be watching you.'

Chapter Thirteen

'See, I told you you'd make friends instantly,' Mum says, as two hours after I thought I'd be home, I finally stumble through the door of The Laurels and collapse at the kitchen table, where Portia is slumped with her head down, and Aston is sitting with his chair pushed back on two legs, his bare feet resting on the stripped pine. 'You're that sort of girl. Instantly popular.'

I'm dying to get my shoes off and my feet up. Mum's Prada trotters might *look* flat and comfortable, but the walk from the station has ripped the back of my heels to shreds in a way that the silver Louboutins never did.

I couldn't face Mum turning up at the school gates in the Cayenne, so I sent her a text to say that some of the girls were going to mooch around the shops after school and had invited me along. What actually happened was I spent the afternoon sitting in class feeling sick, trying to say as little as possible, keeping my head down with tissues spread out on my lap in case anyone accidently on purpose knocked Tippex on my skirt. Then, after school, I hid in the loos until a cleaner came in and threw me out, after which I ran to the station and waited nervously behind a pillar for the train, like some fugitive on the run from the police, worrying that I was going to have stress-induced squits as my insides felt terrible.

'Yeah, it's fine for Little Miss Popular, but I've had, like, a *totally* hideous induction day!' Portia moans, raising her head. 'I've been treated like a leper!'

'You too?' I say, painfully prising my blood-crusted black socks over my heels before taking them off. 'Why?'

Perhaps news has got round that my sister has been sleeping with a married illegal immigrant, although, on second thoughts, most of Portia's friends would think foreign adultery rather exciting.

'Like, people sat on the other side of the common room rather than come over and talk to me,' she continues. 'It was, like, Dad had totally died or something.' She lets her head fall back on to the table with a loud thud. 'We're social outcasts!'

'I've told Portia that people are embarrassed and don't know what to say, so they just avoid us,' Mum says.

'Hardly anyone phoned me after your father confessed. Jonathan Howard has been the only one who's stuck by us. He's been an absolute brick.'

But his daughter has dropped me like a stone, I think to myself.

'I've had loads of calls from girls wanting to comfort me,' my brother grins. 'Chicks like a dude who's down.'

'What sort of day have you had?' I ask Mum, ignoring Aston's leering boast.

'Not great.' She gives a thin smile. 'I went to a few employment agencies, but it seems I'm not qualified for anything and I'm too old to go back to being a promotions girl in a skimpy bikini.'

'You're still a foxy mum,' Aston drawls, picking dry skin off his feet and flicking it on to the floor. 'Oscar Peterson says you're a definite M.I.L.—'

'Yes, well, thank you,' Mum says, trying to sound stern but clearly thrilled that one of Aston's teenage friends thinks she's a hot momma. 'But Oscar's fantasy is not going to help find me a job that gives us money, somewhere to live and food on the table.'

I look at Mum. She's tired, stressed, worried, trying to work out the settings on the Aga. I feel gut-wrenchingly sorry for her, and for the first time I feel really angry towards Dad about what he's done and where it's got us.

I've never felt angry with him before, not even when he stopped me going to a party with Ollie on a school night, or when he made me take back a totally lush sequinned skirt I'd bought on a London shopping trip to Selfridges with Mum, because he said it was too expensive when I was still growing. I was a bit miffed, but I knew he was right. Going to a party during the week wasn't a great idea when I had to get up at six-thirty the next morning, and the skirt would be more of a sparkly bum-bandage than a miniskirt within months. But now I'm so angry towards him I feel scared. If Dad were here now, this would *definitely* be my Gherkin Moment, the moment when I took my blood-crusted socks and wrung his thieving neck with them.

Compared to us, I think as my fingers curl into a fist, *he has it easy.*

I don't mean that being locked in a small cell with thugs is a breeze, but at least for the foreseeable future Dad's got a roof over his head, his bills are paid, he'll be given food and even a job sewing mail sacks or something. He doesn't have to worry about heating bills, where to live or whether he can afford to refill the tank of Mindy Howard's car when it runs dry. *He's* not going anywhere that's needs petrol. I'm also mad that he's hiding in prison, ignoring my letters, refusing to see or contact me.

I never imagined my father was a thief *and* a coward.

The buzzer at the gate goes, and for a moment we all wait for Krystina to bustle in and announce who it is. Then we remember: Krystina's gone off with the lamb chops.

'I'll go,' I say, getting up and padding into the hall.

'Hello?' I say into the intercom.

'Please could I speak to Miss Daisy Davenport, daughter of Mr and Mrs Davenport?'

Good heavens! The woman sounds as if she's calling at Buckingham Palace.

'Who is it?' I ask cautiously, worried it might either be Mel the Mad Pole who's stalked me all the way home, or a deranged footie fan about to kidnap me as revenge for The Dons going bust.

'My name is Jessica Fawcett and I am here on urgent business.'

I press the button for the gates to release, open the front door and wait for Jess to waddle up. But I wait and I wait, and when there's no sign of her, I dig out a pair of flip-flops from the coat cupboard and head down the drive.

A sweaty Jess is standing in the lane on the other side of the gates, which have now swung shut, dressed in mucky cream jodhpurs, a yellow T-shirt with a horse's

164

head on it and, by the lumpy look of her chest, a very badly-fitting bra.

'Jess!' I say through the railings. 'What are you doing here? Why didn't you come in?' Her pink bike is leaning against one of the stone pillars, its white tyres still slowly turning. 'I opened the gate for you.'

'Er, I thought that a butler or someone would come to collect me,' she shrugs. 'I wasn't sure what people do at these big houses.'

'I'll let you in,' I say, stabbing numbers into a keypad by the gate.

But nothing works.

I try every combination of birthdays and anniversaries I can think of, before remembering Mum changed the number when Krystina left, just in case she came back for the family silver or the widescreen TV.

And I can't remember the new code.

'I'll go and get the remote from my bag,' I say, turning towards the house. 'Wait here!'

I'm not actually sure the remote is going to work, as rather than leave *Assertiveness NOW!* in the loos for someone else to find and Mel telling them it was mine, I stuck it in my bag where it soaked into every book, pen and Tampax, and possibly into the dibber's electronics.

'No! No! It's fine!' Jess calls after me. 'There's no need!

I just wanted to ask you whether you'd sell Polly to me? I was hoping to ask you at school today, but I didn't see you.'

'Oh . . .'

'Mum's finally got a job, at a call centre, and the woman who's taking over the stables from Belinda says I can keep her for free, as long as I work there after school and at weekends, so if you tell me how much you want, I could afford to give you say ten pounds a month towards her?'

Polly is worth at *least* three thousand pounds, which would mean Jess will still be paying for the pony when I'm practically forty. Forty!

'Please say yes!' Jess pleads through the bars. 'Please please!'

'I think that would be OK,' I say cautiously. Jess has caught me on the hop and I feel a bit trapped. 'I'll talk to Mum, but the money would be useful, what with the whole Dad-in-prison thing.'

'Some of the girls say you still have money,' Jess admits. 'It's just that it's hidden in Bermuda or somewhere.'

'That's not true,' I say. 'We're broke and need to move out quickly. Mum's looking for a job, so if you hear of anything . . .' My voice trails away as I realize how stupid

I am to even mention job-hunting to Jess. It's not like she'll know of anything suitable.

'Ali G, you know, the man who owns The Kebab King chain, he's opening a new branch in Dickens Road and he needs a manager. I think there's a flat with the job too; I overheard him telling someone when I was in the Copperfield Street branch at the weekend.'

'I'll mention it,' I say. 'Thanks.'

'How was the first day at Bensham?' Jess asks.

'Um, well, I had Melanie Grabowska chaperoning me.'

I fully expect Jess to say: *Oh, isn't she an absolute cow? She made my life a misery, she's a known bully, yada yada yada*, and then we can discuss anti-bullying tactics and solidarity against mean girls, and how we're going to bring down the ultimate Bensham Bitch and be hailed as the girls who saved the school from savagery. What with that and becoming a School Stylist, I'm on to a winner here, I'm sure.

'Oh, isn't she an absolute sweetie?' Jess gushes. 'Some of the others like Sonja and Deeza used to be really mean to me – you know, tripping me up when I went past and knocking Tippex over my books – but when Mel saw them doing it she put a stop to it. She'll look after you.'

Seems like I've been singled out for special treatment then.

'I'm off to the stables now,' Jess says excitedly, swinging a meaty thigh over her pink saddle and putting her feet on the pedals. 'Oh, and one other thing. Thanks for recommending that book, the one by Wanda-May Rubin. I bought it in Smith's and it's great! I'd never have had the courage to come here and ask you about Polly if it wasn't for that book. It's changed my life.'

Chapter Fourteen

'You don't think Mum's, like, totally serious about this kebab job, do you? I'd rather die than— Oh! My! God! Are you preggers? Has Ollie become The Sperminator?'

Portia's done one of her bursting into my room unannounced routines to find me on my knees in the en suite, holding my hair back whilst retching over the toilet bowl.

I've been doing this on and off since about five this morning, which is when I woke up in a panicky cold sweat, my gut engulfed with waves of nausea, my head pounding with terror after a dream where both Melanie and Wanda-May had cornered me in a toilet and wrapped me in loo paper whilst Cheryl Cole stood on the cistern (in a fabulous turquoise minidress) and egged them on.

I've taken a couple of paracetamol for my headache, but chucked them straight back up again.

In a brief lull between retches I managed to get dressed for school, deciding against Chloé trousers, a cashmere sweater and shiny shoes, and ditching the Louis V in favour of a cheap cotton beach bag that still has sand in the bottom. But the sight of myself in my Bensham get-up has started me retching again, even though there's nothing left to bring up but acid and biley foam.

'I'm not pregnant,' I say, wiping my face on quilted loo paper and flushing the loo. 'As if.'

'Mum's fish pie then?' Portia suggests. 'I thought the haddock was like, well dodgy.'

From my position on the cool limestone-tiled floor, I look up at my sis sitting on the edge of the white claw-foot bath, swinging her bare brown legs, not a care in the world, her life at Park sorted whilst I'm due back in the lion's den.

At the thought of walking through the school gates, I retch again.

'Oh, gross!' Portia cries. 'Are you sure luvver boy hasn't got you up the duff?'

I'm quite sure. Since Dad was arrested I haven't even seen Ollie, but after I told him that I'd deleted his text by mistake, he sent a message suggesting we meet up at PizzaExpress in town on Saturday lunchtime. I should be ecstatic but I'm not because I had two other texts last night, *both* from Melanie Grabowska.

The first said Had a gd day? and came whilst Portia was screaming, 'You cannot be serious!' when Mum said she was *very* interested in the position at The Kebab King and would be ringing Mr G today.

The second arrived just before I turned the light out. Sweet dreams it said, which was enough to give me nightmares.

'So, like, what is it?' Portia asks, nibbling at the skin around her thumbnail. 'If you're not with child, what's with the morning chundering?'

Portia and I have never been exactly close. I mean, I love her because she's my sister and we share the same DNA, but that's about as far as it goes. We're not two peas in a pod or anything like that. She thinks I'm boring and has been known to call me Daisy the Dull, whereas I think that she's an exhibitionist drama queen with a big mouth and dubious taste in men, clothes and make-up. So, other than a surname, a double-helix and a father in jail, we have nothing in common.

But I'm desperate to tell someone about what happened yesterday, and I don't want to worry Mum when she's already got so much to stress about.

I put the loo seat down and sit on it.

'Promise you won't tell Mum?' I say. 'Swear on Bentley's life?'

Portia nods gravely, making an elaborate cross over her white T-shirt. 'Promise.'

'You know I said I had a good day at Bensham yesterday? Well, I didn't. It was terrible. The worst.'

There, I've said it! And fessing up actually makes me feel better, less retchy. A bit of minty mouthwash swished around my gob and it will be as if I've never spent the last few hours bent over the bog turning my stomach inside out.

'I thought you went out with some of the chavs after school?' Portia says. 'When Mum told me I fully expected you to come home with a pram and a baby called Tia Maria wearing earrings.'

'I lied,' I admit. 'I didn't go out with anyone. I hid in the loos after school.'

'Really?' Portia raises her eyebrows. 'Pourquoi?'

'To stop Mum picking me up and the girls picking on me. Half the school think I'm a snobby cow, half just blank me and one girl cornered me in the loos, threw my book in the toilet and made me fish it out.'

'What book?' Portia asks, as if the subject matter is really relevant.

'Just a book!' I say. 'A school book.' No point in telling

my sis it was a manual on how *not* to be a pushover.

'Well, at least it wasn't one of yours,' Portia says. 'I'd die if even a droplet of water got near my signed copy of *Twilight*.'

I knew it. Confiding in Portia has been a total waste of time.

Then she says, 'I know what it is, it'll be one of those initiation ceremonies, like when Aston started at Huffman's and he had to run around the quad with an apple in his mouth and a pheasant's feather up his arse. Now you've fished the book from the bog you'll be well in with the charvas.'

'It wasn't,' I say. 'It was bullying. This girl with a head like a pumpkin is supposed to be looking after me, but she's terrorizing me, sending me threatening texts.'

'Well, if there's text evidence, you've got her,' Portia points out. 'Let me see.'

I get up and go through to the bedroom where my phone is on my bedside table. My stomach gives a nervy flip as I see I've got a new Mel message.

Portia follows me.

'She's sent another one,' I say, my heart drumming in my chest. 'She's just sent another one!' I can feel retches begin to roll up my gut.

'What do they say?' Portia asks.

173

I flick through the texts, although I don't really need to read them off the screen. The words of the first two have been going round and round in my head all night.

'*Had a good day? Sweet Dreams* and now, *See you later.*' My voice rises with hysteria. '*Now* do you believe me?'

Portia snatches the phone off me and reads the texts.

'Oh, get a grip, Daisy,' she snorts. 'I thought you were going to say they said something like: *Don't go near a level crossing* or, *You're dead meat, Davers,* but, *Had a good day?* Come on!'

'It's the *way* she's saying them,' I protest. 'She's being sarky. She's taunting me.' I screw my face up and hiss, 'Had a good day?' and then make sucking noises with my mouth. 'She's like that man in *Silence of the Lambs*, the one in the mask.'

'What, she wants to eat you with a glass of Chianti?' Portia asks, putting my phone to her ear.

'What are you doing?' I squeak.

'Ringing her,' Portia says. 'Firing a warning shot over her yellow head.'

Oh. My. God. I want to die. I am going to die. If I don't crumple right here on the carpet Melanie is going to kill me anyway.

I make a lunge for my iPhone, but it's too late.

Portia is through to the bully.

'No, it's Portia Davenport, Daisy's sister? Yah – well, listen here, Pumpkin Head, my sis says you've been like a total bitch to her, sending her, like, totally threatening texts, having a go at her in the toilets, drowning her book and being *really* beastly. I just wanted you to know that, like, any more bog antics and you'll have me to answer to, OK? And I'm, like, dead hard, even though I'm in the sixth form at Park.'

Could my sister sound any more snotty if she tried?

I can hear Mel's voice at the other end of the phone.

Portia's nodding, fiddling with her left earring.

'Right . . . Yah . . . Yah . . . She does . . . Yah . . . She can be . . . OK . . . Yah . . . I'll tell her.'

Portia tosses the phone on my bed.

'She seemed perfectly normal to me,' she says. 'You've clearly got yourself bent out of shape for nothing. She said you were, like, totally flash with the bling accessories at school yesterday and got up everyone's noses by lording it around, talking about Dad's Ferrari and the Louboutins and she was, like, just warning you to back off if you didn't want your head kicked in. She said you got the wrong idea, got all upset with her when she was trying to help.'

'I didn't!' I protest. 'Portia, really I didn't.'

'You can be a bit wimpy, Daisy,' Portia points out. 'Oh, and she said you came on to some lad she had her eye on, which miffed her.'

'I didn't come on to him!' I squeak. 'He just wanted to know if my leprosy was better!'

Portia stares at me. 'God, Daisy, sometimes I think you are *well* weird,' she sneers. 'But if she's still a pain, let me know and I'll punch her lights out.'

Portia wanders out of my room as my phone skitters across the duvet.

It's a text from Mel.

`Just had a v.interesting chat with your`
`sis. Yours, Pumpkin Head.`

And I don't even make it back to the bathroom before I retch into my hands.

'Mum, drop me on the main road, *please*!' I beg as Mindy Howard's Cayenne speeds through the streets towards Bensham High.

'We're already late because of your stomach-ache,' Mum points out, ignoring my pleas. 'I'll drop you right at the front gate.'

My heart sinks as I think of the huge car sweeping up to the school entrance where Deeza, Sonja, Kaylee and Mel will be hanging around, waiting until the last possible moment to go through the gates.

I turn round to give Portia a pleading look, hoping she'll back me up, but she's gabbing on the phone to Mitzie MacDonald, assuring her that compared to her, Kristen Stewart is an absolute troll, it's just that R Patz doesn't know it yet.

'Oh, by the way,' I say. 'Is it OK if Jessica Fawcett, you know, the girl that exercises Polly, buys her off us for a tenner a month? I've said it should be. I meant to ask you last night.' What with the bullying, the Kebab King job and eating dodgy fish, Jess had slipped my mind.

Mum shakes her head. 'Sorry, darling, no can do. Mia Howard is going to be Polly's new owner.'

'*Whaaat?*'

I can't believe what I'm hearing. Mia hates ponies, donkeys, horses, in fact anything that might lift its tail and fart or crap when you're sitting on its back. What on earth does she want with Polly, unless it's cold revenge for Jess and Dom's kebab kiss?

'You sold my pony to Mia without even asking me?' I squeak.

'Daisy, don't cause a fuss,' Mum snaps, even though I've hardly raised my voice. 'Remember, we don't actually own Polly, the receivers do, and Jonathan made them an offer and bought her for Mia. I thought you'd be pleased she's found a good home with someone you know. She might even let you ride her.'

'But I don't want to ride Polly,' I say, feeling close to tears. Ahead of me I can see girls milling around the entrance to Bensham like a shoal of piranha fish waiting for their prey. Me.

'Then there's no problem, is there?' Mum says brightly. 'The whole pony thing has worked out beautifully.'

'Here she comes,' a girl shouts as I walk towards the gates wishing I had a different skirt to the one I'm having to wear. I'll go shopping on Saturday and see if I can find something cheap and shapeless for next week. 'Princess Daisy mixing with us common chavs again.'

My legs are so wobbly I feel sure I must be doing a silly walk, one of those bendy bobbing walks comedians do thinking it looks funny. It certainly doesn't feel funny this morning; it feels as if I'm walking to the gallows. However much I try, I can't summon up any Wanda-May mantras or channel my inner Cheryl.

Someone pretends to bow down as I wobble past.

'Welcome back to Bensham, your Royal Cowness,' she mocks.

'Not just any old cow!' a voice calls out. 'A really posh cow. A pampered expensive cow!'

'Yeah, but they all end up in the same place,' another jeering voice adds. 'Shot in the head in the knacker's yard!'

Acid burns my mouth as I try and choke back a retch that has made it as far as my ears.

To cackles of laughter, I keep walking with my head down until two pairs of wide feet in black flat shoes block my path.

I look up to see flinty-eyed Melanie, her arm around a puffy-faced and sobbing Jess.

'Poor Jess is very upset,' Melanie explains coolly. 'Apparently, you promised her she could buy your pony and then sold it to someone else.'

'I didn't know Polly was already sold!' I squeak. 'I've only just found out myself.'

'You said I could have her,' Jess sobs. 'Last night you stood behind those metal gates at the end of your drive and said I could have her, and then I went to the stables and the new woman said Mr Howard had bought her!'

Jess starts sobbing even more, her whole body shaking as she gasps for breath.

'Are you saying this posh cow didn't let you in?' A gum-chewing Deeza has ambled up with Sonja and Kaylee. Deeza is wearing gold hoops the size of dinner plates in her ears. Sonja and Kaylee are sharing one set of earphones, the white lead connecting them like an umbilical cord between evil Siamese twins. 'You had to stand outside her gates like some stinky zoo animal behind bars?'

Jess nods and sobs.

'It wasn't like that!' I say, looking pleadingly at Jess, willing her to explain the situation. 'I couldn't open the gates. We'd changed the code to stop a Pole pinching a telly and I couldn't remember it.'

Oh God. I am *so* dead.

'Mia's just doing this to get back at me,' Jess cries. 'You know she is. I thought you'd stand up to her. I thought we had a deal. I even told you about a job for your mum.'

'Mia?' Melanie queries. 'Your bitchy bezzie?'

'I was only friends with her because my dad paid me to be,' I say, and then *so* wish I hadn't.

'Seems as if you and this Mia bitch have a habit of upsetting Bensham girls, don't you?' Melanie says menacingly. 'What was it you called me? A chubby continental chav?'

I can hear girls asking: 'What did she call Mel?' and the shocking answer spreading around the group like wildfire.

Then the chants start, slowly at first, getting faster and

faster, louder and louder as girls gather round me, the circle of menacing bodies moving closer and closer.

Rich bitch!

Rich bitch!

I can feel spit on my face.

Rich bitch!

Rich bitch!

Behind me, someone swipes the clip from my hair and tosses it into the air.

RICH BITCH!

RICH BITCH!

My head starts to swim, I feel hot, cold, sick, frightened and totally trapped. I'd like to sink to my knees and put my hands over my head and block out the taunts, but the circle of hatred is so close, there's not enough room. Instead, I'm shoved around like washing in a tumble dryer, bumping off blazers and bouncing off bags.

'Enough!' Melanie shouts, wading through the chanting, spitting girls. Accompanied by the sound of ripping stitches, she drags me out by my left arm and I stagger head-down through the jostling bodies, gasping for air.

The others start to amble towards the gate, muttering, turning back and glaring at me, giving me the evils. Jess blows her nose and follows them, and I'm left alone in the street with Melanie, my tortoiseshell clip trampled to smithereens beneath my feet.

'Thanks,' I gasp, trying to get my breath back, rearranging myself, sticking my fingers under my left armpit and realizing there's a gaping hole along the blazer's seam.

'Oh, I didn't do it for you,' Mel says. 'As your chaperone I have to be on my best behaviour. I did it for me. You and I still have scores to settle.'

'Please,' I say, trembling. 'Please leave me alone. I'll stay out of your way if you stay out of mine. Please, Mel.'

'Been whinging to your snotty sister, eh?' she sneers, leaning against the wall. 'Nice one. But of course, she's at your old school and you're here, so not a lot of help really.' She nods towards my bag. 'Did you bring the swanky shoes in then?'

I didn't. After the incident in the loos yesterday when my Marc Jacobs skirt was sneered at, I didn't think I should start carrying around Louboutins for Melanie to inspect, even if they are dog-chewed.

'But I told you to,' she snaps. 'Don't you *dare* ignore me *ever* again. Bring them in or else . . .'

Her threat hangs heavily in the air as she reaches into her bag, pulls out a can of Coke, shakes it, and then holding it towards my face pulls the ring, drenching me in sticky brown froth.

'Oh dear, what an accident,' she smirks. 'And by the way, it's only Mel to my friends. It's Melanie to you.'

Chapter Fifteen

'So, have you got them?' Melanie asks as we file out of geography on Friday lunchtime.

'Yes,' I say, swallowing hard and opening the beach bag.

I've been carrying these wretched shoes around for over forty-eight hours without Mad Mel mentioning them. I'd rather hoped she'd forgotten and I could go and hide in the library or sit in the loos whilst she went off for a burger with her thuggy mates. So far, complete avoidance of anyone in a Bensham uniform has been an excellent anti-bullying strategy as, other than a bit of gob on a book and some paper flicked at me, everyone's left me alone in my misery. Of course, the downside to this is I have zero chance of making a single friend, not even anyone really ugly who looks like they could do with a friend because they haven't got any. Even really ugly friendless girls are out of my league.

Melanie peers at the shoes, which are nestled between my pencil case and a copy of *Great Expectations*, glittering under the strip lights.

'Nice one,' she nods. 'Let's go to the cloakroom.'

I follow her and we sit on one of the benches whilst I get the shoes out.

'The right one is a bit mangled,' I explain, as Mel kicks off her flats. 'Because of the dog.'

'Hello again!'

It's The One That Got Away, Jake, standing looking every inch The Stud Muffin in his battered black jacket, his rucksack slung casually over his shoulder.

'Oh, hi!' I say, feeling my face colouring.

'How's things?' he asks, ruffling his hair in a frankly super-sexy way. 'Settling in?'

'OK,' I reply cautiously.

I feel really emotional that someone here is actually speaking to me without being nasty, but I can't encourage any further conversation with The Stud Muffin if Mel's not to push my head down the toilet in revenge. She's opposite me, trying to force her feet into Mr Louboutin's dog-eared finest whilst making cow eyes at Jake.

I just sit on the bench and try to look as gormy and uninterested in this sixth-form stunner as possible.

Jake watches Melanie still wrestling with the right shoe.

Then he picks up the left one, which is lying on the floor.

'This yours?' he asks me.

Without smiling or changing my expression I nod.

'Then, Cinderella, you shall go to the ball,' he laughs, ducking down on one knee and presenting the shoe to me. 'But remember, when the bell goes for lessons, the fairytale is over!'

He is sooo funny and super-cute. If only I'd stood up to that shallow cow Izzy Tricket and gone out with him. Not that it makes any difference now of course. I have a boyfriend and a mad Polish stalker.

Jake pulls my school shoe off and slips the silver peep-toe on my foot. I've still got my long black socks on, so, to be honest, it looks well odd, a bit indie/trashy, the sort of thing weird singers might wear on stage. *So* not the sort of classic prepster look I'd usually go for.

'It fits!' Jake declares dramatically. 'Well, I never! It's just like Cinderella and the ugly sisters!'

Before I can bite my tongue or punch myself in the mouth, I giggle.

And then *so* wish I hadn't.

Melanie is glaring at me, her eyes practically glowing

186

red and spinning in their sockets.

'I was just joking,' Jake says to Melanie as some of the other girls dotted around us snigger. 'I didn't really mean you were ugly, just that Daisy is—'

Melanie takes the other silver shoe and throws it at me so hard, I duck as it whizzes past my ear. Then, stuffing her feet back in her flats, she stomps off.

'Oh dear, I think I've upset your friend,' Jake says, retrieving the shoe from under the bench and gently putting it on my other foot, sending shivers down my spine. 'She looked well narked.'

My stomach starts doing somersaults, not because The Stud Muffin has actually touched me, but because I'm thinking of how Melanie is going to make me pay for Jake's ugly-sister comment. Perhaps now is the time I'll be strung from the goal posts and pelted with eggs.

'I read about all the stuff with your dad,' Jake says, sitting next to me.

I'm terrified that Melanie will see us. She's probably watching me right now, seeing whether I'm flirting with Jake or even talking to him, planning to kill me.

'You coping OK?' He gives me a slight and thrilling nudge with his elbow.

I *so* want to talk to him but I daren't, so I just sit there wearing socks and Louboutins, avoiding speaking, looking or interacting in any way with The Stud Muffin.

'If you need to talk, we could go for a coffee . . .'

Oh I want to, but I can't, not if I don't want to be crucified and egged. I need Jake to leg it if I'm not to peg it.

'I can't speak to you.'

I tried to mutter this under my breath without moving my lips, but I've never really practised ventriloquism, so I sound like some rude robot.

'Sorry, for one moment I forgot,' Jake says acidly, getting up and swiping his rucksack from the floor. 'I forgot you think you're better than the rest of us.'

And then he strides away.

I want to run after him and tell him that I really need to talk to him, to someone, to anyone. I want to ask him whether after he left Huffman's the Bensham boys called him names and threw his stuff in the loo. I want to tell him that I'm not snobby and standoffish, just scared.

But I can't. Not only am I a wimp, I need to find my school shoes and they've vanished. They were on the floor, but now the floor is empty, except for a piece of grey gum and some dust bunnies.

Melanie reappears, her face as black as thunder.

'Have you seen my shoes?' I ask, hoping she won't hear the tremble in my voice or the unspoken accusation that I know she's somehow to blame for their disappearance.

'They're on your feet, stoopid,' Mel sneers. 'Are you blind?'

'I mean my school shoes,' I say. 'Please tell me where they are.'

My voice is all weedy and pleady and needy and I hate it, but I don't want to anger Mel or I'll *never* get my shoes back.

'I don't know what you're talking about,' she shrugs. 'But I did notice a pair of shoes in the trash outside the science block.'

The bitch! The absolute bitch! Any minute now the bell is going to go. There's no way can I waltz into French wearing six-hundred-pound shoes, even if one of them is scarred for life by a dog.

I grab my bag and my blazer and set off, running through the corridor, out through the back door, round the back of the building so as to avoid running in silver heels in front of everyone.

There it is . . . the science block . . . the bin is ahead . . . I can see someone throw something in it . . . Oh, gross! Someone's just gobbed in it . . . I have to get there before the bell . . . I have to get my shoes and get to French . . . I will not let that scheming malicious cow win . . . Cheryl wouldn't let anyone nick her shoes, even flat black ballet pumps . . .

And then I'm flying.

Flying gracelessly through the air before crash landing head first on the pavement, feeling as if I'm body surfing on a giant cheese grater.

'So, what I don't understand, Daisy, is why you were running in heels during school time?' Mrs Wilson asks tartly as I sit on the side of the bed in the medical room whilst she dabs my grazed legs and arms with cotton wool and pain-inducing yellow antiseptic.

'Someone stole mine,' I mumble, glancing at Melanie who's leaning against a cupboard, looking all concerned and chaperony. 'They put them in the bin by the science block. I was running to get them.'

'Probably just high jinks,' Mrs W says as she starts dabbing my face, making me wince.

The pain from the graze and the antiseptic isn't the only thing that's distressing me. It's the first time I've met the Head of Pastoral Care and her clothes sense is absolutely dire. How can she relate to Year 10 girls when she's committed the cardinal sin of wearing a flowery skirt with flesh-coloured popsocks? I'm sure she means well, but I can't imagine taking advice from someone who can't get their hosiery right.

'Any idea who took them?' Mrs W enquires.

Now's my chance to tell the truth, to tell her that my first week here has been made a misery by bullies and nip this intimidation in the bud before it gets any worse.

I think of Wanda-May Rubin and her hair, try to let a calm and assertive feeling wash over me – something that is very difficult when it feels as if you're being dipped in acid – and say, 'Well, Melanie—'

'Yeah, I saw a couple of stinky little juniors mucking around with them, and told Daisy,' Melanie jumps in. 'I was just going with her to get them when she tripped.'

As Mrs W concentrates on her dabbing routine, Melanie gives me such an evil glare, any minuscule feeling of confidence I might have had ebbs away.

'Well, thank you for bringing Daisy in, Melanie.' Mrs Wilson smiles. 'You'd better get back to French.'

Mad Mel grins and says breezily, 'See you later, Daisy!' and waltzes out.

Liar! I think to myself. *Crazy bully liar!*

Mrs Wilson stops dabbing and stands in front of me holding the ball of bloody, antiseptic-soaked cotton wool.

'But, Daisy, why did you have those sort of shoes in

school anyway?' she asks. 'What were you thinking of? Were you showing off?'

I start to cry, which is a terrible mistake if your face is one big open sore.

'You're not finding this easy, are you?' Mrs W says softly. 'The change of school, your father . . .' Her voice trails off.

I shake my head and tears and snot fly about. I try to wipe my face with my arm but the nylon jumper feels like a pan scrubber on my exposed skin.

'Has anyone offered you or your family counselling, a chance to talk to someone about what's happened?' Mrs Wilson asks, going to pat my hand, but thinking better of it when she sees my grazed knuckles.

'No,' I croak. 'I've read stuff on the Internet though.'

'Then I think you should learn more about C.O.C.K.S.'

Whaaat? Did I hear right? Did Mrs Wilson actually say that? No wonder Mum didn't want Portia to come here! I'm not sure I'm ready for this either. I mean, I'm only fourteen and have been seeing Ollie for five months, not even that if you count the fact he's blanked me since Dad confessed and the four weeks of Tuscany and Cornwall. And do they think all kids of prisoners go sleeping around and need advice?

'Children of Convicts, Kent Support,' Mrs W explains

without even a slight snigger. 'You're not the first pupil to find yourself with a parent incarcerated. Would you like to go to a meeting? With your mother's permission I could arrange it.'

'I'd just like to go home, please,' I sob. 'If it's not too much trouble.'

Chapter Sixteen

'OK, Mum, you've, like, made your point. Now let's go home,' Portia grumbles. 'We all realize that a life of crime doesn't pay. I'll stop using fake ID to get into pubs and clubs, and Daisy won't steal shoes again.'

'I borrowed them,' I mutter. 'I never stole them.'

'And the whole drugs scenario is totally over,' Aston assures us from the front of the car. 'Once I've been to court.'

'So we don't need to be taught a lesson,' Portia says. 'Joke's over.'

Mum ignores us but the satnav breaks the tense silence with its cheery, 'You have arrived!' as Mum turns the car into Dickens Road.

We crawl along, looking at each shopfront. There's a betting shop, a launderette, an Indian restaurant, a newsagent/off licence, a Chinese takeaway . . .

And then The Kebab King.

Even though the shop hasn't opened I know it's The Kebab King because a man with a horrendous hairy builder's butt is up a ladder painting the letters *KEBAB K* in green in an arc across the window.

Mum stops the car and turns round to face my sister and me.

'This isn't a joke, girls, this is real life,' she says tersely. 'Would you rather I worked here, sell an organ on the black market or work as a prostitute?'

I think of The Laurels, look up at the grubby windows above The Kebab King, and wonder if it's wrong to wish Mum would sell her body so we didn't have to live here.

'Right then,' Mum says, no one daring to answer her question. 'I haven't had a job interview for about twenty years, so wish me luck.'

All three of us mutter something incomprehensible but which clearly isn't *Good luck*.

I'd like to wish Mum well, I really would, but I can't. I just can't encourage her to take a job in a kebab shop. I know she's in a rush to get everything sorted, to get on with life without Dad, but something else, something better than serving pressed meat and chilli sauce has to turn up, surely?

A bell rings as Mum pushes open the door of the shop. It's still being fitted out and smells of paint and woodwork, rather than roasting meat and stale fat.

'Ali Gazidis,' a man announces, bustling from behind the counter. 'But everyone, they call me Ali G or The Kebab King!'

Mr G has a nice friendly face, though a bit weather-beaten, like he's spent too much time in the sun with not enough high-factor sunblock on. He could have looked forty instead of sixty if he'd started on a good skincare routine years ago. He also looks as if he's eaten far too many of his own kebabs.

'Chrissie Davenport.' Mum extends a slim brown hand towards a surprised-looking Mr G, who takes it and shakes it with a hairy-backed mitt. 'We spoke on the telephone yesterday. I've come about the job.' She gestures towards the three of us who are standing in a row like the Three Wise Monkeys. 'These are my children: Aston, my eldest, Portia and Daisy, my youngest.' Mum rolls her eyes as she introduces me to The Kebab King. 'She doesn't usually look like that.'

'I had an accident,' I mutter, picking one of the scabs on the back of my left knuckle. 'I accidentally kissed a pavement.'

I look worse today than I did yesterday, which is tragic given that in a couple of hours I'm meeting Ollie. He hasn't seen me for ages and *never* looking this rank. Long sleeves and jeans cover up my battered and bruised body, but my nose, chin and hands are black, blue, red, brown and shredded, and no amount of MAC make-up can disguise the fact that I look as if I've been rubbed down with coarse sandpaper, taking exfoliation to a whole new level.

Mr G smiles sympathetically at me, unlike Mum who went mental, shouting, 'What is it about you and those ruddy shoes?' when she saw me on the doorstep yesterday afternoon, looking as if I'd been in a fight, wearing a ripped skirt and carrying her broken Louboutins.

Mrs Wilson ran me home, nattering on about C.O.C.K.S. and how it helped a lad in Year 8 whose mother was sent to prison for repeatedly shoplifting Gillette razors from Superdrug and selling them on eBay, whilst I just sat there, shell-shocked, wondering how come one moment I'm zooming around in a Ferrari, going to a posh school and stressing about whether I'd get the Tiffany heart on a chain I want for Christmas, and the next I'm sitting in a beat-up Saab estate next to a woman with dire dress sense, on my way home from Chaverama High, worrying about when I'll next be used and abused by the Bitches of Bensham.

'You came in that car?' Mr G asks in a heavy foreign accent as he looks past our little family group towards the maroon Cayenne parked outside the window. 'You came *here*, for a job, in *that* car?'

'Yes,' Mum says, sounding puzzled. 'Have I parked in the wrong place? Am I going to get a ticket or something?'

'This is a wind-up, yeah?' Ali G chuckles, shaking his head. 'Kosta from Kosta Kebabs has sent you to wind me up. No no! Wait! This is more Ari from The Kolossi Grill!'

Clearly he's finding this an absolute hoot.

Out of the corner of my eye I can see Mum's posture stiffen.

'I can assure you, Mr G, this is no wind-up,' she says tartly. 'You have a job with a flat and all the kebabs, pies and chicken portions we can eat. I need a job, my family need a flat and we'd rather eat kebabs than starve. And for your information, the car is borrowed from a friend.'

'I am sorry, Mrs Davenport.' Ali G wipes tears of laughter out of his eyes. 'You are not a suitable candidate. I am sorry if I've wasted your time.'

Mum looks furious. 'Why?' she demands. 'What's

wrong with me?'

'Don't make me say, Mrs D,' Ali says. 'Please.'

'I told you about my husband on the phone!' Mum snaps. 'And you still agreed to see me! I need to know why you have had a change of heart.'

'Like I said, I'm sorry.' Ali G starts to walk us to the door, clearly hoping that he can usher us out. 'It's not your criminal connections, it's just that you're too English and posh for my business.'

'That's discrimination!' Portia growls accusingly at Mr G. 'If we said because you're a fat wrinkly Greek you couldn't have a job, you'd go ape.'

'And it's illegal,' Aston adds in a menacing voice. 'We could take you to an industrial tribunal and clean you out of cash.'

I breathe a sigh of relief. One day when all this is over, oh how we'll laugh about the time Mum went for a job in a kebab shop dressed in Prada and pearls. If there was ever even a tiny sliver of hope that Mum might be given the job, Aston and Portia threatening Mr G has certainly dashed it.

Mum steps forward and eyeballs Mr G, though she has to bend her legs slightly to do it.

'Listen,' she growls. 'My husband is in jail and is likely to stay there for a long time. In a few weeks we have to leave our house because the bank owns it, along with the cars, my jewellery and even our rocking horse. I have three children, no job, no qualifications and am too old to be a dolly bird sitting on a car bonnet in a fake-fur bikini. I badly need this job, and I am not too proud to admit it.'

Goodness, Mum's wonderful when she's backed into a corner! Even Wanda-May would crumple when faced with Militant Mother in full flow.

'Have you ever done any catering before?' Ali G asks cautiously. 'Any experience of preparing food for the masses?'

'Am *I* used to cooking food for a crowd?' Mum turns to her children as if this is the most ridiculous question she has ever heard. I'm hoping that she's not referring to the dodgy fish pie she knocked up the other night. 'I'll have you know that I have catered for the Ladies' Circle Golf Day, the Oldstone and District Tennis Club Summer Ball and,' she waggles her finger at Mr G, 'many other prestigious soirées.'

This is only half true. She did choose the menus but she didn't do so much as open the oven or brandish a knife. Krystina did all the cooking whilst Mum floated around rearranging the napkins, fretting that the fresh flowers might wilt before the guests arrived.

'And by employing me, you also get my son and daughters into the bargain!' Mum announces triumphantly. 'Your staffing problems are solved in one go!'

Aston and Portia look as if they might faint. I'm wondering if I'll have to wear a uniform and a hairnet like the overweight woman in the Copperfield Street branch does.

'It's either this, selling a kidney or turning to prostitution,' Mum says. 'The choice is no longer mine, Mr G, it's yours. So what's it to be? Selling my body or selling your kebabs?'

There's a pause, then Mr G's battered brown face breaks into a smile. 'Mrs Davenport, we open in four weeks. If you like the look of the flat upstairs, the job is yours for a three-month trial period. I'll help you out until things get going, then we'll see what happens.'

'Really?' Mum says, flushing, and looking shocked that the job she's just been campaigning for is actually hers. 'You mean that?'

'We sometimes get a bit of trouble with drunks coming in after the pubs close, nothing serious, just shouting, demanding extra curry sauce, throwing chips around.' He shakes his head. 'No one would dare argue with you, Mrs Davenport, believe me. You're not just a cook, you're one scary lady bouncer too.'

Chapter Seventeen

One o'clock outside PizzaExpress on the main drag.

I'm waiting for Ollie, feeling sorry for myself, looking a real mess with my scuffed skin and with hardly any cash on me as the money machine swallowed my card. I rang Mum in a panic as I was going to buy a black sack of a skirt for school. In the battle of soft wool v. school tarmac, the tarmac won, but it seems as if it's not just Dad's bank account that has been frozen by the police; we're all being blanked by the bank.

Much to our horror, Mum has taken the job of managing the new Kebab King. The flat upstairs was OK, much bigger than I thought it would be, and it's going to be fitted out with a new bathroom and kitchen. I'll have to share a bedroom with Portia, so she'd better not snore or bring back any weird lads. I'm *so* not happy about the whole thing, but there's nothing I can do, and, as Mum says, let's give it three months, by which time our finances will be sorted out and there might even be enough money left over for us to buy somewhere small, but of our own.

I look at my watch (ten past one) and scan the crowds. Where's Ollie?

I get out my phone and am about to ring him when a text buzzes through from Mad Mel.

Been stood up?

I spin around trying to spot her, but there's no sign of a pumpkin poking above the crowd.

'Daisy?'

I jump.

'Ollie!' I squeal. 'Hi!'

I want to throw my arms around him and snog his face off, but I can't because firstly my arms are really bruised from where I fell down yesterday, and secondly, I know that I'm being watched by a girl who's out to make my life hell, which sort of takes away the passion.

'God, Daisy, what's happened to your skin? It looks like you've got leprosy!' Ollie grimaces. 'Half your face is falling off.'

'I fell on to a giant cheese grater yesterday,' I say, as I carry on whirling around like some demented searchlight looking for the enemy. 'I was wearing silver peep-toes and pretending to be Cheryl Cole.'

'You've been pretending to be Cheryl Cole?' Ollie sounds confused.

'Aye, ah have!'

'And talking Geordie?'

'Why aye. I mean sometimes. By mistake.'

'And why are you spinning round?' he asks. 'Daisy, what is wrong with you?'

'Someone is spying on me,' I whisper, looking up at the shop windows in case Mel's there, watching me. 'A mad Pole with fat feet who looks like a pumpkin.'

Then I have a brilliant thought! I can't see her, but she's clearly watching me, and if she knows that this six-foot tall dark-haired specimen of rugby-playing hunk-hood is mine, she'll be mega jealous.

I launch myself at Ollie, but he takes a step back, which not only shocks me it sends me staggering forwards into the street like some can-clutching drunk.

'Ollie!' I cry, narrowly avoiding knocking over a woman with twins in a pram. 'What's up? Is my skin freaking you out? It's not contagious.'

'It's nothing,' he shrugs. 'By the way, this is for you.'

He digs into his jacket pocket and hands me a package.

So what if he's avoided a street snog because I'm all

manky and flaky? He's bought me a present! He knows how down I am about being at Bensham (I've been leaving moaning messages on his voicemail every day) and he's bought something to cheer me up.

So stick that in your . . . your . . . whatever, Melanie Grabowska!

I wave the bag in the air so that Melanie can see I'm about to be given something fabulous by my fabulous boyfriend. Maybe it's a book of love poems in a gift box, or a set of funny DVDs or perhaps . . .

I pull the present out of its wrapper with a flourish and Wanda-May's photograph stares back at me.

It's another copy of *Assertiveness NOW!*

'You owe me £9.99,' Ollie points out.

'Oh,' I say, feeling deflated. 'There's a bit of a cash-flow problem at the mo. I can't even afford a cheap skirt. But I'll give you the money later. I'll get it back from that scaredy-cat Jess girl I told you about.'

I'd had to pretend the book wasn't for me, but for someone too wimpy to order it for themselves.

'You never really said why you used my name,' Ollie says. He's standing looking hot but awkward, shifting from one black and silver Nike to another. 'Why couldn't you give them yours?'

Now it's my turn to jiggle nervously. 'Well, what with

the whole Dad-being-arrested thing, I thought it best to keep a low profile,' I say. 'There are journos in the bushes and bullies in the window and people out to get me.'

Ollie grabs my shoulders and looks me straight in the eyes. Or at least I think he's looking in my eyes. It could be he's staring at the bruise just above my right eye, which is purple and yellow and the perfect shape of Italy, including a little satellite bruise the spitting image of Sicily.

'Daisy,' he says gravely. 'You've become really *really* weird lately. Do you know that?'

I'm shocked. Weird? Me? Despite what Portia said, I am the least weird person I know. I never dress weird or talk in weird slang. They don't put weird girls in the Park Hill brochure. But I have been under stress, as anyone whose father has suddenly gone to jail would be. Under the scabby skin there are painful monster zits brewing, and what with the daily morning anxiety-vomming, I'm a bit freaked my teeth will fall out with all the regurgitated stomach acid. So what if the stress is turning me into a spotty gummy weirdo? I think Ollie could be a little more understanding, buy me nice presents and meals, pamper me a little. Isn't that what boyfriends are for, not just for snogging?

'I don't know what you mean,' I say, balancing my non-present on the edge of a nearby bin and scratching madly at all the scabs I can reach as they've suddenly started itching. 'I'm fine.'

'I'm serious, Daisy,' Ollie says sternly. 'Spinning, spies, the weird accent, the lies—'

'What lies?' I say, scrabbling at my chin, which feels as if it's crawling with ants. 'I haven't actually been telling people I'm The Goddess Cheryl, if that's what you mean. I've just been pretending to be her.'

Ollie looks really uncomfortable, but then I've just felt blood trickle down my chin so I don't blame him. I dig some pink loo roll out of my bag (with all the sobbing we've run out of tissues at home) and hold it against my face.

'You led me to believe you'd fed the cats when you hadn't, Mia did. You even let me give you a box of fudge from Mum as a thank you.'

I hadn't actually realized that the fudge was from Ollie's mum. I thought it was a present from him.

'When did you speak to Mia?' I gasp. I'm mega-miffed because I'd asked The Weasel to tell Mia not to reveal the change of cat-feeding plan.

'I didn't,' Ollie says firmly. 'There was nothing on telly one night so we ran back the security tape, just for

207

something to watch. We saw Mia come in and out.'

'You have a security camera?' I gasp, remembering how I pretended to exterminate the cats as I chucked salmon at them. 'A camera that records stuff?'

'Yes,' Ollie says darkly. 'And we saw *everything*.' He sighs and shakes his head. 'I dunno, Daisy, you used to be so sweet, so normal, so dependable and now you've turned bonkers. I don't want a girlfriend who lives on Planet Nutter and shoots cats. Perhaps you should see Mum, you know, have a bit of psychoanalysis. I'm sure she'd give you a discount on the fees.'

'I'm just under pressure!' I say, stung that he thinks I'm a fruitcake and wondering how he thinks I can afford a session with a shrink when I can't even buy a cheap skirt. 'It'll all be fine when we're living above the kebab shop.'

Ollie looks aghast. 'You're going to live above a kebab shop?' he says. 'Since when?'

'Since about an hour ago,' I say, still on the lookout for the mad Pole. 'Mum's going to manage a branch of The Kebab King, Aston and Portia are going to work in it and I'm going to wear a hairnet. Let's go and have a pizza and I'll tell you about it.'

Ollie shakes his head and looks grave. 'Daisy, we're moving in different circles,' he says, and for a moment I wonder if he means I'm spinning one way and he's spinning the other. 'I think we should cool it for a while, just until this whole thing with your dad blows over. What with Dad being a judge, I can't really be dating the psycho daughter of a jailbird.'

'You're dumping me?' I gasp. 'Just when I need you and could eat a Fiorentina with a soft egg and extra anchovies, you're dumping me?'

'I think it's for the best,' he says sadly. 'I did send you a text to tell you, but you didn't get it and then Smith's rang about the book so I had to see you. You can post me the money.'

And then he starts walking away.

Just like that.

Five months of going out, snogging and buying him presents and he's dumped me.

Five months of imagining a life with Ollie, living in a lovely house with masses of gorgeous well-behaved children and a full-time housekeeper to wash his rugby kit.

Five months of emergency pussy duty.

Well, he can get lost. I'm not going to run after him and grovel in front of Mad Mel, who's probably seen me get binned. He can go and feed his own cats, and if he thinks I'm going to post him the book money he'll be waiting by the letterbox for the rest of his life! Wanda-May and Cheryl wouldn't put up with this behaviour, and nor will I. He was going to dump me by text! I won't be treated like this. I deserve better than to be used so shabbily.

No I don't.

'Ollie!' I cry running after him. 'Don't go! Please! I'll try to be normal, honestly I will. I won't kill your cats and I can get you a free kebab whenever you want. Or chicken and chips! Load of chips!'

But my now ex-boyfriend's gone, sucked into the crowd of Saturday shoppers.

'Miss! Miss!'

I turn round to see an old woman with a shopping trolley piled with black bin bags, pushing it towards me at such amazing speed, the ears of the scruffy mutt sitting on the sacks are flying backwards.

It's Wee Woman.

'Here you are, dear,' she says breathlessly, handing me Wanda-May's book with a grubby hand as I try not to retch from the smell of stale urine coming from her layers of old clothing held together with a belt of string. 'You left this behind.' She peers at me. 'Did you know you have pink toilet paper hanging from your chin?'

And even though my heart is breaking and I want to

crumple on to my grazed knees in the middle of the street and scream and cry and rant and rave, I smile at the old homeless woman, rip the bog roll from my chin and say politely, 'Thank you so much. That's really kind of you.'

Chapter Eighteen

'Right, four teams, each of seven. Captains: Caro, Bharti, Deeza and . . .' A tracksuited Miss Fullerton, our games mistress, scans the group as I keep my head down.

At Park Hill I loved netball, zipping around the court in my short brown pleated skirt, my yellow polo shirt covered by a Wing Attack vest, sticking my hand up for the ball, knowing that India or Chelsea or Emily would pass it to me. Then I would lob it to Lucy Palmer-Talbot, our Goal Shooter, so she could pop the ball through the hoop, after which we'd all crowd around hugging and giving each other high-fives. But now I'm practically shaking with fear in the changing room on a Wednesday afternoon, dressed in a black skirt, white T-shirt and white trainers. I got out of games last Wednesday by pleading a monstrously (and non-existent) heavy period, but today, when I rubbed my still grazed legs and arms and said that after my fall last Friday I still felt too sore to play, Miss Fullerton brushed off my excuse and told me that a bit of exercise would help ease the stiffness.

'. . . Melanie.'

I'm sunk. As she's still supposed to be my chaperone Mad Mel will obviously pick me first to appear all nice and helpful – then kick me around the court and stamp on my toes.

But Melanie doesn't choose me.

None of the captains do.

One by one, Deeza, Caro, Bharti and Mel call out the names of girls who scuttle across the changing room into their teams, giggling and hugging each other, pointing at their mates in other groups. Even Jess is picked before me. In fact, *everyone* is picked before me. And it turns out that four teams of seven make twenty-eight girls – and I'm numero twenty-nine.

I stand in my skirt, marooned on my own, unwanted, my entire body burning with humiliation.

'Daisy?' Miss Fullerton spots me trying to shrink behind the coats, hoping that I can just hide until everyone has gone and forgotten me. 'Come outside and we'll make sure you get a game. A bit of fresh air and sunlight will help those knees heal.'

* * *

Miss F puts the whistle in her mouth and blows an ear-bleeding blast.

'Deeza!' she yells across the playground, waving. 'Over here!'

Wearing a green bib with WA on it, Deeza Okuma runs over to the side of the court where I've been standing watching the reds (Captain Mad Mel) thrash the greens (Captain Deeza), not because the greens are rubbish, but because Deeza and her friends are spending more time grinning and posing for the lads in the sixth-form block watching from the window, rather than noticing where the ball is on the court.

'Daisy's been telling me she used to play Wing Attack for her old school. Can you give her your bib and let her play the last two quarters?'

Deeza glares at me. 'I'm Captain,' she pouts, jabbing the thin white ribbon draped across her chest. 'I can't leave the team unless I'm injured.'

I have a strong desire to kick Deeza in the shins and *give* her an injury.

'Well, Daisy can be Captain now,' Miss Fullerton says impatiently. 'Come on Deeza, get going. Get the stuff off and give Daisy a run out.'

A sneering Deeza practically rips the bib and ribbon from her body, thrusting it towards me, long sharp fingernails first.

I put the bib on and loop the captain's sash over my head and under my arm, and as I do so, something odd happens. I suddenly forget that I'm gutted over Ollie binning me or permanently terrified of the other girls. The fact that we're moving from The Laurels and Dad's in jail and I still haven't heard from him is pushed into the background. For the first time in ages I feel as if I'm in control, that I can do this and do it well, even with stiff scabby limbs.

'Over here!' I shout to my team as I run on to the court.

The girls huddle around me as I give them instructions on who to watch out for, who to block, who might surprise us with a sudden break and so on.

And in a rare bold move, I also tell them to keep their peelers *off* the sixth-form block and *on* the court.

'Well done, Daisy!' Miss F slaps me on the back. 'I didn't realize we had a netball star in our midst. You should think about trying out for the county.'

'Thanks!' I feel a grin spread across my flushed face. 'I might.'

As we come off the court I feel amazing. I couldn't turn the game around because we were too many goals down when I took over (fifteen to be precise), but there's no doubt that my captaincy meant everyone got better organized on the court and changed the game. Just think what I could have achieved if I'd been made top dog in the first place! I *totally* ran rings round Mel, and on the court the others were fine with me; we seemed to really gel as a team. Maybe seeing me out of the classroom has altered their opinion of me.

Perhaps things are finally looking up, I think to myself as a great wave of relief washes over me.

Miss Fullerton carries the mountain of discarded bibs into the kit cupboard and I go into the changing room where some of my teammates are huddled together, giggling and whispering. Then someone says loudly, 'Did you know Daisy Davenport's had a sex change? She was born a boy called Davie.'

'It's the thighs that give it away,' someone else says in a stage whisper, as I stand rooted to the spot with horror. 'They're big and hairy, like lads' thighs. You can add boobs and shave the stubble, but you can't disguise freaky thighs! No wonder her boyfriend ditched her. He discovered he was dating a tranny!'

Deeza grabs my black trousers from the peg and spots the label: Chloé.

'Ooh, swanky pants!' she taunts, waving them in the

air. 'Normal stuff isn't good enough for our ladyship. Or should I say, *Lord*.'

After the bank kept the card, other than jeans and leggings, Mum's designer trews were the only black trousers in the house. Usually I would be thrilled to swan around in soft wool, well cut around the bum and with stylish turn-ups, but it's been just one more thing to mark me out as different.

Deeza pretends to sneeze into them and blow her nose. Then she throws them at me accompanied by shrieks of laughter. They land on my head, one leg draped over my left eye.

I should ignore them, I know I should, but I can't. I've had nearly two weeks of sneery looks and snidey comments, of girls blanking me or sniggering behind their hands when they see me. Two weeks of having plain flour substituted for self-raising in food tech, my calculator hidden in maths, my books swiped in English and my science projects sabotaged. I've thought of telling Mum about how I'm suffering, but I can't add to her worries, not when she's extra stressed because of the food hygiene course Mr G's sent her on. I've toyed with the idea of ringing one of those bullying helplines to ask for advice, but haven't plucked up the courage to do it, and anyway, they'd just tell me to tell a grown-up, who'd tell stressed-to-the-eyebrows Mum, which would make me feel even worse. I did ring Clemmie and started to tell her that I was finding things tough, but I'd only just got started when she said she had to go as she and the others were about to see a film and could she call later? I clutched my phone *all* Saturday night waiting for her to ring back, but she never did.

I'd like to tell Dad, but even if he would see me, what's the point unless he can order a bully hit-squad from inside? Mum says he's still in a bad way and sharing a cell with a man called Tony who's banged up for pinching lead off a church roof.

Mia seems to have fallen off the face of the earth.

With the Chloés still round my neck, to pointing and jeering I dash into a toilet and look down at my legs.

I've never really looked at my pins in forensic detail, but under the harsh loo lighting I can see the girls are right, there's masses of fine blonde fuzz. Why did I never notice it before? And what's that? An odd bulging vein on the back I've never seen. A really ugly purple knotty thing, like a blackberry wedged under the epidermis.

I spin around examining my pins, which seem to get more and more lad-like with every second.

No wonder Dad told me to take back that sequinned miniskirt to Selfridges. It wasn't because it was too expensive, it was because he knew his man-legged daughter would look like a varicose-veined drag queen in it!

Someone kicks the toilet door, rattling it on its hinges.

'Blubbing again, Davie?' Deeza sneers. 'If you're not, with legs like that, you should be.'

And then a little voice pipes up. 'Deeza, don't be mean. Leave Daisy alone.'

It's Jessica Fawcett. Jess is trying to stand up for me, even though she thinks I sold Polly to Mia just to get back at her. Shy Jess has tried to stand up for me, even though I can't stand up for myself.

Chapter Nineteen

'Daisy?'

Our pretty young history teacher is calling my name from the front of the class where she's been handing back marked history assignments.

At the back of the room I stop picking my spots and slide further down my chair and under my desk. If I slump any lower I'll be lying down. I'm getting more and more like my vertical brother every day, without the dubious druggie habit, of course.

Aston appeared in court a few days ago on the cocaine charge and got a £250 fine, twenty hours of community service in a drug rehabilitation centre and a severe ticking-off from the magistrate, though my bro seemed more humiliated by being forced into wearing a pinstriped suit and red tie by Mum. The other law-related news is that the charges against Mum employing an illegal immigrant have been dropped, and Franco the randy gardener has been deported, much to Portia's delight.

'Daisy?' Miss Appleton queries again. Through a sea of chair backs and blazers I can just about make out her blonde head swivelling around. 'Is Daisy off *again*?'

This isn't an unreasonable question as my attendance rate at Bensham is running at 54.3 per cent. As well as the odd afternoon where I've had to leave for (fictitious) emergency root canal treatment and an infected ingrowing toenail, I've pretended to be at death's door many times in the last few weeks on days when I've woken up and just couldn't face going in.

So far Mum's fallen for the *I've got a painful period* lie, *This is the world's worst headache* excuse (complete with major groaning and the wearing of mega sunnies) and several strange non-specific viruses. There have also been mornings when I've genuinely been retching my guts out, from cold fear rather than a bug. But this morning, Thursday, Mum was unreasonably suspicious of my fictional flu, despite my cunning ruse to snort freshly ground black pepper to bring on realistic sneezes. She forced me to come in, even dropping me right at the gate in Mindy's *Look At Me I'm Loaded* Porsche. Not only was that a total bummer, my nose still itches.

'Davie's at the back,' Sonja says, turning and pointing at me.

This is it.

I'm sunk.

In front of the entire class I'm about to be exposed as a fraud and a cheat, just like my dad.

At Park I took a lot of time and care over my homework, creating pretty-coloured fonts and lovely borders on the laptop. But what with everything going on, quite frankly I couldn't be bothered to explain in three thousand words or less why World War One ended in 1918. In fact, I was really tempted to write *Because we won*, and leave it at that.

So I cheated.

I found someone on the Net called Podz666 who'd posted his own essay on a website. Then I went berserk with the cut and paste keys, moved things about a bit, stuck a few of my own words in, and because the whole WW1 thing was so depressing, found a poppy in ClipArt and put it in the margin to brighten things up.

Miss Appleton smiles when she sees me. I love Miss Appleton, in a non-lesbionic way of course. She's one of the few teachers here who knows how to dress and is on first-name terms with hair-glossing serum. I can relate to Miss A, unlike the walking clothing catastrophe that is Mrs Wilson.

'An excellent piece of work, Daisy, the best in the class. Well done.'

My face starts burning. I feel like a slug for being praised for something I haven't really done. A slug slithering even further under a piece of furniture, hoping to hide somewhere cool and dark.

Around me there's a hum of disgruntled mutterings.

At Park, whoever got the highest mark would get a round of applause. I remember standing up and bowing to cheers when I got the top grade for my project on fashion icons of the twenty-first century. True, Izzy Tricket had chosen Lady Gaga, but the signed photograph of Cat Deeley that Cat's PA sent me after I'd written the white-toothed one an admiring letter, gave me the extra winning mark.

Miss Appleton hands a bunch of paper to someone at the front of the class. Slowly it's handed back. Nuri, a lad with sticky-out ears sitting in front of me, passes it over his shoulder. When I take it, my fingers touch something wet and sticky.

Right across the front page someone has scrawled *Posh Swot* in bright pink lip gloss and stuck a piece of gobbed grey gum in the centre of my poppy.

Ahead of me I spot Sonja putting a pink tube back in

her pencil case as she nudges Deeza.

And then the fire alarm rings.

Again.

This will be the fourth fire drill we've had in the three and a half weeks I've been at Bensham, and none of them have been real *burn down the school*-type fires – unfortunately. It just seems there are some kids who are unable to pass a red box saying 'In Case of Fire – Break Glass' without doing so.

'All right! All right!' Miss Appleton calls out above the noise of the fire alarm ringing and kids shrieking. 'File out quietly.'

We're supposed to leave everything behind, but I can't risk getting back to find my things nicked or trashed so, abandoning the forged essay, I grab my bag and slink towards the door.

Outside on the landing, shrieking bodies are swarming along the corridor and down the stairs, pushing each other around, clutching their phones, Facebooking the imaginary fire.

I accidentally bump into Deeza.

'Ugh!' she screams, exaggeratedly brushing her blazer. 'Davie the leper has touched me! I'm contaminated!'

We spill outside, but the moment we do, the alarm stops and everyone groans.

'Back to class!' teachers start shouting from all directions. 'Come on! Get a move on.'

But when I get back to my desk, my history assignment is missing. Everyone else's desk is cluttered with stuff, but my desk is Clearasil clear.

I look under the desk and around the chair, but it's vanished.

So many people could have taken it. So many people taunt me or blank me or hate me. It's probably crumpled in a bin outside, or hidden at the bottom of Melanie's school bag.

Then Miss Appleton comes over to my desk, puts her hand on my arm and, whilst I'm thinking what lovely glossy pale-pink nails she has, says very quietly, 'Daisy, could we have a chat after class?'

'Bensham takes a very strong line on bullying,' Big Bird squawks as I sit opposite her in her office.

Popsocks woman is next to me, legs crossed, a sliver of pale hairy calf spilling over the top of one of her tan knee-highs.

'We won't tolerate it,' Mizz Birch continues. 'Bullies are *severely* dealt with.'

Both women glance towards the shrunken head.

Wow. They really do take bullying seriously if they

put mean girls' heads on sticks.

I smile as I enjoy a little fantasy about Melanie and co. being shrunk and displayed on a bookshelf. I'm not into housework, but how great would it be to flick a feather duster in their shrivelled faces!

I've been smiling much more since I fessed everything to Miss Appleton last Thursday. Turns out it wasn't the Bensham Bullies that had pinched my work, but the teacher. When I'd left because of the fire alarm, Miss A had seen it on my desk complete with its gloss and gum graffiti, pulled me aside later and asked what was going on, and, faced with someone so kind, lovely *and* stylish, I told her *everything*. Well – not quite everything. I didn't fess up that it was Podz666 that wrote most of the assignment rather than me. She'd have had to be wearing top-to-toe Prada for me to open up about *that* one.

At first I was seriously freaked that just like Portia having a go at Melanie, telling Miss Appleton would make everything a zillion times worse. But now it's Tuesday lunchtime, no one has harassed me, and I've felt *much* better. I wasn't even sick when I woke up this morning, a first for weeks.

'I've spoken to all the girls you mentioned to Miss Appleton, and Sonja and Deeza agree they've gone too far,' Mizz Birch says. 'They won't do it again . . .'

I can feel there's a *but* coming . . .

'. . . but when I spoke to Melanie, it's clear that you've not been entirely innocent in this sorry tale, Daisy.'

My blood freezes in my veins. I can't be hearing this right. Is Big Bird saying I'm somehow to blame for having had my life made hell?

'What?' I squeak.

'Let's see.' The headmistress flips open a pad of yellow paper. 'Calling Melanie a chubby continental chav; flashing expensive clothes and accessories around school; telling her you think you're wonderful; bragging about how much your shoes cost; getting your sister to threaten her and call her Pumpkin Head; flirting with her boyfriend; pretending you have leprosy to ditch someone because he was short and overweight, calling me . . .' she coughs, 'Big Bird.'

'It wasn't like that!' I gasp, horrified as the charges against me are read out.

'So you didn't bring in a bag or shoes worth hundreds of pounds?' Mrs Wilson asks.

'Yes, but—'

'And you admit you laughed at Melanie because she's not as slender as you?' This is Mizz Birch having a go.

'I didn't start it!' I protest.

'And you've been keeping away from everyone, not

making any effort to try to make friends?'

'Yes, but because—'

'And did your sister threaten Melanie and call her after a large orange vegetable?'

'And did you accept money to be friends with someone?'

'Did you really say you were wonderful?'

'Even better than Cheryl Cole?'

The accusations come thick and fast.

Between Mizz Birch and Mrs Wilson I feel as if I'm being interrogated in court. Shouldn't someone be here to defend me, if not a barrister, at least Mum?

'I can explain . . .' I try.

But I can't, because I'm beaten.

I start to cry, salty tears stinging my scabby spots.

'You see, bullying can work both ways, Daisy,' Mizz Birch says as I wipe my nose on my blazer sleeve. 'And when bullies are found out and confronted, they're often unable to stand up for themselves so they turn on the tears and crumple.'

Big Bird and Popsocks Woman are staring at me. Quite frankly, Mrs Wilson's stare looks more as if she's trying to hold a fart in her bum than appear stern, but Mizz Birch is another matter. It's very scary to be glared at by someone who resembles a giant feathered Muppet.

'Perhaps at your old school Mrs Channing tolerated an atmosphere of bragging and bitchiness,' Mega Muppet says through her pursed beak. 'Maybe adopting a superior attitude to others was even encouraged. But as you can see from the reaction here, snobbery and snootiness is not welcome.' Mizz Birch shuffles in her chair and adjusts her boobs with her elbows. 'What goes around comes around. If you treat people with disdain, mockery and contempt, Daisy, you must expect similar treatment.'

It takes me a few seconds to realize what Mizz Birch is getting at.

And then it hits me.

She's saying *I'm* a bully. Melanie Grabowska has persuaded them it's *me* who's been a bitch. Me, Daisy Davenport, the sort of girl who wouldn't dare say boo to a goose in case it turned round and pecked me.

Mizz Birch sits back on her perch and watches me weep. 'I have to say Daisy, Alicia Channing gave me a totally different impression of you when we spoke. She said you were a beacon of enthusiasm: polite, helpful, a team player, a real asset to the school. There was even mention of you being a hamster monitor.'

But she still chose Portia over me for the bursary, I think bitterly.

'This is just a warning shot,' the headmistress growls.

'But if Melanie comes to me with *one* more complaint about your behaviour...' Her eyes dart to the shrunken head, '... the school will be forced to take further action.'

I walk out of the headmistress's office and, through blinding tears, start running.

It's almost time for afternoon lessons to begin so I'm struggling against the crowd, banging against bodies, elbowing people out of the way, ignoring the shouts of kids who tell me to watch where I'm going or to eff off.

I run past the library with its strict no food or drink policy, where every lunchtime I hide behind a shelf of physics textbooks, pretending to be interested in particle fission whilst trying to quietly eat a fruit and nut bar without leaving telltale crumbs.

I speed by the toilets, where during breaks I sit on the back of the loo with my feet pulled up, my heart hammering, hoping no one will look over the top and see me cowering, only to come out and find someone's written *DDs a leper* in lip-liner on the mirror, something I found very upsetting, and not just because they missed out an apostrophe.

Then it's round the back of the gym store where I wait after school until the coast is clear, even though it stinks of pee because some of the rugby lot can never be bothered to take their boots off to go inside and use the toilet.

I've had it with Bensham High. Even if it upsets Mum, I'm leaving and I am *never* going back. They can shout and rant and threaten, but no one is going to stop me running out of those school gates to freedom. No one.

'Yeow!'

Except possibly a gorgeous sixth-form Stud Muffin called Jake. I've just barged straight into him.

'Watch where you're going!' Jake snaps, picking up his rucksack, which has fallen off his shoulder in the collision. Then he stares at me and says softly, 'Daisy? Have you been crying?'

I snort back snot, rub my eyes and hang my head.

'Come on, what's wrong?' The Stud Muffin presses. 'You can tell me. Are you OK?'

Well, as he's asked.

'I'm picked on, blanked and jeered at; I wake every morning and am sick with nerves; I sit in lessons unable to concentrate because my gut is churning; my father's in jail and doesn't want to see me; we're moving from a humungous Georgian house in the country to a titchy flat above a kebab shop in town; my old friends are ignoring me; I have no new friends because I have to hide from the bullies all the time; my boyfriend has dumped me cos he thinks I'm a nutter; you think I'm a snotty cow; I'm *covered* in spots; and, to cap it all, the teachers think I'm a bitchy bully and want to shrink my head. So, I think that would have to be a big fat *No*, Jake, I'm *not* all right!'

Good heavens! I temporarily forget to feel wound up and tragic as I realize I've said the word *No* out loud, in public, in front of a frankly gorgeous specimen of male DNA.

What a breakthrough! I mean, I haven't said it in an assertive way as in, *No I will* not *let you have twice as much space in the wardrobe, Portia, just because you're older*, but it's a start. I should keep practising.

'No. No. No. No.' I chant out loud, thrilled at the way the word is now so easily tripping off my tongue. 'No! No! No!'

'Do you want to talk about it?' Jake asks. 'It might help.'

'No. No . . .'

And then I realize I've said *No* to Jake, by mistake.

This is terrible! I used to always say *Yes* when I meant to say *No* and now I'm saying *No* when I mean *Yes*.

'Sorry, I mean, yes. I was just practising saying the word no, you know, no, *non*, *nein*, *nyet*.'

232

OMG! First Geordie, now Russian. No wonder Ollie thought I was weird. Jake's probably thinking *nutter* at this very minute.

He looks at his watch. 'Look, I'm almost late for double chem, but how about meeting after school, say at The Cappuccino Club?'

Ooh! I've heard some of the girls talk about the coffee shop near here where they go after school. Can you imagine if I sauntered in with Jake? Melanie's chin would drop into her chocolate-sprinkled froth!

Of course, when he'd gone and I was on my own with her, she'd stick my head under the steam machine and blast it.

'No . . .' Good heavens! There's no stopping me now. 'I can't. I mean, I'd love to but I've got to deliver leaflets announcing a Kebab King is opening in Dickens Road on Friday evening. Mum's running it and we'll be living there.'

This isn't a lie to get out of having my head boiled; it's true. I've volunteered to troll the streets and push leaflets through letterboxes encouraging people to taste *Gourmet Kebabs from The Kebab King*.

Taking the doner and shish upmarket was Mum's idea and Mr G went for it. She said that kebabs shouldn't be just for when you've had six pints of lager, but could be in the same league as a good Indian or Chinese, something that you can order when you can't be bothered to cook, or you've given your staff the night off. So as well as the standard stuff, we're also offering Blackened Chilean Sea Bass kebabs, a venison Bambi Burger and an organic lamb doner with rocket salad drizzled with parmesan and balsamic dressing, all of which can also be delivered by Aston on Ali G's son's moped with an insulated box strapped on the back. We're even doing online ordering; Portia's designed a fabulous website with animated kebabs.

'Well, I could help you,' Jake suggests. 'We could walk and talk at the same time.'

So I say *Yes*, arrange to see him at the shop at five, and because I really don't have anything to do until I meet him for leafleting, go back into school and arrive slightly late for English lit, grinning from ear to ear.

Chapter Twenty

'So, what do you think?' Mum asks as I push open the door of The Kebab King.

She's standing behind the counter wearing a green and white bandana around her head, a matching apron tied over her blindingly white T-shirt and a broad smile.

'It's fabulous!' I gasp as I look around.

I'm not just trying to make Mum feel better about our fall from grace, I really mean it; the place looks amazing.

Mum and Ali G have been busy since I was last here, the day Ollie dumped me, and no, I haven't sent him his £9.99 yet. If he wants the cash he can come and get it, though at the moment I haven't got it.

The raised counter and kitchen stuff was already here, but now there are smart metal tables and chairs; a window seat lined with green and white stripy cushions; green and white wall tiles; laminated menus dotted around; a magazine rack full of glossy mags and some frankly rather weird pictures of fruit and veg on the walls.

Just a few weeks ago when Mum was sobbing in the coat cupboard with a Croc up her bum, I thought she'd either crumple at the thought of our fabulous lifestyle disintegrating and turn to swigging gin for breakfast, or marry a doddery ninety-year-old multimillionaire with a dicky ticker, just to keep us all in Louboutins and Ferraris.

Boy, was I wrong.

I know there are still tears because I've seen her wiping her eyes as she opens another bill or finds some other account Dad hasn't settled, but now she's helping to expand a business, organizing Mr G, thinking about sales and profits.

I'm so proud of her and when I tell her, her eyes glisten, though she pretends it's because she's been chopping onions for the freezer.

'Now, remember, don't just drop them in the nearest bin or put four through each letterbox,' she says, handing me a stack of leaflets. 'Each one is a potential customer. Portia's doing the streets as you turn left out of the shop, so can you turn right? Daisy, are you listening?'

I am listening, but I'm also looking at the door and

hoping that at any minute Jake will walk through it. We said five o'clock, but the smart chrome clock on the wall says it's five-fifteen and there's no sign of him.

Clearly I've been stood up.

It's revenge, I think as I start trudging miserably along the road, stuffing leaflets through letterboxes, sending dogs mental, nearly losing a fingertip on one particularly vicious spring-loaded brass flap-on-a-box. The Stud Muffin is standing me up as revenge for the leprosy lie. He's probably sitting in The Cappuccino Club right now, flirting with loads of girls, telling them what he's done, laughing at me.

'Daisy?'

It's not Jake; it's Mad Mel. She's either found out about the kebab shop or she's stalking me again.

I ignore her and keep walking.

'Apparently you've been upset at the way you've been treated,' she says, trotting beside me. 'Seems like we got off to a bad start.'

Still I blank her.

'Jess told me you were opening on Friday. I'll help you deliver those if you like.' She sticks out her right hand. 'Go on, give me half. We'll get it done twice as quick.'

I don't want her here, but I can't have her telling Mizz

Birch I snubbed her offer of help or it won't just be a chunk of meat that will be stuck on a stick.

'OK.' Grudgingly, I hand her a stack of leaflets. 'Thanks.'

'Let's go over there,' she suggests, nodding towards the other side of the road. 'There are loads of houses round the back.'

We pause at the zebra crossing, wait for the traffic to stop and start to cross.

And then just as we're right in the middle of the black and white lines, it starts raining Kebab King leaflets.

'Oh dear.' Mel shrieks with laughter as the glossy rectangles swirl around, bouncing off my shoulders and hitting the ground. 'I dropped them by mistake.'

'Like hell you did. I saw you deliberately throw them in the air.'

This isn't me being all Wanda-May assertive. It's The Stud Muffin who's crept up behind us.

'Look, I'll pick them up,' I say, ducking down. Cars are starting to beep and flash their lights and Melanie doesn't show any sign of doing anything except pout at Jake.

'No, let her do it,' Jake says, pulling me back up with a strong grip. 'She tossed them.'

I'm tempted to keep bobbing down just so he'll

keep hauling me back up.

For a moment I think Melanie's going to be all stroppy, but then she starts scrabbling around my feet collecting the leaflets, handing them up to me and Jake before rushing off down the street.

'Now,' he says, shuffling the paper into a neat pile. 'Are you going to tell me what's been going on?'

'We're back!' I say, laughing as I push open the door of The Kebab King, followed by Jake.

Once we got rid of Mad Mel, I've laughed non-stop, even when I've been telling Jake about the mean girls. Somehow he manages to see the funny side of even the blackest situation. For instance, he pointed out that something wet and sticky on my history assignment could have been *far* worse than lip gloss, and his take on the book in the loo was that at least I didn't find any nasty bio-waste wedged between the pages. We've swapped phone numbers so that if there's an emergency such as Deeza tying me to a bus stop, I can call him. Is it wrong to secretly wish Deeza *will* tie me up but leave my arms free, just so I can ring him?

'Look who's here!' Mum says brightly when she sees me.

Jonathan Howard is sitting on one of the new tables.

Next to him, still in her Park Hill uniform, is Mia.

Half of me is thrilled to see Mia, the other half is totally freaked. Just when I'm allowing myself a little fantasy about Jake asking me out and the two of us meeting Ollie in the street and me saying, *Do I know you?* in a really condescending voice when oily Oll says *Hi*, cupid has chucked Mia and Jake together. If Mia turns on her lad-snarfing charm, the two of them will be out of the door on a date faster than I can say Bambi Burger, and I'll be left trudging the streets with leaflets all on my tod, peering round corners, waiting for Mel to pounce on me and tip me headlong into a wheelie bin.

Except Mia doesn't look cute or lost, she looks nervy, ill and haunted. When she sees me, a brief smile flickers across her face before she sets her features into a completely blank look.

'Er . . . this is Jake,' I say.

'Hi!' Jake smiles.

Mia says nothing.

'How are things?' I ask her.

'OK,' she shrugs, looking at the floor.

'Will you tell Daisy the fantastic news, Chrissie, or shall I?' The Weasel says, looking smug.

'Tell me what?' I say excitedly. 'Is Dad coming out

of prison? Can we stay in The Laurels? Have we won the lottery?'

Mum puts her hand on Jonathan Howard's arm. 'Jonathan has made the receivers an offer for The Laurels, which the bank has accepted, and, as they're going to Barbados at Christmas, Jonathan has agreed we can stay on in the house until the New Year. Isn't that fabulous news?'

'*You're* moving into *our* house?' I gasp. It's bad enough losing The Laurels without The Weasel moving in.

'Daisy!' Mum snaps. 'I thought you'd be pleased. Jonathan's also agreed to take Bentley. We really can't keep him in a flat. It wouldn't be fair when he's been used to so much room.'

'NO!' I yell so loudly, it makes even me jump. 'First my pony, then my house and now my dog! Well, no! I'd rather live on the streets and smell of wee than lose him. If you won't let me take Bents I'll become Wee Woman only with a pedigree Labrador in the front rather than a scruffy mongrel. I'll spend all day pushing him round, picking up bits of wire and eating out-of-date sandwiches.'

'DAISY!' Mum looks absolutely horrified at my outburst. 'What on earth has happened to you? Are you on drugs or something? Jonathan and Mindy are the only

241

people to have stuck with us through this mess. If it weren't for them, we'd need to be out of The Laurels in a few weeks. This gives us breathing space.' She turns to The Weasel. 'I'm *so* sorry Jonathan. It's not like Daisy to be difficult.'

'I'd better get going,' Jake says, looking embarrassed at being involved in a family spat. 'Good luck for the opening on Friday.' He waves at no one in particular and lopes out.

The Weasel stands up, rubs his nose and stretches. 'Well, we must be going too. We're off to a dinner party later, at the home of Judge Simons.' He sounds smug at the prospect of hobnobbing with a legal eagle. 'Mia is *very* friendly with his son, aren't you?'

'You're seeing Ollie?' I gasp. Weirdly I don't feel gutted, just surprised. Ollie always claimed he couldn't stand Mia; too emotionally exhausting, he'd said.

She shakes her head. 'He's seeing Izzy Tricket now. They're only friendly cos we feed their cats.' Her voice is flat and hoarse, practically a whisper, as if all the life has been sucked out of her.

Jonathan Howard kisses my mother on both cheeks and starts heading to the door, Mia in tow, her head down, her shoulders hunched.

'Jonathan, I'm sorry about Daisy.' Mum shoots

me evils. 'Teenagers!'

'Not a problem, Chrissie. Mia's going through a very difficult phase too, aren't you?' He pokes Mia in the arm and she flinches.

'And thank Mindy, won't you,' Mum gushes. 'Tell her I'll get the car back to her when I can sort something out, and if you fancy ostrich nuggets and chips, you know where to come!'

As they leave, Mia turns and glances over her shoulder.

I can't be sure, but I think she looks frightened.

Chapter Twenty-One

'This is, like, so mental!' Portia says, handing over another yellow polystyrene box containing a high-class kebab and a portion of crispy fries. 'You'd think these people had never eaten.'

It's Friday evening on the first day we've opened, and Mum's gourmet kebabs are a roaring success. The shop is packed, a queue is snaking out of the door and the phone is ringing off the hook with people wanting orders delivered. As well as Portia and Mum serving behind the counter and Aston out on deliveries, Mum's roped in Krystina, who's chopping lettuce and tomatoes like a Pole possessed. I'm splitting my time between clearing tables and slitting pitta breads, whilst Mr G, who is supposed to be serving, is standing around beaming, telling his mates Kosta and Ali that gourmet kebabs to go was all his idea.

I'm thrilled for Mum that everything's going so brilliantly. Jake (sigh) and some of his friends popped in; Mad Mel turned up and bought a Bambi Burger without stuffing it in my face, and even Portia is managing service with a smile rather than a sneer.

'Oh my God, it's true!' a girly voice shrieks above the noise of the fans and fryers. 'I thought it was just an ugly rumour, but here you are!'

Izzy, Bee and Clemmie are standing in the shop, dressed up to the nines, gawping at me.

I haven't forgiven Izzy for not inviting me to her barbie and I'm miffed she's made a move on Ollie, but it's great to see the others.

'Hi!' I say, waving a pitta bread in the air and rushing over.

'Oh God, don't come too close,' Izzy gasps, wrinkling her Dannii and taking a step back. 'I, like, don't want to stink of chip fat all evening or get grease on my top.'

'We're going to a party at Dom Harper's,' Clemmie explains. 'Everyone's invited *except* his parents. It should be wild!'

'I thought you hated The Bull?' I query. 'He's a total letch! He jumps on girls and snogs them.'

'Duh, Daisy! His parents have just had a pool installed,' Izzy says condescendingly. 'I'll be bezzies with anyone who has a private pool.'

So that's *why she was friendly to me*, I think. Because I had a pool she could parade around in her tiny bikini, flaunting her unnaturally concave stomach.

'You must feel gutted you can't come,' Bee says gravely. 'Staying here, frying chips or whatever it is you do.'

'Oh, Mum won't mind if I go for an hour or so,' I say, wondering how I'll feel if I actually see Ollie and Izzy together, and whether I'll be able to stop myself drowning them in The Bull's new pool. 'But I don't have a bikini.'

'Er, like, what are you doing?' Bee gasps as she watches me struggle to unknot my apron.

'Coming with you,' I reply, wondering if my underwear is good enough to pass as a bikini. I've a feeling it doesn't match, that I'm wearing Miffy underpants and a Hello Kitty bra, a sort of body battle of the characters. Then I realize it doesn't matter. I won't get in the pool now I know I've got man thighs.

Izzy looks me up and down.

'*You* can't come,' she says witheringly. 'You're no longer in The Glossy Posse. You party with the chavs, not the cream.'

She peers up at the menu board behind the counter. It must be a risk for her, bending her neck back like that. Isn't she worried her giant head is going to snap off and

246

roll across the floor? If it did, the way I'm feeling right now, I'd kick it out of the door and shout, 'GOAL!'

'I'll have a tuna kebab with lettuce and no hint of pitta bread,' she barks at Portia. 'Even sniffing carbs makes me swell.'

'Make that two,' Bee calls out. 'But maybe without the tuna. Just salad in a box, no dressing.'

'I'll have a doner and chips,' Clemmie says, licking her pale glossy lips. 'With chilli sauce.'

Izzy and Bee gasp with horror. 'A doner on the lips, a lifetime on the hips!' they chant disapprovingly.

'You don't want to be touched by the blubber stick, do you?' Izzy adds darkly.

'Just a vegetable skewer then,' Clem says glumly.

Portia's dropped the smile and is now scowling as she slams the order into the till.

'Oh, we don't have to pay,' Izzy says confidently. 'Remember we're, like, top bezzies with your sis, aren't we, Daisy?'

They all look at me expectantly with their mascara-drenched cow-eyes.

Other than Clem's *chaverama* text on the first day at Bensham, not one of them has been in touch to see how I am or whether I'm having a hard time. My Facebook pokes have been blanked, my texts have been ignored and my chat room conversations frozen out. I'm not good enough to go to their swanky pool party, but they expect free nosh. They've kicked me out of their lives and now in an act of delicious revenge, I'm going to kick them out of our shop.

'You're not my friends,' I growl, 'so either pay up or get lost!'

As the three witches show no sign of getting their D&G or Mulberry purses out, I march over and show them the door.

'Go on, go!' I say. 'Take your fake noses and your bobble-heads and bog off!'

The girls gawp at me. Although I've started to say *No* more often, even I'm astonished at my use of the phrase *Bog off*. I seem to have taken assertiveness to a new level.

'God, Daisy, what's happened to you?' Izzy sneers. 'Oh I forgot. Daddy's gone to jail and you've gone to Bensham.' She flicks her head towards the others. 'Come on, girls, let's go and party amongst our own kind.'

And just as I think I've got rid of one set of problems, in walks Melanie Grabowska, who announces in a loud voice, 'My Bambi Burger has mouse shit in it.'

The shop falls silent.

'I bought this earlier and when I got it home, I found mouse droppings in it,' she announces to the queue. 'The place must be infested with vermin.'

Mum and Mr G dart from behind the counter as, with a theatrical flourish, Mad Mel lifts the bread lid off her burger.

There are certainly mouse droppings: three dark mini-torpedoes to be precise. But why would a mouse crap so neatly, right in the middle of a slice of tomato? It looks like some weird excrement garnish. They're even at right angles to one another.

And then I glance at Melanie, and whilst her face looks innocently shocked at finding an unwanted topping in her tea, her eyes are cold and hard and calculating. It's the same look she gave when she deleted my texts and stole my shoes. I bet she looked like that when Big Bird Birch tackled her over the bullying and she blamed me.

'She's lying,' I say to Mum who's turned deathly pale. 'She's doing this to get back at me.' I look over at Portia, who's taken the opportunity of a sudden drop in sales to reapply mascara using the stainless steel door of the microwave as a mirror. '*This* is the girl I told you about. The ringleader of the Bensham Bullies! She's planted the poo!'

'Yeah, tell that to the environmental health people,' Melanie sneers, turning on her heel and walking out, still clutching the poop-filled bun.

I dart after her.

'Hey! I haven't finished with you yet!' I yell down the street. 'You're a lying cow and you know you are!'

Lit by street lamps, I can see Melanie the Mad Pole wave her hand dismissively in the air as her pumpkin head bobs down the road.

And that's it. It's my Gherkin Moment. The red-mist moment Wanda-May Rubin warned me about. The moment when the worm turns. It's just a good job this worm is holding a wholemeal pitta bread rather than a loaded gun.

I fly down the road and catch up with her.

'I said, I hadn't finished with you,' I yell in her face. '*You* put mouse poo in that Bambi Burger didn't you?'

'Prove it,' Melanie shrugs, trying to step past me. 'You know you can't.'

She's forgotten that although she's wider than me, I'm better at netball than her, so pretending her body is an air-filled bag of rubber, I dart and block her path.

'Listen, you bitch,' I snarl, still ducking and diving. 'You can tease me and taunt me and make my life a living hell, and do you know what, I no longer care what you or your thuggy mates do to me. But do not, I repeat, do *not* drag my poor mother into this. She's worked hard to get that place off the ground and I'm *not* going to watch some lowlife like you wreck it without a fight.'

And then . . .

Ohmygod. What have I done?

I'll tell you what I've done. I've just slapped Mad Melanie bang in the middle of her chest with a pitta bread. Half of it is still in my hand, the other half is dangling from a button on her black jacket.

We both stare at this strange bread-based brooch.

For one awful moment as Melanie raises her hand I think she's going to punch me, splattering my nose all over my face. I'll end up like Izzy Tricket, choosing my celebrity beak from a catalogue. Obviously I'll go for a Cheryl.

I screw up my face and wait for the killer blow, but instead of sending me flying, Melanie just removes the bread, brushes crumbs off her coat and says tersely, 'No one has ever done that to me before.'

I'm not surprised. It's not every evening a mad teen goes roaming around the streets armed with a piece of flatbread looking to confront her bully.

'Well, you deserved it,' I say defiantly. 'I've had enough.'

The two of us stand there in the street, pitta breads drawn, waiting to see who'll make the first move. I'm standing stock still, not because I'm squaring up to

Melanie, but because behind my fierce stance I'm actually bricking it and feel rigid with fear.

Then in a voice just above a whisper, Melanie says, 'I know. I'm sorry.'

Wow, I didn't expect that! I never dreamt the ultimate mean girl would apologize, but now she has, the least I expect is for her to grovel on her hands and knees, wailing that she's ashamed of herself and will carry my books around for the rest of the year as penance.

'Is that all you have to say for yourself?' I gasp. 'You've tried to destroy me *and* my family, and you think everything will be OK with just a simple sorry?'

'*Very* sorry?' Melanie suggests.

Then she chucks her pitta-half on the ground along with the contaminated Bambi burger.

Didn't fighting knights throw their swords down as a sign of defeat? Is Melanie dropping her food on the ground to show she's thrown in the (sort of) towel, and will now leave me alone? I chuck my pitta on the ground too, not because I'm admitting defeat, but because I'm feeling rather silly standing on a busy road brandishing half a piece of bread, not to mention wearing a green and white striped apron, a matching bandana and a hairnet.

'Why?' I ask. 'Why have you made my life hell? Just because of that stupid day in Starbucks? I told you, it wasn't me that dissed you, it was my ex-bezzie, Mia.'

Melanie leans against a low wall and kicks the bricks with her heels. I have a feeling that those bricks could have been my head.

'It wasn't just that. I mean, a bit, but there was other stuff.'

'Like?' I'm not going to let her get away with this. I want answers. Good ones.

Melanie chews her lip and shrugs. 'Dunno really. Deeza and that lot always run close to the edge, but I've never been mean to anyone before. I was going to give you a second chance and then you waltzed in with your designer stuff, looking the mutt's nuts, thinking you're Cheryl Cole, Jake slobbering all over you, everyone giving you attention. You narked me.'

I suddenly realize what this has all been about. 'You're jealous!' I gasp. 'You're jealous of me!'

'Maybe,' Melanie shrugs. 'A bit.'

'What's there to be jealous of?' I ask. 'My dad's inside, we've lost everything and I was so nervous on my first day at Bensham I had to pretend to be The Goddess Cheryl just to pluck up the courage to walk through the school gates!'

'I didn't know that,' Melanie says, hanging her head. 'I just thought you were a typical snobby Park Hill cow who thought we were all brain-dead chavs and bitches at Bensham. I thought you needed teaching a lesson.'

I'm about to tell her she's wrong, when I realize that Melanie Grabowska is right. Underneath the fake Cheryl-confidence I was cripplingly nervous, but underneath the nerves I *did* look down on the Bensham girls, because that's what Park Hill girls are taught to do. Mizz Birch had a point when she said Mrs Channing encouraged Park Hill girls to feel superior. My ex-headmistress didn't even let Gloria sniff the butts of dogs that weren't pedigree breeds.

'Well, if I came over like that, I'm sorry,' I say. 'I didn't mean to. But I still didn't deserve to be bullied. No one does. *Ever.*'

'I know and it's over,' Melanie says. 'I'm sorry I've been such a bitch. But Jake has the hots for you though, you can't deny that.'

'Well, he's never made a move,' I say. 'I think after our ski-snog I've put him off girls for life. I think I've turned him gay.'

And then we laugh. Both of us. Together. Laugh and laugh hysterically until I'm in danger of wetting my knickers.

'Melanie, you do know if you don't fess up about planting the mouse poo they'll close us down,' I say as we head back towards The Kebab King. 'Mrs Chmielinski will lose her job and we'll be homeless, again.'

'It wasn't mouse poo,' Melanie admits. 'It was hamster crap, but I'll say sorry. And you've learnt a Polish surname!' She gives me a nudge. 'I think you'd better call me Mel from now on.'

Chapter Twenty-Two

'Daisy, you coming to The Cappuccino Club?' Sonja asks as we amble out of school on Wednesday, almost two weeks since I assaulted Mel with bread.

Wow! This is the first time anyone has suggested I join the frothy coffee clique. I thought that I might have blown my new and still very fragile friendships after a rather tense netball match earlier where, as Captain, I yelled at Deeza because she kept stopping to roll up her waistband to make her skirt even shorter.

I glance across at Mel, who smiles back.

'Yeah, I'd love to,' I say, rummaging in my bag for my phone.

Five missed calls, all from the same unrecognizable non-moby number and all in the last ten minutes. It's been on vibrate, and I haven't felt it buzz as it was wedged between piles of books and files.

I'm not going to ring it back; I can't afford to. The money-munching iPhone has gone, so now I'm paying as I go and having to ration my communications.

But *five* missed calls? Someone's keen to track me down. What if it's Dad in prison? Maybe he's finally got his head straight and is contacting me.

I press dial. It rings and rings and then, 'Yes?' It doesn't sound like a prisoner picking up the phone in a cell block. It sounds like an anxious young woman.

'Um, who is this?' I ask.

'It's the public phone at Park Hill School. Who's that?'

I instantly recognize Mia's impatient voice at the end of the line.

'It's Daisy,' I say. 'I think you've been calling me.'

'I won't be a minute!' I call out as the Bensham girls swarm into the café and I stand outside, my phone pressed to my ear. 'It's just Mum.'

I don't want them to think I'm being snobby and standoffish the first time they've invited me to join them, and taking a call from the Park Hill girl that dissed Mel would permanently slam the coffee shop door in my face.

'Look,' I whisper. 'Can you ring me later? I'm out with friends.'

Ooh, how great that sounded. *Out with friends*.

'Daisy, I really need to see you,' she hisses.

Oh, it's just like the old days; Mia expecting me to drop everything to deal with some major catastrophe such as a shop selling out of her size of jeans, or a disastrous pedicure where her big toenail has been filed too short.

Except that it's not the old Daisy. I'd bend over backwards for a true friend, someone I could rely on, but not one who dropped me like a pair of hot hair-straighteners the moment my life took a dodgy turn. And the only reason I was friendly with Mia in the first place was because Dad told me to. Well, now he's in jail and can't even be bothered to answer my letters, he's in no position to tell me what to do any longer.

'I'm busy,' I say. 'It'll have to wait.'

'It can't,' Mia whispers. 'It's urgent. I *have* to see you. Meet me in the third changing-room along from the left on the right-hand side in Topshop in an hour, OK?'

There's no *way* I'm going on a mercy dash to Mia. She can bug someone else with her selfishness. It's been three weeks since her weasel of a dad announced he's buying The Laurels and not once has she been in touch, not even to ask whether I'm leaving the *Glee* poster she covets.

'Mia, I'm sorry. I can't.'

Ooh, very calm and assertive. Ms Rubin would be proud of me. I might even think about getting my hair to do the whole Wanda-May V-sign thing.

'You have to, Daisy,' Mia hisses down the phone. 'This time it really is a matter of life and death.'

'Er . . . there's somebody already in that one!' a sulky assistant calls out.

'I *know*,' I say defensively.

In the spirit of my new-found assertiveness, I pull back the changing-room curtain with a flourish.

'Oh! God! Sorry!'

I've got the wrong cubicle. Instead of skinny minnie Mia waiting for me, there's a whale of a woman in a whiteish-grey bra and vast flesh-toned pants, struggling to zip up a teeny red dress.

Ignoring the *told you so* glare of Sulky Girl, I take a deep breath and cautiously put my head round another curtain.

This time I've got the right place.

Still in her Park Hill uniform, Mia's sitting on the floor facing me, her head down, her knees up to her chin, her heels drumming the carpet. This is a level of Mia-stress I've never seen before, a level right off the scale. When she glances up, I notice she's got a ciggie in her mouth and is wearing very large, very dark sunnies.

'You can't smoke in here!' I hiss. 'You'll set the sprinklers off. And what's with the indoor shades?'

'It's not lit,' Mia shrugs, taking the fag out. 'I just need something in my mouth.'

I sit on the ground at right angles to her, then seeing the rank state of the carpet, wish I hadn't. I'm also beginning to wish I hadn't lied to the girls about why I had to leave The Cappuccino Club. What if they see me in here and realize Mum hasn't crashed the Porsche into a coffin-filled hearse, the first excuse I could think of at short notice, and only because a funeral went past when I was on the phone. And at the back of my mind, I'm annoyed with myself that I've fallen for that whole Mia-emergency scene again. No one will have died, be about to die or even be remotely ill. Perhaps it's time to reread *Assertiveness NOW!*

'So, what's all this about?' I ask irritably. 'What's the big secret?'

Mia bites her lip, there's a pause and then, 'My dad's been blackmailing your dad.'

Well, I didn't expect that! But it does explain the missing money and why the Howards were planning Christmas in Barbados whilst we were staying in Kent.

Mum's planning to put Christmas dinner on a skewer on the shop menu in December: turkey, stuffing, a sprout, a roastie and a parsnip all on a stick garnished with holly. Buy two and get a cracker and a sprig of plastic mistletoe free.

I tear my mind away from crazy festive kebabs. We're here to talk about blackmail, not takeaways.

'So Dad's innocent?' A vision of me at the prison gate throwing my arms around Dad pops into my mind. It's *The Railway Children* all over again. I might even shout out, 'Daddy! My Daddy!'

'No, he's not.'

I mentally shoo Dad back behind the prison gates.

Mia beckons me closer, and I shuffle over on my bum.

'When Dad did Davenports' accounts he discovered your dad had been nicking money from the company, fiddling the VAT and stuff,' she whispers. 'Dad wanted to send me to Park Hill but we couldn't afford it, so he threatened to shop your old man unless he got hush money. It just started as school fees, but then Dad demanded more and more until there was nothing left. *That's* why your dad had to pull out of the club; he couldn't afford to run it *and* pay off Dad, especially when he wasn't selling many cars. But when he dumped The

Dons, Dad freaked in case someone started digging around and found out the truth. You don't know who tipped off the cops, do you?'

My head is spinning. I'm just thankful that I'm already slumped on a manky carpet or I would surely faint at Mia's revelation. 'I don't know who told the police,' I say. 'But how do *you* know all this?'

'I overheard stuff, snooped around a bit, guessed something was up when he banned me from seeing or speaking to you, took my phone off me and locked me in my room in the hols and at weekends. Then a couple of days ago I confronted him in the kitchen.' Mia frantically rolls the unlit cigarette across her palms. 'I told him I thought he had something to do with your old man going to jail; that he was jealous of your money and the house, the pony, the dog, even your mum.'

'And how did he take it?' I ask. 'Did he fess up?'

She takes off her sunglasses.

'Oh. My. God! Mia!'

I'm shocked. Her left eye is swollen and closed, its socket a rainbow of purple, red and yellow bruises.

'Your dad punched you in the face?' I gasp, horrified.

'No . . .' She lightly touches her eye and winces. 'I threatened to shop him if he didn't lay off Mum, so he

262

threw me against a cupboard and I caught my face on the door handle.'

'Your mum?' I think of nervy little Mindy Howard, a shrew married to a weasel. 'He does the same to her?'

Mia nods. 'He bullies her. Calls her names like Mindy the Minger and throws food at her if he doesn't like what she's cooked. He's even hit her with a copy of the *Telegraph* just because she couldn't do the quick crossword.'

Mia starts sobbing, her whole body shaking. I don't have a tissue, so I hand her one of the tops I've brought in as a decoy. It seems a shame to snot on fuchsia-pink silk, but this is an emergency. I'll worry later about how we hand it back covered in tears and nose slime to the sulky assistant.

'After he pushed me into the cupboard and stormed out, Mum told me I was right. She'd known about the blackmail for months, but was too scared to say anything.' Mia wipes her nose on the top. 'She said she thought when your dad confessed he'd drop Dad in it, he'd go to jail and we'd both be safe. But your dad's stayed schtum, and now we're moving into your house with your dog on robbed money.'

Mia ups the sobbing level.

Sulky Girl looks suspiciously round the curtain.

'She's been dumped,' I explain. 'Left preggers at fourteen.'

'So, tell the police!' I whisper, once SG has scuttled off. 'If you don't, I will.'

'No!' Mia shakes her head. 'Dad's a monster, but he's a clever monster. He'd know Mum and I have said something. If he got bail or got off he'd kill us.' She's hyperventilating with fear. 'The only person who can give evidence against him is your dad. I don't know why he hasn't named and shamed him, but when you next see him, ask him to do it, please, Daisy.' She grabs one of my hands and clings to it with sweaty fingers. 'We're desperate. *So* desperate.'

'I have never heard of anything more ridiculous in my life,' Mum snaps, waving a large and scarily sharp-looking knife at me. 'Don't you *ever* repeat such a vicious allegation ever again.'

Hmm. It was probably a mistake to question her over The Weasel being a wife-beating bully as well as a conman just as she's cutting up chunks of lamb, but I couldn't wait to tell her all about Mia's changing-room confession.

To say she hasn't taken it well is somewhat of an understatement. I'd have bet my Mulberry bag on it that she'd be straight on the phone to David Cohen or to the police, turning the bullying weasel in and putting out the bunting. Never for one moment did I think she'd defend him, refuse to believe Mia or me *and* threaten me with a wide-blade blood-stained Sabatier.

'Jonathan Howard has been a total rock to me, to this family and to your father. Look at how he's letting us stay on at The Laurels until we get this place sorted out.'

'It's a cover-up,' I say. 'Mia wouldn't make this up. You should have seen the state of her! She had a black eye and was snotting on silk!'

Mum gives a dismissive snort. 'That girl is a drama queen.'

'Well, if you won't tell the police, I will,' I say, knowing full well I can't because Mia has begged me not to. 'Someone has to.'

'You will not.' Mum slams the knife's silver blade into a hunk of bloody flesh. 'If it's not true we'll be left high and dry without Jonathan's help, and if it was true, don't you think your father would have mentioned it when he was arrested?'

Now I've found out where the missing money has gone, the one remaining mystery is why Dad didn't drop The Weasel right in it.

'Well, ask him,' I say. 'When you next see Dad, ask

him whether there's any truth in what Mia says. If you don't, I will.'

'I've told you. He doesn't want his children to see him in jail,' Mum says tightly.

But I want to see Dad. He might be a criminal about to be put away for years, and I'm angry with him for what he's done, but I'm even angrier that he's such a coward he can't face his own children over a prison table.

'This isn't about him any longer, it's about me!' I yell. 'I'll *demand* to see him.'

Mum looks up at me sharply. 'Daisy, don't be ridiculous.'

'I will,' I say defiantly. 'I'll stand outside the prison and scream and scream until they let me in, or I'll chain myself to the railings!'

I don't actually have any money to buy a chain, but perhaps someone can lend me a bike lock or something.

Mum puts down her knife, walks over to the door and turns the sign to *Closed*.

'Sit down,' she says, gesturing to a chair. 'We need to talk.'

There's something in Mum's voice that signals this time I should do as I'm told. It's also a tone of voice that makes me feel a bit scared.

'I haven't been exactly straight with you – or with Aston and Portia come to that,' Mum admits. 'The thing is . . .' She swallows hard and rolls her eyes backwards, as if she's trying to blink back tears. 'I haven't seen your father, not since he confessed he was guilty.'

'Whaaat?' I don't believe I'm hearing this. Mum's been trotting off once a week, taking my letters with her, saying she'd spent the afternoon at the prison drinking lukewarm coffee, eating stale digestive biscuits, telling Dad our news.

'But you gave him my letters,' I croak. 'You said he didn't feel up to seeing us.'

Mum bites her lip and fiddles with the strings on her apron.

'You said he was sharing a cell with Tony the lead burglar and the food was OK.'

'His solicitor told me those things. I couldn't face seeing him,' she admits. 'I kept meaning to, but when it came to it, I couldn't walk through those prison gates and see my husband behind bars.'

'So, where did you go?' I ask.

Mum seems to be sinking further and further down in her chair. 'I drove to Dover, sat in the car looking out at the sea, watched the ferries sail in and out, trying to make sense of it all.'

'And did you?'

'No,' Mum says quietly. 'No, I didn't.'

'I thought he was too much of a coward to see us,' I say, pouring a mound of salt on the table and tracing my finger through it. 'But still, he could have written to me.'

'He did.' Mum grinds her eyes with her palms. Then she gets up, walks over to the freezer and pulls out a polythene bag. 'I'm sorry. I didn't know what else to do with them.'

She hands me the icy package. Beneath the fogged plastic I can just about make out Dad's sloping handwriting. In the damp bag there are letters, loads of them, not just addressed to me but to Portia and Aston too.

'I intercepted the post,' Mum explains. 'I didn't want him to have anything more to do with you.'

'Why?' I ask.

Mum just stares into space and then says, 'To make him feel as desperate and alone as I do. I'm sorry, Daisy, I shouldn't have used you against him. I thought if I got a job quickly, made a real success of our life, showed him we could be fine without him, I'd feel differently, that I could hold my head up as I walked through those gates. But I don't – not yet.'

And then she slumps back on a chair and starts to cry.

And the thought of my mother sitting alone, in a borrowed car, looking out to sea whilst her husband is in prison, breaks my heart.

I drop the soggy letters and wrap my arms around her. She used to smell of Chanel Nº 19 and hairspray, but now it's chip fat and burnt meat, and at the back of her head, behind the green and white bandana and under the hairnet, grey roots are creeping along her once pristine blonde parting.

'I really want to go and see him,' I say. 'You don't have to come with me, but I need to go.'

Mum kisses me on the cheek. 'I know,' she says heavily. 'I can't see him, Daisy, not yet, but if you want to go I'll arrange a visiting order. You can ask him about all this crazy stuff with Jonathan Howard.'

Chapter Twenty-Three

My butt has turned to a block of ice and I am absolutely blue-lipped freezing, but I can't go inside even though I'm desperate to thaw out and go to the loo because Sonja, Deeza, Kaylee, Mel and me are sitting on the wall outside the sixth-form block, listening to music on Mel's phone as Kaylee and Sonja both want to catch a glimpse of a couple of sixth formers who they think will come out for last break. I don't think they'll come out, because it's too cold, they've got their own snug common room, and faced with walking past a row of Year 10 girls who are likely to give each lad a score out of ten, why would they? But whilst I'm still trying to prove I'm not a snobby rich bitch but one of the girls, I need to stick with them, even if my buttocks get frostbite.

'Dais,' Sonja says. 'It's my birthday this Saturday. Me and the girls are going shopping, having a pizza, going to the flicks. Do you wanna come?'

Want to come? Of course I want to come! More than anything I want to wander around town with a group of girls who are still wary of me, but might one day become real friends. But I've already got plans for Saturday 18 October. Plans I can't change.

'I can't . . .'

'Oh well, if she's already got a better offer,' Deeza says sarcastically, jumping off the wall and standing in front of me. 'What is it? Some fancy schmancy cocktail party?' She pretends to sip a drink with her little finger sticking out. 'OK, yah, yah, top up the Bolly!'

Deeza's still sarky towards me, not even slightly friendly. I'm pretty sure that if Big Bird Birch hadn't told her to back off, and Mel hadn't decided I'm not a snobby cow after all, she'd still be on my back. It's no big deal. I don't have to be friends with everybody, just a few people will do.

'Actually, I'm going to see my dad in prison,' I say. 'For the first time.'

The girls look cold, but impressed.

'I went to see my mum in jail,' Kaylee says. 'She nicked something from the Lancôme counter in Fenwick's and they banged her up for three months.'

Wow! This is the first time Kaylee's mentioned

her mum's a klepto jailbird. If only she'd said something earlier we could have bonded over crimes and sentences.

'Seems a bit harsh,' I say. 'Sending her to prison for taking some mascara or lippy.'

'Nah, it wasn't the slap she nicked,' Kaylee says. 'It was the till. You OK with going?'

'Yes and no,' I admit. 'I might have to go on my own.'

Four visiting orders came, but I'm the only one going. Mum says she'll take me but she won't come in, Portia's keeping clear because she's still angry with Dad, and Aston is staying here because he's got to paint the walls at the drug rehab centre with a woman he's got the hots for.

'I'll go with you,' Mel offers. 'It'd be cool to see inside a prison, as long as you're not banged up, of course.'

I'd love Mel to come with me, but she can't. 'You'd need a visiting order and it's made out for Portia,' I point out. 'You need to show ID and everything.'

'So,' Mel shrugs. 'I'll pretend to be your snotty sister. With the right accessories I think I could do stroppy rich bitch rather well.'

'You won't get in without someone who's over eighteen,' Kaylee says with the knowledge of someone who's been there, done it and seen the handcuffs. 'You've got to go with an adult.'

This is a blow. None of us had looked at the small print in the long letter that came with the orders. I just assumed that I could swan in, interrogate Dad about The Weasel and get Mr Howard banged up. If Aston won't break his painting date, I'm stuck.

Then I have an idea.

What's the point in having a number for emergencies if you don't use it in an emergency? And this is about as serious as it gets.

I get out my phone and scroll through the phone list.

'Jake?' I say as the others clap their hands over their mouths to stifle screams and giggles. 'You know you said you'd help me out if I needed something? Do you think you could pretend to be my brother Aston and go to prison with me?'

'This is mental,' I whisper, as we shuffle forward in the queue outside Her Majesty's Prison Dover Court, a mass of rectangular boxes that look as if they've been built from red Lego bricks topped with a grey roof. 'We'll never get away with it.'

I can't believe that only a few months ago I wouldn't say boo to a goose, and here I am trying to smuggle my friends *into* jail. Portia's bet me the bigger wardrobe that

I won't get away with the scam, and Mum's said that if I get caught, she's not visiting me in prison. Jake and Mel wisely decided not to tell their parents they were spending their Saturday afternoon in jail pretending to be someone they're not.

Mum said she'd run us here, but I couldn't bear the thought of sitting in Mindy Howard's swanky car, knowing Jonathan Howard had bought it with money he's stolen from Dad, so we came by train. After Mel had stopped pouting over the fact that Jake was mean to her on the zebra crossing but only because she'd been mean to me, we had a good laugh.

Jake shoots me a sidelong heart-melting smile, pats my arm and I smile back, even toss my hair a little. Then I feel confused as Jake is supposed to be Aston, so I'm sort of flirting with my brother, which is sick on so many levels.

'I think I look just like a snobby rich bitch,' Mel says, running her hands down her hair as the queue shuffles forward. 'Loads of people are drooling over my bag.'

In a vain attempt to make large Mel resemble my slim sister, we've used a whole bottle of smoothing serum, straightened out the pumpkin hair, and for an authentic rich-girl-gone-wrong look, added a pair of sparkly chandelier earrings and my cracked silver leather Mulberry Bayswater bag. She looks absolutely fantastic, but I don't think I'm ever going to be able to wrench that Mulberry off her shoulder.

Jake's hair looks a bit like Aston's photo, blonde and shaggy, but other than that, we'll just have to pretend he went through a car window and has had to have major reconstructive surgery in the last six months.

A man with a red face and long nose and chin leans through a window cut into the grey concrete wall. 'Order and ID,' he barks.

He looks just like Mr Punch. At any moment he might start wrestling with a crocodile and start shouting, *That's the way to do it!*

I get out my visiting order and my passport.

Mr Punch looks me up and down, makes some notes on the other side of the window and then snaps, 'Order and ID.'

Jake passes over his Aston paperwork and is ticked off the list without a murmur.

'Order and ID?'

I nudge Mel, who hasn't handed over either.

'Order and ID!' Mr Punch barks again.

If Mel's not careful he'll be leaning out of the window and beating her about the head with a truncheon. That will hurt more than being slapped in the chest with a wholemeal pitta.

'The man wants your passport and Dad's visiting order,' I hiss, my heart beating so loudly I can hear it echo in my head.

'Oh yah, so sorry,' Mel drawls in a *completely* false-sounding accent. 'I was just, like, thinking how *totally* lovely my *very* expensive bag looks in the sunlight. My sister Daisy gave it to me, you know.'

Oh lordy. She's taking this whole pretend-posh-sister thing a bit far.

Mel/Portia dips into her bag and gets out her ID.

I can hardly breathe for fear. Here it is, the moment Mel's going to be arrested for fraudulent use of documents along with me and Jake for being an accessory to the crime. No wonder son-of-a-judge Ollie dumped me; he clearly realized he'd be sucked into a life of fraud and deception whether he wanted to or not.

The man looks at the passport, then at Mel, then back at the passport.

My legs feel as if they're about to buckle from under me.

Mel coughs and looks embarrassed. 'I've . . . er . . . put a bit of weight on since then,' she says in a low voice. 'Too much comfort eating of fig rolls when Daddy went inside.'

'Go through,' the man orders.

I want to jump with joy and do a high-five with relief. Thank goodness Portia cut her hair and dyed it black *after* she had her passport photo taken. As it is, she's only fourteen in the snap and is staring out from the photo booth with straight shoulder-length blonde hair and a sulky 'cross me if you think you're hard enough' pout, exactly like Mel. And not only have we fooled the guards, I've won the bet. The bigger wardrobe is mine!

'I didn't realize there'd be so much waiting about,' Mel grumbles. 'It's not as if we're into Lego and Stickle Bricks.'

Saturday afternoon must be family visiting time. The room we're sitting in is packed with kids running around, making things, screaming. It's like being in a very weird nursery, a scary nursery watched over by prison warders.

So far we've done nothing but queue: queue to be searched by a lesbionic-looking woman who I'm sure took longer over patting my back jeans pockets than was strictly necessary; queue to take our boots off; queue to give our names *again*; queue to join the queue in the family room.

'Keep away from the quality,' Mel growls at a small

dark-skinned girl who's come near us holding a lump of modelling clay. 'Touch my bag and I'll get you put away for life!'

The little girl runs away and hides behind a woman in a red coat who's sitting on a chair crying into a piece of kitchen roll.

'Have you noticed,' Mel says, looking around, 'that some uniforms make even scroats look sexy, whereas others would make even someone sexy look a scroat?'

It's not something I've ever given much thought to, but then I look at Jake, who's helping a boy with a buzz cut create a ladder out of Meccano, think of him in a uniform with shiny buttons and feel quite faint with lust. This is such a waste of a delicious thought because, as I said to Mel on the night I assaulted her in the street, I seriously think I've turned Jake off girls for life.

I see him around school and he waves, and he eats gourmet kebabs several times a week and we have a laugh and a chat, but there's not even the slightest hint of romance between us, not even an electric deliberate-but-let's-pretend-it's-accidental brush of hands or bump of hips. Loads of the other girls fancy him and get all giggly and hair-flicky when he's around but, as far as I can tell, he's not seeing anyone, not even a leggy sixth former doing chemistry.

A guard with a massive bunch of keys swinging round his tree trunk of a left thigh starts calling out names.

'Tracey Clarkson, Timmy Clarkson and Bibi Clarkson!'

'Cathy Ryan and Rosie O'Malley!'

People start to get up and move towards and through the door. Visitors who haven't been called begin to gather up toys and pack their bags. The woman in the red coat tucks the kitchen roll in her bra and furiously rubs some make-up on to her blotchy face.

'Aston Davenport. Portia Davenport. Daisy Davenport!'

That's us. Well, me and my pretend sibs.

I feel sick. *Seriously* sick. Barfing all over the floor sick. That would cause a stir in the waiting room, wouldn't it, throwing up all over the Thomas the Tank Engine clockwork railway set. It's going round and round next to me as my stomach goes round and round with it. Any minute now one of the little trucks is going to be filled with a liquid cargo. What a disaster, not just for the next kid who plays with it, but because I'll be vomming in front of Jake, which will totally put him off me, gay or not.

'I can't go in,' I croak, clutching my gut. 'Honestly, I can't.'

Mel grabs my arm a little too firmly.

'Where's the plucky girl who attacked me with bread?' she says. 'Come on, sister, you're going in, even if I have to drag you.'

Chapter Twenty-Four

All three of us sit on one side of a table, waiting for Dad. There's a sign taped to the fake-wood top reminding us not to kiss, touch or take drugs during the visit. Sounds like the sort of thing Mrs Channing used to say before school discos at Park, not that Portia took any notice.

I'm so nervous, I realize that I'm sweatily holding Jake's hand on one side, and before you get all excited that a flame of romance ignited as we went through the metal detector and Jake isn't gay after all, I should point out I'm clutching Melanie's paw on the other.

And then Dad comes into the room, hesitantly at first, glancing at all the other tables and visitors. He looks amazingly well, better than just before he went to prison, though the pale-blue sweatshirt and white bib he's wearing don't suit him.

Then he sees me, his face lights up and he waves as he walks briskly towards us.

I've run this scene through my mind so many times since Dad was taken away that late August morning. I thought that I'd run to him and he'd swing me round like he did when I was little. I thought we'd hug and kiss and maybe cry. I thought it would be like *The Railway Children*. But now he's here I'm being reminded that if I so much as touch my father, the visit will be ended *immediately*. I can't be thrown out before I find out the truth, and I need to get to the truth before the prison guards get to us – if not for illegal hugging then for illicit visitors.

'Daisy!' he exclaims, sitting opposite me and my fake brother and sister. 'It's *so* good see you.' He goes to extend his arms across the table towards me, but his hands brush the list of rules and he pulls them back. Then his eyes alight on Jake and Mel. 'Who are you?' he asks.

'Well, that's just great!' Mel says dramatically. 'You've been absent from our lives for so long, you don't even recognize your own son and daughter! What sort of a father are you?'

Oh. God.

Mel's in a particularly stroppy mood because they've

made us leave our stuff in a locker outside. The prison guard had to practically wrestle the silver Mulberry off her; she only let it go after he pointed out that the bag would be effectively under armed surveillance, and therefore safer here than anywhere else in the country.

'Just so as you know, I'm your son,' Jake mumbles, not particularly convincingly. 'Hello, Dad.'

'What's going on?' Dad looks confused. Well, you would be, wouldn't you, if you get put behind bars for two months and then find two of your three children look completely different when they finally visit you.

'This is Aston and Portia, remember?' I say to Dad, urging him not to cause a fuss and have us all thrown out. 'Mum and *the others* couldn't come.'

I stress the words *the others* and do quite a lot of eye-rolling for added effect.

Dad's bewildered gaze flickers from left to right. 'Well, son and daughter,' he says to Jake, who's looking gorgeous but sheepish, and Mel, who's still channelling her inner Portia and looking posh and sulky, 'maybe you could get us all a cup of tea?' He nods towards a machine in the corner. 'White and two sugars for me.'

'So?' Dad raises an eyebrow as he watches his pseudo-kids head off. 'Any clues?'

Around the edge of the room the guards are leaning against the walls, watching us, jangling their keys, chewing gum.

'Look, Dad,' I whisper. 'It's great to see you and all that, and I'll tell you all the news in a mo, but before we get thrown out, I need to know one thing . . .'

'Why I did it?' Dad sighs, shakes his head and runs his hand across his sweaty forehead. 'Daisy, I was a desperate man.' He leans forward and looks at me with earnest eyes. 'The business was failing, the football club was haemorrhaging money, so was the house. Then there was your school fees, the dry cleaning bills, your mother's endless colonics . . .'

'So it wasn't because Jonathan Howard was blackmailing you?'

I thought I'd cut straight to the chase, not just because I need to get to the truth, but because I've just seen a granite-faced prison guard escort Jake away from the drinks machine and through the swing door.

'I don't know what you mean,' Dad says, folding his arms and assuming a poker face.

'Yes you do,' I hiss. 'Mia's told me she knows her dad was bleeding you dry. Why didn't you tell the police Jonathan Howard was blackmailing you?'

Dad stares at me. 'Is this the only reason you've come?'

he says coolly. He starts brushing imaginary crumbs off the table. 'To cross-examine me?'

I'm furious that Dad is being so awkward, and now more convinced than ever that Mia is telling the truth.

'I want to know why you're protecting that weasel,' I say. 'You've *got* to tell me or I'll cause a scene.'

Dad sits back in his chair and blows air between his lips. 'You've changed,' he says sadly. 'You were such a quiet little thing. What's happened to you?'

'What's happened to me?' I gasp. 'What do you think has happened to me, Dad? Look around you! Look where I'm visiting you! What do you think has happened to Mum, and to Portia and Aston?'

'Well, Portia and Aston have obviously changed too,' Dad says sarcastically. 'I hardly recognized them.' He laughs at his own joke, a smile breaking out across his face.

I know violence against parents is never *ever* justified, but right now I'm in serious danger of being thrown out of prison for slapping my dad straight in the chops.

I tuck my hands under my thighs and clamp my legs to the chair.

This wasn't how it was supposed to be on so many levels. I thought I'd be here with my family, urging Dad to keep his pecker up, assuring him that we'd all be waiting for him to come home and that by the time he was released we'd have a whole empire of kebab shops and a fleet of delivery mopeds. Instead we've fought, I've tried not to hit him and I've smuggled a potentially gay non-boyfriend and an ex-bully into jail with fake IDs whilst they pretend to be my family.

Tears sting the corners of my eyes. I bite my lip to try to stop them but it's no use. There are no beads or nipples to count, nothing to distract me from the grim reality of visiting Dad in prison. I can't even summon up the tiniest amount of Goddess Cheryl to help me through.

'Daisy, *this* is why I couldn't tell the police everything,' Dad says, choosing his words carefully. 'When I saw you run down the drive after the police car and looking so distraught, I knew I couldn't wreck another family, put them through what I've put you and your mother through. I pleaded guilty straightaway so that there wouldn't be a long trial to endure, and to get some time off my sentence.'

'Well, I'll ask Belinda Trotter,' I say defiantly. 'I'll track her down and get her to dob that weasel Jonathan Howard in it.'

'The arrangement was between Belinda and me,' Dad says crisply. 'Anything else I may or may not have done, she knew nothing about it.'

'If you won't report him, I will!' I shout, calling Dad's bluff. 'He's not going to get away with this!' My voice has pierced the low hum of the room. A prison guard stands next to me, his finger over his mouth, telling me to button it. When he's gone, Dad leans towards me.

'Daisy, it's all over,' he says in the same 'don't mess with me' tone of voice he used to use to order Portia to her room. 'There's no more money for anyone to take. Even if what you're alleging can be proved, it wouldn't affect my sentence. Whatever might have happened later, I *did* commit fraud. I'm not giving evidence against anyone and that's that.'

I sink down in my seat and drum my feet on the floor in frustration. I've got my chestnut Uggs on, so there's just the dull thud of distant galloping horses from beneath the table.

'Mia's got a black eye from her dad,' I mutter. '*And* he beats Mindy with the *Telegraph*.'

'Mia's a troublemaker,' Dad reminds me. 'You said it often enough.'

Mel and Jake appear, each carrying a couple of cream-coloured plastic cups. They've obviously been keeping their distance to let me talk to Dad, not that it's done any good.

'You could have told me I had a drug habit and a criminal record,' Jake whispers as he sits down next to me. 'They've searched me everywhere, and I mean *everywhere*.'

With Mel and Jake there, Dad starts to witter on about everyday things. How his cellmate 'Tony the Lead' is actually a really nice guy. Have I settled into my new school? Has Bentley's chronic flatulence problem got any better? etc. etc.

I don't really feel like talking, so I just nod and say, 'Yup' at appropriate points, other than when he asks me if I'm still seeing that worm Ollie, when I say a firm 'Nope', and try not to blush in front of Jake.

A bell rings and people start to get up and say their goodbyes.

'Daisy, will you come again?' Dad says urgently. 'And talk to your mum, and the others?'

'I'll think about it,' I shrug. 'I can't speak for the rest.'

Jake and Mel nod at Dad and head towards the door.

And then we both stand awkwardly on opposite sides of the table, though the distance seems much wider than a lump of plastic fake-wood.

'Daisy,' Dad says, 'don't let this come between us, please, I beg you. It's all over with the Howards. There's nothing left to take and now you're at a new school, you

288

don't even have to see Mia.'

I look up sharply. What a complete turnip I've been! I've been here all this time and there's one thing I haven't mentioned.

'You don't know that Jonathan Howard has bought The Laurels, do you?' I say. 'No one's told you he's sniffing around Mum?'

Chapter Twenty-Five

'Hot choccie?' Mel asks as we all dump our bags on one of the tables at The Cappuccino Club and start whipping spare chairs from under the noses of non-Benshamites, ignoring their cries of 'Teenage thugs!' and 'Hooligans!'

'Please!' I say.

Since the prison visit, Mel and I have come to an arrangement whereby we share joint custody of the silver Mulberry, in return for which Mel buys me hot chocolate with whipped cream and chocolate dusting whenever we go to The Cappuccino Club after school, which is three days a week, the non-café days being because I play netball for the school and need to either be at a match or practising for one. This suits me because I don't have the money to regularly buy luxuries like hot chocolate, and Mel because she can afford to stand me three sugary hot drinks a week, but not to buy a silver Mulberry handbag.

'Daisy! Just the girl I've been looking for. Fancy a drink?'

The girls start giggling and nudging each other as they look at the man towering over our table.

'Ooh!' Sonja sniggers. 'You gone and got yourself a Sugar Daddy, Dais?'

'Given up on Jake then?' Kaylee nudges me in the ribs. 'Going for someone more experienced and with *way* less hair?'

Terry Strain grabs Mel's empty chair.

'That's taken,' I snap, dumping my bag on it just as Spud Head begins to lower his butt.

'You could sit on my knee,' Kaylee suggests, suggestively.

'Ignore him,' I order. 'He's a journalist. He writes lies and then doesn't apologize.' I look up at his hovering bulk. 'I've got nothing to say to you, other than, keep away from me and my family.'

'So no quote then,' Spud Head says. 'You won't give me a quote about—'

'Actually, I will give you a quote,' I cut in. 'I've changed my mind. Get your notebook out.' And then because you still need to be polite, even if you're being stroppily assertive, I add 'Please.'

Terry scrabbles around in the pocket of his jacket and pulls out a small black book and a four-coloured pen. He looks disgustingly eager and overexcited.

'A horse, a horse, my kingdom for a horse! Richard III, Shakespeare. There, you wanted a quote and I've given you one.'

I smile triumphantly at the giggling girls, delighted that I've not only managed to put the sneaky journo in his place, but done so with wit and intelligence.

'Well, that's very apt,' Spud Head says, his voice dripping with sarcasm. 'Given the fact your dad used horses as a cover for his money-laundering operation.'

Suddenly, I don't feel quite so smug. I feel as if he's slapped me in the face with his grubby little notebook.

'Can't blame you for keeping quiet though,' Spud Head continues, putting his notebook back in his pocket. 'You've learnt the hard way the old wartime saying: Loose lips sink ships. Or in your case: Rich bitch lets slip.' He roars with laughter.

'I didn't tell you anything!' I snap. 'You're making it up. Trying to provoke me into saying something.'

'Didn't you realize it was *you* who tipped me off as to what your dad was up to?' Terry says. He glances around at the café, which has fallen silent. 'Are you all sitting

292

comfortably?' he asks the gawping crowd. 'Then let me tell you a story.

'I'm not just a journalist, I'm a lifelong Dons fan too, so when this young girl's dad pulled out of the club and she and her toff-head brother sat in their Ferrari, swinging swanky shoes and sneering at some of my friends, I decided to do a bit of digging. I was looking for something embarrassing; you know-a car sold to an arms dealer or whether Jim Davenport was shagging his secretary. I didn't find anything like that but I did discover that Mr D was very supportive of the equine sports, sponsoring his lovely daughter here as part of a showjumping team that required the purchase of dozens of expensive horses, horseboxes, travel overseas, a big indoor arena, saddles, vet's bills; all expenses run up by a stables who then invoiced Davenport Motors, who paid the bills.'

'And did you?' Mel asks me. 'Did you have all these horses?'

I'm too horrified to say anything.

'Well, Daisy here was very helpful in confirming that instead of a string of posh ponies there was only one, even letting me know where the mule was stabled, didn't you?'

My face burns as I remember the day in the garden

when I grabbed Terry by his bits and dragged him out of the undergrowth. I thought I was putting everything right by talking to him, but I just made things a zillion times worse.

'So then I went to Pegasus, saw the owner who said that all the horses were abroad competing, and then met a stable girl who hadn't a clue about any show jumpers or swanky horseboxes. She showed me Daisy's pony though. Flashy mare.'

Jess. Jess must have shown Polly to Terry the Spud.

'In other words, Daisy, your dad was paying money to Belinda Trotter for stuff that didn't exist, and then she was giving your dad the money back, less a cut for her. Biggest scoop of my life and you led me straight to it.' Terry looks smug. 'Thanks, Daisy. I even got a promotion out of it.'

I don't blame Spud Head for feeling angry towards my family or even writing the story, but it was Dad, not me, who committed a crime and I don't deserve to be humiliated in front of a packed coffee shop. I know I said I wouldn't, but I can't keep it back any longer.

'How dare you!' I explode. 'Dad wasn't keeping all the money, he was giving it to Jonathan Howard who was blackmailing him! *That's* why Dad was stealing! To pay off The Weasel!'

Mel puts her arm around me and growls at Spud Head, 'Bog off, journo-boy, and yes, you can quote me on that.'

'So you must feel pleased that Jonathan Howard's under arrest,' Terry says. '*That's* why I was hoping for a quote from you. He was charged with fraud and blackmail at lunchtime today.'

CALLED TO ACCOUNT

THURSDAY 23 OCTOBER

Terry Strain: Crime Reporter

Police confirmed last night that Jonathan Howard, 41, of Berry Close, Potter's Bottom, has been charged with conspiracy to defraud James Davenport and HM Customs & Excise.

No pleas were entered when Howard appeared in court and bail was refused.

Representatives of the Davenport family and Aspland & Stratton, the firm of chartered accountants that employed Howard, declined to comment.

A date for the trial has yet to be set.

Chapter Twenty-Six

Mel stops dead outside the school gates and bristles like a dog in attack mode.

'It's her!' she growls, lunging forward. 'Let me get her and I'll sit on her head.'

'Leave it!' I order, dragging her back by her coat.

'Well, just give me the word,' Mel says menacingly, glaring at Mia, who's standing on the other side of the road. She's dressed in jeans and a grey jacket, but she doesn't look like a Park girl playing truant; she doesn't even look like Mia. There's no nervous leg-twitching or foot-tapping or even a cigarette in her mouth. Unusually for Mia, she looks super-chilled.

'Go on, I'll see you at The Cappuccino Club,' I say, pushing Mel in the direction of the coffee shop and away from Mia. 'I won't be long.'

'So, how are things?' I ask as a smiling Mia ambles

across the road to meet me. 'I read about your dad. I tried to call but—'

'The police still have all the phones,' she says as we walk back to where she was waiting. 'Look, I'm not really supposed to see anyone who might be involved in The Monster's case, but we just wanted to say *thanks*, to you *and* your dad.'

She flicks her head. Some way down the road I can see Mindy Howard at a bus stop, surrounded by kids from Bensham. When Mindy sees me looking in her direction she nods and gives a furtive wave.

'He's pleading not guilty and the case is going to trial, but your dad has given the cops everything they need. They're pretty sure of getting a conviction,' Mia explains.

'Cool!' I say, though it's odd to be congratulating someone on their father going to jail. 'Have you seen him since he was arrested?'

'No and I won't,' Mia says firmly. 'You seen yours?'

'Just the once,' I say. 'Now he's done the right thing. He's up for sentencing in a few days so he'll probably be moved to another prison, further away.'

'I'm sorry,' she says, reaching forward and squeezing both my hands. 'Now The Monster's gone, things can only get better for me and Mum, but it must be rough for you and the others. I know your dad did wrong, but

297

I can't help feeling somehow mine's to blame.'

'It's OK,' I say, not entirely convincingly. 'Things are working out, slowly. I guess you won't be going to Barbados for Christmas though.'

Mia giggles. 'Mum and I never wanted to go in the first place, not if *he* was there. But no, the Caribbean is off. Probably just Mum, the Queen's speech and me. I can't wait.'

'And school?' I ask. 'Will you have to leave Park Hill?'

'I hope so.' Mia drops my mitts and pulls a face. 'I've had enough of those snotty Glossy Posse bitches. Did you hear Izzy is going out with Dom?'

'No!' I gasp. 'What happened to Ollie?'

'The Simonses don't have a pool,' Mia says wryly. 'She dumped him by text.'

'Typical Izz,' I laugh. 'So, where are you going?'

Mia bites her lip and raises her eyebrows. 'Um . . . I was rather hoping I might come to Bensham. We'd be back together, you could show me around, introduce me to everyone. It would be just like old times, what do you think?'

I think of Melanie and Deeza and Sonja and Kaylee. Despite Mel claiming I'm the only one she's ever bullied and she'd never do it again, it was all I could do to keep her from jumping on Mia a moment ago. It would be a full-time job keeping the Bensham Bitches away from her. I'd never get any work done. I'd fail my GCSEs from being on constant high alert.

I know I'm supposed to be the new assertive Daisy but, 'Well . . .' is all I can think of to say.

'I'm not the girl I was before,' Mia says softly. 'If that's what you're worried about.'

'Nor am I,' I admit. 'Looks like we've both changed.'

I look into Mia's eyes. They're still rimmed with heavy black eyeliner and she's gone OTT with the mascara, but they're no longer flinty, hard eyes. She says she's changed and I believe her. Now her bullying dad isn't around to make her anxious and bolshie she's been set free. And whilst no way would I ever want my father to be in jail, in the end Wanda-May was right: what doesn't kill you *does* make you stronger.

For a moment, neither of us move, and then we both throw our arms around each other and hug.

'Oh, I've just remembered something,' Mia says, breaking free and rooting around in her bag. 'Can you give this to Jessica Fawcett for me?'

She hands me a stiff A4 brown envelope.

'I've given Polly to her,' she says. 'As a gift. It's all signed and witnessed and everything. I'd rather Jess had her than anyone else.'

CAR DEALER JAILED FOR FRAUD

TUESDAY 11 NOVEMBER

Terry Strain: Crime Reporter

A wealthy car dealer who fraudulently obtained and laundered money has today been jailed for two years along with his accomplice in the scam, said to be worth hundreds of thousands of pounds.

James Davenport, 49, and Belinda Trotter, 55, were sentenced at Maidstone Crown Court yesterday after pleading guilty to several counts of conspiracy to defraud, and deception.

Davenport and Trotter falsely claimed expenses for equine services, including the purchase of horseboxes, horses and overseas travel.

David Cohen, acting on behalf of James Davenport, lodged an immediate appeal against the sentence citing new evidence involving an alleged blackmail plot.

Chapter Twenty-Six

CHERISH. CHARITY. CHUCK.

I look at the handwritten signs stuck on my bedroom wall under which are positioned three large cardboard boxes.

And then I look at the pair of silver Christian Louboutin peep-toes I'm clutching, and dither over which box to toss them into.

I certainly don't cherish them; they're tainted by being the shoes in the paper, the shoes at school and anyway, one of them is totally wrecked.

I could give them to the charity shop, but what are the chances of someone who has lost their right leg and doesn't have a replacement false one, popping into the Cancer Research Shop for a single sparkly designer shoe, size six?

This leaves me with *Chuck*, but I feel physically unable

to toss out such shoes of beauty, even dog-eaten ones.

I throw them on my bed along with all the other things that fit into the fourth, unboxed, unlabelled but largest category of *Undecided*.

As the sale of The Laurels to the Howards is off and the house and most of its contents are about to be sold at auction, we have to pack up and leave by the end of the week, so I'll be spending all weekend sorting through my life. It's only Saturday lunchtime and already I'm exhausted and depressed, not just at the amount of stuff I've got, but at the money I've wasted. I've found clothes I've never worn, books I've never read and far too many gloopy lip glosses to count. And just how many Beanie Babies does a girl of my age need?

There's no room to lie on the bed, so I sit on the floor, my back resting against the mattress. From my lower vantage point I can see a mouse just under a chest of drawers. Not a real mouse, obviously, or I would be up and out of the room in a nanosecond, but the velvety-soft pink mouse Ollie gave me for my fourteenth birthday. After a cake in the shape of a handbag at home, I went for milkshakes in town with the Glossy Posse. I had my new Mulberry, the girls shrieked when I showed them the cute mouse, and we christened it Pinky by sprinkling its head with strawberry syrup, a tragic mistake as his fur has never recovered.

Last July I thought I had it all: the It bag, the glam girlfriends, the swanky house and a hunky boyfriend. I never realized that life can unravel in an instant and how quickly things you take for granted can change. Four months later I'm sharing the bling bag and a bedroom, I'm still feeling my way on the new friend front, and as for Ollie, I hope he lives a sad and lonely life and keeps getting dumped.

I get up, retrieve a dusty Pinky and toss him in the charity box. Then I grab the Louboutins off the bed, go out on to the landing and shout, 'Here you are, Bents! Finish them off!' as I lob the silver shoes over the banister to Bentley, who's sitting looking forlorn in the hall. He's not the brightest mutt in the world, but even he knows something's going on, what with the packing cases dotted around and strange men coming in and taking away Dobbin along with the other antiques.

Seeing Bents' hangdog expression makes me feel weepy. We're taking the hound on the condition that one of us walks him every night and every morning, but still, he's another Davenport who's going to have to cope with being cooped up, at least for now.

My phone rings and I amble back into the bedroom and retrieve it from underneath a pile of knickers.

It's Jake.

'Hi!' I say, looping a thong over my hand and wondering what on earth possessed me to buy a piece of underwear with a smiley face sewn on the front. 'What's up?'

This is the sort of relationship I now have with Jake. Not a heart-hammering knee-trembling stomach-fluttering type of relationship, just the sort of casual friendship I have with some of the Bensham boys. I see him around school or in the street, and he often comes in for a kebab, but he's no friendlier to me than to Mel or the others, so I've completely given up my fantasy of the two of us starting up where we left off in Méribel. It's not as if he hasn't had the chance to ask me out or make a move. When he walked me back to the kebab shop after we'd visited Dad and I was feeling a bit low, then would have been the ideal opportunity for him to put his arm around me and give me a comforting sympathy snog. Instead he said, 'Your blood sugar's probably a bit low with skipping lunch. Go and have a burger and you'll feel better.' And then he bought chips and went home.

'You sound a bit down,' Jake says. 'Everything OK?'

I look around at the chaos. 'Not really,' I sigh. 'The packing isn't going well, I've got stacks of boxes to take to charity, Mum's at the shop, Portia's had a tantrum about moving and gone to Mitzie's, Aston's on a date and I'm mega fed up.' I throw the thong in the air and it lands on top of my bedside lamp. 'And we're moving at the end of the week.'

'Well, I could come and help you if you like,' Jake says. 'I passed my driving test yesterday and Mum's let me have her car.'

Jake! Here! In my house! In my bedroom! Forget what I said earlier; my heart's hammering, my knee joints are bending and a whole swarm of butterflies have come to life in my gut.

'Oh, congrats! That would be great!' I say as casually as I can. 'The more the merrier.'

And then I give him my address, put the phone down and go absolutely mental trying to decide what to wear.

I can hear a car crunch up the drive. I know it's Jake because he had to press the gate buzzer, so, ignoring the fact it's freezing outside, I've artfully arranged myself by one of the bay trees, hoping that my lip gloss doesn't look freshly applied and freaking that even with thick black tights my denim skirt isn't too short if I have to bend down to help Jake pick up a box. I'm pretty sure the girls were just being mean when they said I had man thighs, but I've still got my doubts, which is why I've started shaving my legs, *all* the way up.

A silver VW Golf manoeuvres slowly up the drive . . . full of passengers.

'You said the more the merrier so I brought reinforcements!' Jake calls out cheerily, as two vaguely recognizable sixth formers clamber out after him. 'You know Ben and Vinod, don't you? They've come to help too.'

'That it?' Jake asks, as Ben and Vinod stagger downstairs either side of a particularly large and heavy box containing books and china animals.

'I guess so,' I say, slumping on the bed and looking despondently around the room.

There's still masses of stuff to sort out, but it's amazing how much you can get done if you've got a Stud Muffin and his friends standing in your bedroom waiting for you to decide whether it's worth keeping a plastic water bottle, just because it reminds you of your first date with an ex-boyfriend who turned out to be a loser.

Jake has taken several carloads of stuff to the Cancer Research Shop, and now my once lovely room looks dreadful, like some sort of trashed student squat.

'You're not finding this easy, are you?' Jake says, which is something of an understatement.

I'd really like to do the whole *A house is just bricks and mortar, a home is the people in it* spiel, but the truth is, this is the only home I've ever known, and I really don't want to leave it to live above a kebab shop on a main road sharing a bedroom with my stroppy sister. I'm pleased Mia and her mum have escaped from the wicked weasel, I really am, I'm just sorry that the Davenports don't seem to be enjoying such a neatly happy ending.

'No.' I shake my head. 'I'm not.'

'It'll be OK,' Jake says gently, sitting next to me and squeezing my hand. 'Everything will work out brilliantly, I just know it will.'

Suddenly I feel nuclear furious.

'How can you say that?' I shriek, jumping up and rounding on him. 'You don't know if everything's going to be OK, none of us do! I didn't know any of this was going to happen, did I? Dad's in prison near Birmingham, we're stuck in a flat down here, we've got minus money, and you sit there and announce it's all going to be OK! What are you, a ruddy mind-reader with a crystal ball?'

I'm horrified at my outburst. The words have ricocheted off my tongue before I can stop them. One minute I can't lose my temper, the next I can't keep it.

'I know it's going to be OK because you're the strongest

girl I've ever met,' Jake says evenly, getting off the bed and fishing his car keys out of the back pocket of his jeans. 'I think the way you've dealt with all this and the stuff with the bitchy girls at school is wonderful. I don't have a crystal ball, but you're definitely a girl *with* balls.'

For a moment I stand there oscillating between feeling gutted at how badly I've behaved towards a Stud Muffin who's given up his Saturday afternoon to help me, and thrilled that Jake thinks I'm a gutsy gal.

Assertiveness NOW! is poking out of my *Cherish* box. I've given the pristine copy away to charity, but I've kept the one that's stiff and curled from its dip in the toilet as a reminder of the day when I should have stood up for myself instead of letting Melanie push me around. I pick it up, look at Wanda-May's water-wrinkled face and I giggle. Only a few months ago I was too scared to even buy the book and now Jake thinks I have balls! And it's not the book that's turned me from wimp to wonderful. I've done it all by myself. Still, I should apologize to . . .

'Jake?'

He's gone. I was so busy congratulating myself I hadn't noticed he'd left.

I bound down the stairs, two at a time, and out of the front door where The Stud Muffin is about to get into his car.

'Wait!' I shout. 'There's something I need to say!'

He turns to look at me, one trainer-clad foot in the car, one on the gravel drive.

'I'm sorry that I was such a stroppy cow,' I gasp. 'I didn't mean to be.'

'That it?' Jake asks.

'Er, no.'

Ben and Vinod are looking out of the window. My heart is going wild and I can hardly breathe. I clutch Wanda-May to my chest. 'I wonder if you fancied going on that date we talked about? You know, start off where we left it in Méribel?'

There, I've said it, and it wasn't so bad, was it?

'Where we left it?' Jake asks.

'Something like that.' I giggle nervously. 'Unless you've turned gay or something.'

There's an awkward pause and then Jake laughs. 'I'm not gay,' he says, shaking his head, 'but I can't go out with you, Daisy. Sorry.'

My insides lurch as I realize with butt-clenching horror I've just been knocked back in front of Ben and Vinod. How excruciatingly humiliating to be shot down in front of the others! Wanda-May didn't warn me this might happen. Where was her Dealing with Rejection chapter?

'Oh!' I say, totally deflated. 'I just thought, you know,

what with all the kebabs and going to prison for me. Sorry, I should have realized we're just friends. Good friends.'

'I'd like to be far more than a good friend, but I can't risk you getting leprosy again,' Jake says.

I thought he knew I was lying over the medical emergency, but perhaps not.

'I wasn't really ill,' I admit, my cheeks burning. 'It was just—'

'You thought you deserved someone better than me.' Jake cuts off whatever feeble excuse I was trying to come up with.

'No!' I protest. 'I didn't!'

He leans against the car. 'In the coat queue one of my mates overheard your friend telling you what a minger I was and that you deserved better.' His voice is coolly calm. 'I told him you wouldn't listen to your friend, that you'd still go out with me. Then the leprosy text came through and I was gutted. I might be taller and thinner nowadays, but I'm still the same Jake from the disco in France you snogged and then snubbed. I can't risk going through all that again. Sorry.'

He gets in the car, closes the door, fires the engine and starts off down the drive.

Oh. My. God. All this time he's known what Izzy

Tricket said. No wonder he never asked me out! He thought if he did, I'd knock him back again.

'JAKE STOP!' I race after him, hammering on the window using *Assertiveness NOW!* as a battering ram, its pages scattering on the drive. I no longer care about making an idiot of myself in front of Ben and Vinod, but I do care about just how much I hurt Jake by listening to Miss Bossy from The Glossy Posse. 'LET ME EXPLAIN!'

Jake stops the car and opens the window.

'Listen,' I gasp, leaning through the window, clutching the door. 'If you don't want to go out with me now, that's fine, but you should know that I *never* thought I was too good for you. I just did what a shallow bitchy bobble-head told me to and I was stupid to listen to her. I never used to stand up for myself. I do now. I'm not the girl I was in Méribel. I'm no longer a wimp!'

'That's quite a speech,' Jake says.

'Well, it's true,' I say.

'In that case,' Jake says, 'I think we left it here . . .'

Then he leans through the window towards me and kisses me. It's a soft, gentle kiss, *definitely* not the sort of kiss you'd give to someone who's just a friend, even a *very* good friend. It's far too long and *much* too loaded and causes my limbs to tingle so much I drop what's left of Wanda-May on the drive.

311

And as Vinod and Ben start pipping the car horn and whooping I realize that Jake is right.

Things might be rough right now but, in the end, everything is going to work out brilliantly.

About the Author

Helen Bailey was born and brought up in Ponteland, Newcastle-upon-Tyne. Barely into her teens, Helen invested her pocket money in a copy of *The Writers' and Artists' Yearbook* and spent the next few years sending short stories and poems to anyone she could think of. Much to her surprise, she sometimes found herself in print. After a degree in science, Helen worked in the media and now runs a successful London-based character licensing agency which has worked on internationally renowned properties such as Snoopy, Dirty Dancing, Dilbert and Felicity Wishes. With her dachshund, Boris, and her husband, John, she divides her time between Highgate, north London and the north-east. She is the author of a number of short stories, young novels and picture books.

www.helenbaileybooks.com

Questions and Answers with

Helen Bailey

Can you write anywhere or do you have a special place where you like to write?

Years of writing advertising copy to tight deadlines means I can write anywhere there's a keyboard, a pen and paper, or, at a pinch, my arm and a lip pencil.

What do you do if you get writer's block?

Take the dog for a walk. It's amazing how inspiration can suddenly strike when you're scooping the poop.

What is your favourite memory?

A warm day on Ullswater in the Lake District in the late 1970s, pottering about in our inflatable dingy with my brother John, and our dachshund, Rusty. Very *Swallows and Amazons*. I think I remember it fondly because most of our family holidays seemed to be spent in a car park, peering out of rain-lashed car windows hoping the weather would clear up.

Describe your teenage self in five words.

Anxious. Anxious. Anxious. Anxious. Anxious.

If you could give your teenage self one piece of advice, what would it be?

Relax. It will all turn out OK in the end, I promise you.

Are today's teens different from how young people were when you were a teenager?

From the emails and letters I receive, it seems that the stuff I was stressing about in the seventies (school, boys, exams, boys, parents, boys, clothes, boys, friends, boys, the shape of my legs, oh, and boys) are still being majorly stressed about in now.

What do you think is the hardest part of growing up?
Perhaps once I feel grown up I could get back to you on this one?

What book do you think every girl should have on their shelves to get them through their teenage years?
A securely padlocked diary, or, if further security measures are required to avoid prying sibling or parental eyes, padlocked and hidden at the back of a knicker drawer. Being a teen can be tough, and writing things down can help relieve the pressure of life, at least it did for me.

What songs would you put on the soundtrack to *Running in Heels*?
Uptown Girl: Billy Joel. Life is just peachy for pampered Daisy.
Illuminated: Hurts. Our heroine realizes her cushy life is built on deception.
Welcome to the Jungle: Guns N Roses. Perfect for Daisy's first day at her new school!
Boulevard of Broken Dreams: Green Day. The title says it all.
Better Days: Goo Goo Dolls. The Davenports face a new and uncertain future.
Shine: Take That. An uplifting track to end the book. Go Daisy! Go!

Can you run in heels?!
Generally I'd prefer the upper speed limit whilst wearing heels to be more of a power walk, though I daresay if I found myself in a field with a charging bull whilst wearing a pair of spiky heeled Christian Louboutin's, I could run like the wind; I'd probably end up face down in a cow pat pretty quickly though.

LIFE AT THE SHALLOW END

INTRODUCING **ELECTRA BROWN**

Electra's family is falling apart. Her dad's moving out, her mum's given in to her daytime TV addiction, and her little brother (aka The Little Runt) has just been caught shoplifting. Even the guinea-pig's gone mental.

Where can a girl turn in her hour of need? To her best friends, of course. Together, they think up a plan: persuading the class geek to stalk her dad seemed like a good idea at the time ...

The first in the fabulous Electra Brown series.

978 0 340 94538 4 £5.99 Pbk
978 1 444 90372 0 eBook

www.helenbaileybooks.com
www.hodderchildrensbooks.co.uk

OUT OF MY DEPTH

Electra's totally out of her depth. Everyone's giving her the third degree!

Freak Boy's dad wants to know whether he's being bullied. Sorrel's interrogating Electra about Lucy's private life. Even her dad is cross-examining her about her mum's love-life, over his Deep Pan Super Supreme.

And all Electra can think is, *How far can you get a piece of melted cheese to stretch without it breaking?*

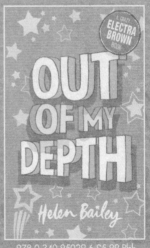

978 0 340 95029 6 £5.99 Pbk
978 1 444 90373 7 eBook April 2011

www.helenbaileybooks.com
www.hodderchildrensbooks.co.uk

TAKING THE PLUNGE

Electra's finally taking the plunge. After all, her friend Lucy did it in France, Sorrel thought she had but hadn't after all, and Claudia, who's done it loads of times, has bet Electra she won't.

She will, though. She's going to go out with the first boy who asks her. But what if he turns out to be a frog and not a prince?

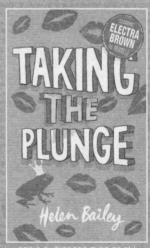

978 0 340 98922 7 £5.99 Pbk
978 1 444 90375 1 eBook Jun 2011

www.helenbaileybooks.com
www.hodderchildrensbooks.co.uk

FALLING
HOOK, LINE AND SINKER

Electra's head over high heels in lurve! She's fallen hook, line and sinker for a testosterone-packed hunk. He's cute, he's cool and he's been expelled from school. What more could a girl want?

There's only one minor problemo: she already has a boyfriend. She should do what's right and walk away. But will she? As if?

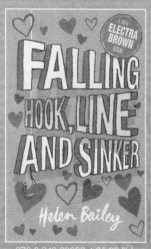

978 0 340 98923 4 £5.99 Pbk

www.helenbaileybooks.com
www.hodderchildrensbooks.co.uk

Want to know more about the fabulous
Helen Bailey and her books?

Check out
www.helenbaileybooks.com
for information on all her books,
fun quizzes, and all sorts of info on
Helen herself.

Don't forget to sign up and receive
regular newsletters featuring competitions,
previews and all the gossip!